I squeezed the trigger of the Special in my hands and the slug barreled out into the night, roaring, striking home. *This wasn't the way it was supposed to happen, man*, he'd have said had the bullet not destroyed his larynx and then the spine at the base of his skull. "Lou-eeeee," his brother cried as the kid's body crumpled in midair and fell, thudding, frozen like a bowling trophy on the ground.

SAY GOODBYE TO APRIL

SAY GOODBYE TO APRIL

Ken Pettus

Knightsbridge Publishing Company
New York

Copyright © 1991 by Ken Pettus

All rights reserved. Printed in the U.S.A.

Publisher's Note: This novel is a work of fiction. Names, characters, places, and incidents either are the product of the author's imagination or are used fictitiously, and any resemblance to actual persons living or dead, events, or locales is entirely coincidental.

No part of this publication may be reproduced or transmitted in any form or by any means, electronic or mechanical, including photocopy, recording, or any information storage and retrieval system now known or to be invented, without permission in writing from the publisher, except by a reviewer who wishes to quote brief passages in connection with a review written for inclusion in a magazine, newspaper, or broadcast.

Published in the United States by
Knightsbridge Publishing Company
255 East 49th Street
New York, New York 10017

ISBN 1-56129-185-4

10 9 8 7 6 5 4 3 2 1
First Edition

To my wife, Alice

With special thanks to Larry Alexander

SAY GOODBYE TO APRIL

1

The telephone woke me up. My electronic alarm clock / radio / calendar / thermometer / barometer played quiet music, told me it was 9:07 A.M. on June 20, that the temperature was 65 degrees Fahrenheit, 18 Celsius, humidity 54 percent, and the barometric pressure was 29.98 and rising. I called it Helen's clock. She'd given it to me as a birthday present five years before. And she had another present for me that day—an announcement that she was going to file for divorce.

As talented as this home weather bureau was, it didn't tell me who was calling. I had a strong hunch it was Frances. I was wrong.

It was Checkers.

Not Checkers himself. Jasmine. Checkers always had her place his calls. He didn't do it to make an impression. He did it because he was too damn lazy to press the buttons himself. He was, without a doubt, one of the world's most avid conservers of energy.

His own.

"Mr. Cage?"

"Who the hell do you think it is?" I growled.

"Mr. Checkers calling."

Her voice was as frosty as Nome in November. I

wasn't one of her favorite people. Nor she mine. It had been mutual dislike at first sight. Her last name was Cavallo. That's Italian for horse. In Jasmine's case, a Clydesdale. She was secretary for Checkers, Wilbur Stuckey, and old Doc Hooper with whom Checkers shared a second floor suite in a geriatric office building on the west side of Los Angeles. Stuckey was a kid who'd just squeaked by his bar exam and was doodling on a yellow legal pad waiting for his first client. Doc Hooper had given up whatever practice he'd had and was writing a column for a short string of weekly newspapers. It was called "Hooper's Health Hints." That from a guy who was an alcoholic with emphysema, arthritis, and a heart problem.

Checkers came on the phone. "Hallo, Tug!" he boomed.

"How're doing?" I asked.

"Fine, fella, fine."

And no doubt he was. I could see him lounging back in his swivel chair with a back as tall as city hall, in his shirt sleeves, his stockinged feet propped on the desk, windmilling one arm, then the other. A big man, Checkers sweat with the best of them. He could also come right to the point when he wanted to. He asked me to meet him at Ito's for lunch.

I tried to think of an excuse to beg off but nothing came to mind before he said, "I got a job for you."

"What kind?"

"Missing persons."

I didn't say anything. Looking for a missing person is often as stimulating as sorting mail. And not as remunerative. Checkers sensed my ennui.

"Only there might be a lot more to it than that," he said, trying to sound portentous.

"Such as?"

"How about meeting me at Ito's at one, and we'll talk about it?"

I agreed.

I took my car out of the basement garage of the apartment house in Marina Del Rey, where I was paying more rent than I could afford, rationalizing it by telling myself it was cheaper to stay put than to move.

It was a hazy, bleached-out day. The sun above the overcast gave it a fluorescent quality. I drove to Lincoln Boulevard and got into the left-turn lane. Waiting for the light to change, I remembered, irrelevantly, that it was four years to the day since I'd left the Los Angeles Police Department.

I'd been with the LAPD for ten years and was working the Hollywood Division, two years in narcotics, most of them as an undercover agent, and then with robbery/homicide, teamed with Checkers. He was a sergeant, a veteran of twenty-five years. He'd have made captain if he hadn't rejected further upward mobility to escape being chained to a desk. Although a sedentary soul, both by nature and design, he preferred the unpredictable freedom of the streets to the confinement of a squadroom or office. He'd already spent fifteen years in Hollywood and knew every scabby inch of it.

On that night four years before, Checkers and I were heading back to the station on Wilcox just south of DeLongpre. We crossed La Brea at Sunset a little short of the witching hour and picked up a call for all cars in the vicinity. A fast-food joint was being hit. We were minutes away. We rolled, were the first unit on the scene, and were climbing out of our car when two men came backing out of a Burger King. We shouted at them, identifying ourselves as police, ordering them to freeze. They whirled and started shooting up the parking lot.

Checkers was on the leeward side of the car and took cover behind it. Me, I was caught in the open and had to do a swan dive headfirst toward an inconveniently situated dumpster. That's when I took the first slug. It went tearing into my back on the right side, piercing the soft tissue between the lowest rib and the pelvic wing, coming out the front with a picturesque spray of blood and mashing against the metal.

The word is you're too busy to feel any pain when something like this happens to you. The word is wrong. All of a sudden I knew why my old man howled the day the kidney stone he didn't know he was incubating knocked on his back and said, "Surprise!"

I might also mention the force of the impact, which propels you headlong in the same direction as the bullet.

In the old days, when a pair of low-life bastards like these were caught pulling a low-grade heist like this —no matter how they were armed—the fire fight nine times out of ten was on the sane side. Assuming your definition of "sane" was a fast exchange of shots, a few pings, and a quick hands-in-the-air trick accompanying an "okay, hey, easy, nobody needs to get their bowels in an uproar, you know what I mean? Okay?"

Yesterday's news.

Now? A whole new morality. Who cares how many innocent bystanders get in the line of fire? These dudes, be they gang-bangers or *vatos* or surfer punks from Pacoima up in the Valley, they don't have the good-old Joe Friday zip gun. They've got the State of Israel's best Uzi, or one of Mother Russia's finest Kalashikovs. In lieu of those, hey, how about a nice AK-47 and a dozen easy-install clips?

Sport a handful of modern automatic firepower like that, sport, and you begin to get the feeling that you are wearing an invisible shield. Who can pierce the spray you can surround yourself with as you make your getaway? Certainly not a pair of dumb Detective Division cops who have to make do with a couple of lousy .38s.

Maybe a .357.

Maybe a backup .22 at the ankle.

Maybe.

Considering the fact that backup was on its way— the undulating sirens of at least three and maybe four black-and-white units come a-running from Sunset and Cahuenga boulevards was beginning to fill the air stereophonically—you'd think that an experienced flatfoot like me would play duck and cover, using his index finger as a pointer when the cavalry arrived. I mean, how long would the perps be gone, ten seconds?

Thirty?

Maybe my brains were located halfway between my lowest rib and the wing of my pelvis, I dunno. What I do know was that Checkers somewhere behind me was shouting something like, "Are you crazy? Get down! Tug!" And to my own horror I was doing just the opposite.

I guess I was mad in both senses of the word— angry and nuts. One of the fuckers'd shot me, dammit, and, dammit again, my adrenaline was erecting my own invisible shield. The desire for instant vengeance, it's called.

There was this old-fashioned fire escape overhead, attached to the back of an old-fashioned brick building three stories high. The kind of back-alley Hollywood the "Fun Bus" tour guides avoid, which Universal and Fox and Warner Brothers TV use for cop shows when they don't want to spring for the Big Bucks it costs to go east to New York, or Chicago. If I could scramble up and get a better bead on the punks, I dimly remember thinking, I can pay them back for whatever they'd done in the Burger King.

For making me hurt.

The fact was, they were scrambling now that they'd laid their carpet of lead, the intention obviously being to leap the chain-link fence that divided the alley in two, preventing cars from using it as an interblock shortcut. Once over the top, on the far side, hey, they could vanish into the night and rendezvous anywhere between here and Compton, or East L.A., or Granada Hills. Then it'd be the forensics boys with their fingerprint kits and the dour looks. Another manila folder in the unsolved file.

Fuck that.

The clang of shoe leather on metal was coming from the rungs beneath my feet and the simultaneous clang of high tops on chain link was coming from the fence. Everybody was going up, holes in their sides or no holes in their sides, and to hell with the red Jackson Pollack splatters dripping irregularly onto the pavement below. One good thing about this: It's hard to shoot and climb, which meant that even though one of the assholes got off a couple of new rounds in my direction, his aim was off.

Well, off enough. My face did get peppered with

sharp little shards of brick and my ears suddenly rang with the sound of the ricochets but I was still all-too-mobile. And soon on the first landing of the fire escape, dashing to the far side and ignoring the creak of the bolts and the shimmy of the slats. If the damn thing stayed put during the '33 Long Beach 6.2, the '71 Sylmar 6.6, and the '87 Whittier 5.9, it'd stay put for me, even when I lunged forward, belly-flopping against the far rail without an American Flyer named Rosebud, my hands together over my head clutching my piece. One well-aimed shot was all I needed. One of the two hoods was all I needed.

One would make the other, either as part of a deathbed confession or in front of the stenographer in the interrogation room. The trouble was I only had one chance now, the first of the pair having already made it over to the sanctuary on the dark side of the fence.

No sweat. His colleague was now precariously balanced at the top of the thing looking like King Kong facing the biplanes. The perfect target.

I squeezed the trigger of the Special in my hands and the slug barreled out into the night, roaring, striking home. The kid—he was a kid—gurgled one story below me, a shocked look on his face. *This wasn't the way it was supposed to happen, man*, he'd have said had the bullet not destroyed his larynx and then the spine at the base of his skull.

Slow motion? No. Stop-action. Frame by frame by frame, illuminated by the red, blue, and amber gumballs of the units screaming up on either side of the barricade. I shall never forget the wail that came keening out of that circus of light, not from the kid but from his brother—it was his brother—frozen like a bowling trophy on the ground. "Lou-eeeee," I think he cried as the kid's body crumpled in midair and fell, thudding. "Noohhh!"

A new wave of gunfire, aimed upwards . . . an entire clip's worth savaging the bricks and the glass in the windows and the slats of the fire escape beneath my feet. It was a miracle that only three of them struck me, making a grand total of four. Of the four only two are worth noting—the one they extracted from my lung and the one that shattered my left kneecap.

Lou-eeeee was dead. Lou-eeeee's brother was in the hospital ward down at the county jail. I, in the orthopedic wing of Queen of Angels in intensive care, and agony, could take comfort from that. Cold comfort.

"Well, what did you expect after playing 'Rambo Goes to Hollywood'?" Dr. Arnold Shafer, orthopedic surgeon, asked in his best bedside manner, a Rodeo Drive label on every garment, every sparse strand of hair blow-dried by Vidal Sassoon. Shafer didn't speak much English after that. He communicated in the medical professional's equivalent of speaking in tongues. But, with some persistence, I extracted a few more sentences in the vernacular.

I would, he said, experience some recurring pain in my knees, a permanent stiffness, and a slight limp.

Bye-bye Dr. Shafer.

Bye-bye career.

The limp wasn't slight enough for the LAPD to ignore, especially after a department medical examiner looked at the X rays of my knee and saw the three large staples holding it together. A gimpy cop who could, at best, only trot after the nearest scofflaw just wouldn't do, so I was forced to apply for a disability pension, filling out enough forms to overload a shopping cart, then went home to stare at the gaping hole in my life.

It was an empty time. I was trapped in the Horse Latitudes of indecision about my future. I saw no one, talked to no one. Even my relationship with Checkers was put on hold except for an occasional phone call. I wanted time to think. I'd drifted into becoming a cop a couple of years after serving with a Combined Reconnaissance and Intelligence Platoon in Vietnam. But I'd been reasonably content with the job, satisfied to leave advancement in the ranks to time and circumstance.

After two or three weeks of pick-and-shovel cerebration about what to do with my remaining years, I decided to return to UCLA—I'd graduated with a degree in police science—and enter law school. I knew I wasn't really serious about it. But the thought was comforting, liberating. My lethargy lifted. I felt a freshening breeze fill my sails. No matter what my destination, I was underway again.

Slowly.

2

"Retire?"

Checkers nodded.

"You're kidding."

He shook his head. "I've already turned in my papers."

He'd appeared at my apartment unexpectedly that evening, a bottle of Jameson Irish Whiskey in tow. We'd reduced the contents of the jug by a third, talking about nothing in particular, before he broke his news. He sat in my easy chair, shoes and jacket off, tie and collar loosened, drink in hand. I stared at him incredulously. I had never, I suddenly realized, thought of Checkers as being anything but a cop. He'd been born one, he'd die one. I asked him why he was throwing in the towel, so to speak.

Because, he said, he was coming up on twenty-six years of serving and protecting the citizenry of Los Angeles. That was enough. Everything was a rerun. He'd been there before.

"What'll you do?"

"Loaf."

I snorted. Not that he didn't have the disposition for it. Or the talent. When the mood was on him, he could raise it to an art form. Still, he'd given the department full measure. And maybe a little more. But loitering on the department's time without being caught was a game he played. On his own, the sport would be gone.

"You'll be climbing the walls in a week," I told him.

"Think so?"

"I know it."

He took a pensive pull at his drink, then said, "What about you? You just gonna schlep around this apartment, drawing your disability?"

I told him I was making plans.

He lumbered to his feet, went to the Jameson, and poured another drink. "Maybe you'd like to come in with me."

"Come in on what?"

He went back to the easy chair and made himself comfortable. "The private investigation business."

As I remember, I responded with something pertinent. Like: "Huh?"

Checkers drank. I waited. He drank some more. I waited some more, finally demanding: "What the hell're you talking about?"

He'd been thinking about it for some time, he said finally. A year or more. And he'd done some ground work. He'd approached Seaboard Life and Casualty Company. He knew the chairman of the board. Or the president. One of the honchos, anyway, and had proposed that the company put him on a retainer to do what investigative work it might need. They didn't have a staff of investigators, hiring freelancers as the occasion demanded. He'd shown Seaboard how he could save them money.

"We dickered over the dough," he continued. "But

the company farted around. I'd damn near forgotten about it. Then I got a call from a guy named Snyder. Executive vice-president. He said the company'd just got its ass burned by Jack Matson. Know him?"

I said I'd heard of him. He was a private detective.

"Crooked as a hockey stick. He double-crossed Seaboard on a case. Sold 'em out to the plaintiff's lawyer on the q.t. and then skipped town. Cost Seaboard a bundle. Anyway, Snyder made me an offer. It didn't send me dancing in the street, but I took it. Three thousand a month plus two hundred an hour when I'm doing an investigation for 'em."

"Not bad."

"It's a start," he said. He was already thinking ahead. He had a wide acquaintanceship in the Los Angeles Bar Association. Lawyers whose practices often required the use of a private detective.

"That's where we go. Where the money is. No nickel-and-dime stuff. Woman comes in. Husband's whoring around. Wants us to catch him with his nappies down. She's thinking maybe fifty an hour, tops. We tell her to go down to the corner. Talk to the guy with the white cane and tin cup. Fifty an hour's his speed . . . How about it?"

"I don't know," I replied.

"What's the matter?"

I said I'd been thinking about returning to school and going for a law degree. But what was really the matter was that I'd spent four years working for Checkers. Not *with*. *For*. He'd been the boss. If we hadn't agreed on how to move on a case, we did it his way. He'd never pull rank. He wasn't the sort. He'd cajol, bluster, manipulate, pout, using whatever tactics fit his mood. But he'd always prevail.

"Jesus Christ," he said scornfully, "what this country doesn't need is another lawyer."

I bristled. "What the hell makes you think it needs another private detective?"

And that started it. The argument went back and forth. Through the rest of the Jameson. Through a half bottle of Haig & Haig I found in a kitchen cabinet. On and on. But, finally, too drunk and too tired to argue about it further, we struck a compromise of sorts. I agreed to work for him if and when I could spare the time from whatever else I decided to do. Thinking about the agreement the following morning, remembering how satisfied Checkers appeared to be, I knew I'd been had by him.

Once more.

Ito's was another world in another time—a Japanese inn evoking the era of shoguns and samurai. A place of aged timbering and wood paneling, rich and deep. Of shoji screens and tatami mats and a miniature stream tumbling into a pool encased in bamboo and stones, ancient and worn. There wasn't a false note in this peaceful, unhurried haven from the fortissimo life outside its door.

The *bijutsuka*, the artist, who'd created it, was Ito Kuroda, the restaurant's owner. He and Checkers had been friends for years. More than friends, actually. Checkers occupied the second floor apartment in a converted garage that Ito had behind the restaurant. Checkers' tenancy dated from a time when Ito had a problem about his liquor license, the answer to which had become mired somewhere in the bureaucracy's sclerotic arteries. Checkers offered to look into the matter. He prided himself on being an unerring pathfinder through the government's cabalistic maze. It was no idle boast. Within days, Ito no longer had a problem. And from then on, Ito housed and fed Checkers on the cuff.

Ito greeted me, escorted me to a table, brought me a Bloody Mary, and we caught up on each other's health until Checkers arrived. He moved toward us, putting me in mind of a sea-going tug plowing through rough water under full steam. He was sweaty, as usual. And just as rumpled. Even though he didn't scrimp on the price of his suits, they looked as if the alterations had been made over the phone.

"Hey, you're lookin' good, fella," he said and turned his attention to ordering miso soup, shrimp tempura, and a bottle of Kirin beer. I stayed with my Bloody Mary.

"How's your time?"

"In relation to what?"

"This missing persons job I mentioned."

I waited while he gulped some of his beer.

"Like I said, there might be more to it than a guy just disappearing."

"Who?"

Checkers dipped into a pocket, came up with a Polaroid snap, and handed it to me. It was a medium-close shot of a man in his thirties with a thin face, longish brown hair, wearing slacks and a Harris tweed jacket over a turtleneck sweater.

"Him," Checkers said.

"Who is he?"

"Name's Paul Bennett." His soup and tempura came and he dug into it. "He's from Seattle," he said with his mouth full of shrimp. "A lawyer. Has his own practice and doing okay. At least that's what she said."

"She?"

"April Tyson."

"Who's April Tyson?"

"Part-time typist, full-time girlfriend, and his client."

"She sounds well connected."

"Funny you should say that."

I didn't know what I was going to run out of first: my Bloody Mary or my patience. But I played the straight man once more. I asked why it was funny I should have said that.

"Name of Price Medford mean anything to you?"

It did.

If you lived in Southern California—even if you arrived the day before yesterday—there were certain names you just couldn't help but get acquainted with whether you wanted to or not. Doheny, for instance. Chandler. Mulholland. The founding families, as it were, along with the founding scandals. The bombing of the Chandler *L.A. Times* (which almost got the great Clarence Darrow disbarred), the murder of film director Desmond Taylor, and the scandalous "Coke bottle" trial of the silent screen's "Fatty" Arbuckle.

In with them all, albeit perhaps with not as much notoriety, was the Medford clan. Price was, if the rumors were true, the last of the line, which stretched back to old Simon. Simon Medford, who'd arrived in Los Angeles at a felicitous time: the land boom of the 1880s. He had the money to invest in real estate. He did, heavily, and cashed in—either through luck or squinty eyed New England acumen—before the boom went bust. He went on from there, profiting greatly in land development after Los Angeles rousted the farmers of the Owens Valley and stole their water. Simon became one of the plundering pashas who hawked the ideology of growth at any price, secure in the knowledge that there would be a bumper crop of Angeleno suckers to pick up the tab.

But as wealthy as he became, Simon was a shadowy figure on the roster of buccaneering businessmen of the day. His name seldom appeared in the newspapers. Nor did Price's. Not until the old man's death in 1925. He was sixty-five and a widower when he died, and a few days after his funeral it was revealed that he'd had an affair of several years' standing with a young movie actress. She was Rene Shaw and she gave an exclusive interview to the rambunctious *Daily Enquirer*, suggesting that Simon hadn't died a natural death. He had, Rene avowed, been feloniously dispatched to prevent him from changing his will, naming her an equal beneficiary with Price.

It's hard, in this permissive time, to credit the firestorm of scandal ignited by the actress' accusation. It commanded the front pages of the city's newspapers, several of them thundering demands that Simon's body be exhumed and trundled to the coroner for an autopsy. It was Price, of course, who was trapped in the middle of the tempest. His father's estate was valued at over twenty million, a more than tidy amount in the 1920s. If Simon was going to bestow half of it on the comely Miss Shaw, Price had ample motive to kill the old gentleman before he could take pen in hand. The less inhibited of the daily journals made that point.

But in vain.

Price, a religious young man of twenty-five and a member of a small but militantly evangelical sect known as the Soldiers of God, remained sequestered, ignoring the rowdydow. At the same time, mysterious and well-heeled forces moved across the troubled waters, stilling them. The coroner said he could do nothing about retrieving Simon's mouldering corpse from its grave until the district attorney obtained a court order directing him to do so. The DA said he was awaiting a police investigation. The police refused to comment until the coroner determined that Simon had died of something other than natural causes. It was an early-day version of a catch-22. Over a half-million dollars changed hands in the production of this charade. Or so it was rumored. Whether true or not, the ink-stained Furies soon raced off after fresher game.

Price came out of hiding, living quietly, bestowing on the Soldiers of God several million dollars, more than enough fertilizer to nourish an explosive growth in its membership. The head of the sect, one Cornelius Bell—said to have the ring of a cash register—was off and running, racing Aimee Semple MacPherson to the wire for the hearts and minds of Angelenos. Rene Shaw was the only one who wasn't laughing at the conclusion of this opéra bouffe. Invoking the morals clause in her contract, her studio cut her adrift and her career sank faster than the proverbial rock. Her lovely face was never again seen on a silver screen.

Forty years later, the *Los Angeles Times* published a retrospective on the strange case of Simon Medford when Rene was found dead from alcohol-related causes in a scruffy Hollywood bungalow where she had lived with a dozen cats and a million cockroaches. The story appeared ten years after Price had become the "Los Feliz Hermit," and it speculated on why he had secluded himself in the mansion his father built early in the century on an acre of ground abutting Griffith Park. It offered two theories. One was that he had retreated out of grief over the death of his wife, Lora, who was killed in the crash of an airliner. The second notion was that he'd become a recluse following his estrangement from his daughter Julia over her marriage to one Alex Tyson, whose net worth could be carried in his vest pocket. But whatever the reason, Price Medford locked his doors against the world, turning his house into a self-imposed prison.

Checkers disposed of more tempura while I asked what Paul Bennett and his typist-cum-lady friend had to do with Price Medford.

"She claims she's Medford's granddaughter. Says her mother was Julia Medford before she married Alex Tyson."

"Where's her mother now?"

"Dead," Checkers said. "Died a coupla years ago."

"And Tyson?"

"Dead, too, for all the girl knows. Says he deserted her mother right after she was born. Just took off. Never heard from him again."

"So what does she want?"

"To find Bennett."

"What does finding Bennett have to do with her being Medford's granddaughter?"

"That's why he came to Los Angeles."

"Because April Tyson is Medford's granddaughter?"

"You got it."

Only I didn't. The fog was descending to ground zero. I suggested he go back to the beginning and tell it the way it happened, one, two, three.

"Okay," he agreed, signaling for another bottle of beer. "Yesterday afternoon . . . late, about five-thirty or six . . . I get a call from the lady. She says she's calling from a pay phone at Parker Center. Says Detective Sid Tobin suggested she contact me. I ask what about. She says she'd like to see me right away. Could she come to the office? I said sure. With traffic, it's close to seven before she gets there."

"What's she like?"

"What the hell difference does it make?" His Kirin came. "Good-looking, nice figure, kinda nervous."

"How old?"

"You wanna talk, or you wanna listen?" he growled, pouring the beer into a glass. "I don't know. Thirty, maybe. Around there." He drank and went on. "Anyway, she tells me she's from Seattle and who she is and who Bennett is and how she works for him part-time and they're real close friends and all that. She says Bennett came to L.A. to see if Medford was still alive and try to talk to him."

"What took so long?"

"Whaddya mean?"

"Why hadn't she tried to contact Medford before?"

"I dunno. She didn't say."

"Are you sure she's really Medford's granddaughter?"

Checkers gave me an indignant look. "Course I'm sure."

She'd shown him a fat envelope full of proof. It included her mother's birth certificate as well as her own, snapshots of Julia Medford with Price and Lora, and letters her mother wrote to Medford after Alex Tyson deserted her, telling her father that he'd been right about Tyson and asking to be forgiven. The letters had been returned marked "Return to Sender." April told Checkers she'd shown the proof to Bennett a few weeks ago, and he'd talked her into letting him contact Medford and try to arrange a meeting between her and her grandfather. She'd refused at first, but Bennett kept bringing it up and she'd finally agreed.

"When was this?"

"She said Bennett left Seattle a week ago last Monday. He called her on Thursday. Said he had an appointment to see Medford's lawyer the next afternoon and he'd call her after the meeting. But he didn't. And when she called him . . . he was stayin' at the Airport Hotel down by LAX . . . she was told he'd checked out that morning."

"That was last Friday?"

"Yeah." Checkers tweezered up some tempura crumbs with his fingers. "And she says she waited around, thinking he'd call or show up. When he didn't, she flew down here. Got in yesterday afternoon and went to Parker Center to file a missing persons report. But Tobin wouldn't take it because she ain't related to Bennett. Told her to contact me."

"What've you done?"

"Nothing. Haven't had time." He looked at me irritably. "After the lady left, I called you. Where were you?"

"Frances and I had a date."

"Who's Frances?"

"A girl."

"I hope so."

"What do you want me to do?"

"Find Bennett."

"What're you going to be doing?"

"I'm goin' down to San Diego this afternoon. Moffitt's trial starts tomorrow. I don't know when I'll go on the stand. May have to hang around for a few days."

Moffitt was agent for Seaboard Life who'd spent several years writing policies for fictitious clients, paying the premiums, then collecting on them after a suitable lapse of time. He covered his tracks with fast footwork and a blizzard of forged paper and false identities and took the company for nearly a million dollars.

"I phoned Miss Tyson this morning, and told her you'd see her about three," Checkers said.

"Where?"

"Santa Monica. The Pacific View Motel on Ocean Avenue. Room twelve. Can you make it?"

"Yeah."

"Good."

"You think Bennett being missing has anything to do with the fact that he was trying to get Medford and the Tyson woman together?"

"Could be."

"What's Miss Tyson think?"

He shrugged.

"Can you tell me anything else that might be helpful?"

He ignored my sarcasm. "You know everything the lady told me."

"Then what does that leave me to talk to her about?"

Checkers was comforting. "You'll think of something."

He was wrong.

I hadn't thought of anything by the time I reached the Pacific View Motel, a place that might have aged gracefully if someone had left well enough alone. Instead, it had undergone a face-lift to make it look—that awful word—"trendy," turning it into a garish mongrel of bad taste.

I parked my Volvo near room twelve and sat for a few minutes, hoping for inspiration. It was futile, and I decided I'd have to settle for making reassuring noises to Miss Tyson. I might even quote statistics about the number of people reported missing vis-à-vis those who eventually turn up safe and in reasonably good health. I had no idea what the ratio was, but Miss Tyson certainly wouldn't either, so I figured it'd be safe to fake the numbers.

I went to the room. A "Do Not Disturb" sign hung on the doorknob. Since I was expected, I knocked and waited. And waited, knocking again with the same lack of response.

"Who're ya lookin' for?"

I turned. A middle-aged woman with the shape of a truncated telephone pole approached. She identified herself as the manager, repeated her question, and I told her I'd come to see Miss Tyson.

"Miss Tyson?"

I jerked a thumb at the door. "Number twelve."

"She's gone."

"Gone?"

"Checked out."

I looked at the "Do Not Disturb" sign. The manager anticipated my question.

"Gentleman checked in 'bout an hour ago. Said he drove straight through from Dallas without stopping and needs sleep."

"Did Miss Tyson say where she was going?"

"No."

"Did she leave any messages?"

"No."

"What time did she check out?"

" 'Bout one-thirty."

Ms. Phone Pole moved on, going into the office. I went to a pay phone, dialing Checkers' office number, hoping to intercept him before he left for San Diego. Jasmine answered with her inimitable growl. She sometimes varies her greeting with her incomparable bark.

"Let me talk to Checkers," I said.

She knew my voice. But being a student of slow torture, she asked who was calling.

"Tug," I said through my teeth.

"Mr. Cage?"

"Damn it, Jasmine, is Checkers there?"

"No."

"Has he left for San Diego?"

"Yes."

"Where'll he be staying?"

"Why?"

"I want to call him."

"He isn't there yet."

"I *know* he's not there yet! I want to know where to reach him when he does get there!"

There was a moment of silence while Jasmine enjoyed my frustration. Then she told me. Frostily. "The Ocean Lodge."

I slammed down the receiver as hard as I dared without being charged with the willful destruction of phone company property. The sun had burned through the overcast. It was hot. Muggy. I went to the Volvo, pulling off my jacket. Paul Bennett was gone. April Tyson was gone. Checkers was gone. The whole damn world was somewhere else. And I wasn't sure where I was.

Or why.

I went to my apartment, dialed the number for the Ocean Lodge, left a message for Checkers, then had a shower. A long one. It helped. I put on a pair of swim trunks and took a book and a bottle of beer out on the balcony. I tried to read, but my mind kept gnawing at the question of why April Tyson checked out of the motel without letting Checkers know. The only answer I could come up with was that she'd somehow located Bennett and decided to skip out on even the small tab she'd run up for Checkers' time. But it wasn't a satisfactory explanation. Checkers never worked on spec. There always had to be some up-front money. It could be modest, but it had to be bankable. Of course, this might have been an exception proving the rule. A combination of an attractive young lady pleading poverty and giving him a story about being the granddaughter of an old moneybags like Price Medford could have triggered a lapse of judgment by Checkers.

A soft westerly, usual for that hour of a June day, sprung up and was herding a distant fog bank toward shore. I downed the last of my can of beer, decided to have another and to stop fretting about April Tyson. She was Checkers' problem. As I was crossing the living room to the kitchen, the phone rang. I thought it was Checkers returning my call. It wasn't.

"Mr. Cage?"

It was a feminine voice, soft and shaky.

"Yes."

"This is April Tyson."

It took me a few seconds to swallow my surprise. "Hello?"

"I said, "You were supposed to see me this afternoon."

"Yes."

"Why'd you check out of the motel?"

"I was going to call Mr. Checkers but . . ." Her voice trailed away. I waited. "I can't explain on the phone. Can you meet me?"

"Where?"

"I'm in a bar on Ventura Boulevard. It's called Duncan's. It's on—"

I cut her off. I knew Duncan's. I suggested she come to my apartment.

"Meet me here . . . please." It was a plea, and I didn't argue. I should have.

3

It was the time of day known as the Children's Hour, and Duncan's was crowded with overage juveniles lapping up the booze as if it were two hours to the Holocaust and counting. The noise level was several decibels above that of Chavez Ravine during a ninth-inning Dodger rally.

April Tyson was waiting inside the door. She was tall, slender, her skin toast brown, hair a lustrous black worn in a chignon. But as lovely as she was physically, she beamed a strong and immediate signal—even through obvious fear—that the most important part of her was something out of view. Something she didn't easily share. Whether it had to do with strength or vulnerability, I couldn't guess.

We needed no introduction. Eye contact took care of that.

"Thank you for coming," she said and looked despairingly at the raucous lounge.

"We can't talk here," I told her.

We went outside. On the sidewalk, away from the dimness of Duncan's, her eyes betrayed the redness of recent tears. And the tears started to well up again.

"What is it?"

She took a deep breath. "Paul's dead . . . murdered."

She raised a hand to stifle a sob rising from some cold, hollow depth within her. I took her arm, escorting her to the Volvo. In the car, I said nothing until her reservoir of tears ran dry.

"I'm sorry," she said.

"Take your time."

"I'm all right now."

"Then tell me about it."

"Paul called me about one o'clock."

"How did he know where you were?"

"Marian Neff. She's his secretary. I called her when I got down here and told her where I was staying. Paul said he called her and she'd told him where I was. He told me he was at the Valley Crown Motel on Ventura Boulevard and asked me to come there as soon as I could. He said he thought we should go back to Seattle. I packed and checked out. I was going to call Mr. Checkers but—"

She broke off with a shiver. I took her hand and told her to take it easy.

"He said he was in room ten," she went on. "I went to it and knocked. There wasn't any answer. But the door was unlocked and I went in and . . . saw him." It was growing dark. April stared out the windshield, her face dimly reflected in the glass, remembered horror replacing the shock and sorrow in her eyes. "He was on the floor. There was a lot of blood." She trembled at the memory.

"And you ran."

She nodded.

"Why?"

"Why?" She looked at me as if I had two heads, neither of which was working. "Paul was dead."

"And you were afraid."

"I still am."

"Do you have any idea why he was killed?"

"No, except—" She stopped again.

"Except what?"

"There were clothes and papers all over the floor."

"You think he walked in on a burglary?"

"I don't know."

"Or was someone looking for something after he was killed?"

She didn't know that, either. I tried another question.

"When he called, did he tell you why he checked out of the hotel near the airport?"

She shook her head.

"Or why the two of you should go back to Seattle?"

"No."

"Did you ask him if he'd seen Price Medford's lawyer?"

"Yes," she replied, "but he said he'd tell me about it when he saw me."

"What time did you find him?"

"About two."

"What were you doing from then until you called me?"

"Driving around. I started for the airport. I was going to go back to Seattle, but I decided that wouldn't do any good. I went back to the motel. Paul's motel. I just drove past it. I thought the police might be there."

"But they weren't?"

"I didn't see them."

"You'd have seen them."

"I drove around some more, then I stopped here and had a drink and called Mr. Checkers' office. His secretary told me he wasn't in. I didn't know what to do. Then I remembered you. Mr. Checkers gave me your phone number."

I brought the car to life.

"Where are we going?"

"To the motel."

"Where Paul is?" Her voice foundered in near panic.

"Yeah."

"No!"

"You can stay in the car."

"But what if the police are there?"

"Then we forget it."

"But why do you want to go there?"

"I'll explain later," I said, even though I suspected I never could.

I made a run past the Valley Crown. It was obvious the management and guests were unaware of the corpse in their midst. So I made a U-turn and drove back, parking across the street. April sat with her head slightly bowed, eyes averted. I asked her if she'd touched anything in the room. She said she hadn't, except for the doorknob. I left the car, telling her I wouldn't be long.

Unlike Santa Monica's lovely Pacific View, the Valley Crown was a back-to-basics establishment, old but tidy, a memento to a bygone day when motels simply offered a night's sleep and hadn't yet aspired to being vacation spas. It was a one-story structure with a venerable olive tree centered in the parking lot. A "Vacancy" sign burned, and a young man in the office was engrossed in a television sitcom masquerading as entertainment. I limped past unnoticed. Dim light bulbs burned outside the doors to the rooms bordering the parking lot, which was shaped like a squared-off horseshoe. I went to number ten. There was no car parked outside it. I guessed Bennett came by taxi. I used my handkerchief on the door and entered the room.

The drapes over the window looking out on the parking lot were drawn so that the dim bulb outside did nothing to relieve the inner darkness. I waited for my eyes to adjust, and the outline of the dead man faded in slowly. I didn't go to him immediately. Instead, I went to the bathroom and snapped on the light and pulled the door to within a few inches of closing, giving me enough light to poke around the room. Bennett was sprawled on the floor faceup. His jacket was off, his white shirt front was stained with dried blood, and it was obvious that the three holes in his shirt had been made by a knife.

Someone had ransacked the room—someone in a hurry. Or a frenzy. The bed was torn apart. The contents of a carry-on suitcase—shirts, shorts, socks, pajamas—had been thrown about helter-skelter. And so had the papers from a briefcase. The drawers of a chest stood open. They'd apparently yielded nothing. A wallet was on the floor near Bennett's body. I assumed it was the dead man's even though credit cards, money, driver's license, and anything else that might've been in it were gone. I opened the closet. In contrast to the room, it looked undisturbed. It held a sports jacket, a pair of slacks, and two shirts on hangers. I went through the pockets of the jacket. They were empty except for a slip of paper with three telephone numbers on it. No names. Just numbers. I stuck the slip of paper into my billfold and started to look through the papers on the floor, when I was stopped by the sound of a car pulling up outside.

I turned off the bathroom light, crossed to the window, and peeked through the draperies. A man and woman exited the car, entered the next room, and I could hear their muffled voices through the wall. I decided it was time to leave. I turned to the door and gave the room a last, quick appraisal. Except for the piece of paper in my wallet, I was satisfied homicide would find the room in the same condition I had. And then I left, asking myself why I'd come in the first place. I didn't answer it.

I couldn't.

April eyed me inquiringly when I got back to the Volvo. I didn't answer the look. There was nothing to say. I still didn't know any more about Bennett's murder than she had told me. So I drove in silence to a filling station in the next block and stopped beside the public telephone, left the car, got a North Hollywood Division operator, and asked for homicide.

Almost immediately I heard, "Sergeant Wilson."

"A man's been murdered in room ten of the Valley Crown Motel on Ventura Boulevard," I said.

Wilson demanded, "Who is this?"

"Room ten, Valley Crown Motel," I repeated and hung up.

As I drove out of the gas station, April asked where we were going.

"To my apartment."

* * *

I took April's luggage into the bedroom and grabbed a robe, pajamas, and slippers and told her I'd sleep in the den. That's what the building manager called it when I rented the apartment. It was as acceptable a description as any, I suppose. A small, secluded room. That's the dictionary definition. Mine was small and secluded. It was also dark. It had one window with an unobstructed view of a brick wall about a dozen feet away. I'd furnished it with a couch, desk, two walls of bookcases, and a leather recliner. Having no claustrophobic tendencies, I found it a satisfactory place to concentrate. No tempting distractions, although I occasionally caught myself counting the bricks in the wall next door.

I used the phone and called Joe Zajic's service station on Lincoln Boulevard. Joe'd kept my Volvo running beyond its allotted years. He did a good business because he did favors. I asked one. Would he go to Duncan's parking lot and bring April's rental car to the Marina, relaying the license number from the rental agreement she'd given me? Joe didn't need an ignition key. He'd once made his living as a repo man but quit because the worst thing—more heinous than murder —one man could do to another in Los Angeles was take away his wheels. Although Joe may have grown a little rusty, I'd give odds he could hot-wire a 747 in less than thirty seconds.

I went into the living room and asked April if she wanted something to eat. She said no. I asked her if she wanted something to drink. She said no again. So I fixed myself a vodka and tonic and checked my answering machine. There was a message from Checkers. I returned his call.

"Hiya, Tug! How we doin'?"

"We've got trouble," I said.

"That so?"

"That's *very* so."

"What's the problem?"

I told him.

"Holy shit!" This was followed by a short silence. Then: "I'm going on the stand in the morning. I might be on it for a coupla days. I'll check the airlines. See if I can get a plane up there and back tonight. I'll get back to you."

I hung up and turned from the phone. April was standing in the bedroom doorway.

"Mr. Checkers?" she asked.

I said it was and explained he was tied up as a witness in a trial in San Diego but was going to try to fly to Los Angeles tonight to talk to us. April crossed to the sliding glass door to the balcony. It was open and she looked out over the marina's main channel to the lights of the restaurants and gift shops of a complex called Fisherman's Village.

"I think I should go to the police," she announced.

I didn't say anything.

"If I don't, it'll seem as if I have something to hide. And I don't," she added firmly, glancing around at me. "Do you believe me?"

"I don't know enough to have an opinion," I replied. "If I had to guess, I'd say I do."

"Then why didn't you take me to the police?"

"Why didn't you call them when you found Bennett?"

"I was afraid."

"You were still afraid when I met you." She didn't challenge me, so I went on: "Wait until we've talked to Checkers. It won't make any difference whether you go to the police tonight or in the morning."

"Won't it?"

"No."

"The police know I'm in town. And if they contact Paul's office, Marian'll tell them she told him where he could reach me."

"But she can't tell them whether he did or not."

"I don't like to lie."

"You don't have to like it," I replied. "Just do it. Homicide won't know you were at the Valley Crown unless you tell them. All they're likely to find out is that you were at Parker Center to file a missing person's report and were told they couldn't accept it and Sergeant Tobin suggested you contact Checkers. But Tobin doesn't know whether you did or not. All you have to say is that you didn't know what happened to Bennett until you read it in the newspaper."

April thought about it, but I could tell she wasn't ready to applaud the idea.

"Look," I said, "when you come right down to it, what can you tell the police? That you don't have clue one why Bennett was killed, right?"

She nodded.

"So there you are."

It took her a minute to accept that, then she said she'd have a drink after all. I made her one, and she sat on the edge of the couch sipping it, her eyes fixed contemplatively on the coffee table in front of her. I tried to guess what she was thinking, but it was futile. I finally broke the silence by asking her how well she knew Bennett.

I could hear mental file drawers open and close and received the impression that her dossier on the man was rather skimpy. And I was right. She said he hadn't talked much about himself. He was born in San Jose. His parents were dead, but he had a married sister still living there. She didn't know why he'd moved to Seattle but he had, graduating from the University of Washington law school. She said she'd met only a few of his friends, and his relationship with them seemed superficial.

"How long did you know him?"

"About four months."

"And that's all you know about a guy you were in love with?"

"I'm not sure I was."

I changed the subject: "Why didn't you come here with Bennett to contact your grandfather?"

"I wanted to, but Paul said it might make me look too . . . eager. That all I wanted was some of his money."

She saw the question in my eyes.

"And it isn't. All right, I wouldn't turn it down if he offered me some. But the most important thing is to see him, talk to him. He's the only family I have left."

"And what if he won't see you?"

"Then nothing."

The phone rang. It was Checkers. He said he'd arrive at Burbank on Delta at eleven-thirty. "Meet me."

I said I would.

"Alone."

I glanced at April.

"She listening?"

"Yes."

"Alone," he repeated and hung up.

April asked me if that was Mr. Checkers and was he coming up from San Diego, and I said yes and I was meeting him at the airport and she'd had a bad day and looked beat and why didn't she get some sleep.

"Isn't he coming here?"

"No."

"Why?"

"He didn't say. He just said he wants to see me." I hesitated and added, "Alone."

"Why?"

"Will you stop asking why?" I sounded testy. I felt testy. I softened my tone. "He's got his reasons, so let's go along with them, okay?"

She eyed me warily. "How do I know I can trust you?"

"Trust? What's to trust?"

"I'm the one who's in trouble."

"We went through that. You're *not* in trouble."

"I want to know what's going on."

"So do I. And as soon as I find out, you'll know."

Our eyes held. I considered taking her with me until I saw the resentment and suspicion recede from her face. She dropped onto the couch, and I again suggested she get some sleep.

"I couldn't sleep."

I went into the bathroom and came back with a vial of Amytal I kept on hand for those nights when my knee was in a sour mood. I told her to take one. She hesitated, then reluctantly agreed, asking if I'd wake her when I got back. I promised I would, and she disappeared into the bedroom. I went into the den and sat at my desk, taking out the slip of paper I'd removed from Bennett's jacket. I dialed the first number written on it. I let the phone ring a half-dozen times, got no answer, hung up, and dialed the second number.

"Woodman and Associates," a woman's voice answered.

I tried to sound puzzled. It wasn't difficult. "Woodman and Associates?"

"Yes, sir."

"Not Manny's Delicatessen?"

"No, sir. This is the law firm of Woodman and Associates. This is the answering service."

"Sorry."

I hung up and consulted the phone directory. Woodman and Associates was listed with an address on the Avenue of the Stars in Century City.

I went to the third number and was taken aback by a recording of a choir enthusiastically singing "Onward Christian Soldiers." The singing faded to the background, and a woman's voice, buoyant as a cork, came on the line.

"This is the Soldiers of God Temple," she announced on tape. "Our office hours are from nine A.M. to five P.M. Please call back during that time. Or if you wish to leave your name and number, you may do so after hearing the sound of the tone. God bless you." The choir came charging back with "Onward Christian Soldiers." I put the phone down.

Reverently.

4

Burbank Airport was comparatively deserted. As I circled toward the parking lot, I spotted Checkers in front of the Delta terminal. I pulled up and honked, and he heaved his bulk into the seat beside me.

"The bars're closed in there. Let's find a place where we can get a drink. Make it close. I'm catching a twelve-fifty back."

As I drove off, I asked what the big secret was.

"No secret. I figured we oughta have a private talk about what we've got ourselves into here and decide what we're gonna do about it."

"We might not have a choice."

"Whaddya mean?"

"April made noises about going to the police. I persuaded her to hold off until I talked to you. But tomorrow morning. . . ?" I shrugged.

"What's she gonna say to 'em?"

I said I'd asked her and she agreed she knew no reason why Bennett was killed. "But she's worried it'll make her look bad if she doesn't come forward."

Checkers huddled in the far corner of the seat and stared into the night. Headlights and street lamps ran by. Finally, he said, "She wouldn't be in much trouble. Maybe none."

I was going to say I hoped so, but I didn't get around to it, because I saw a palsied neon sign in the window of a hole in the wall on Hollywood Way. The sign twitched out the word "Arnie's." I parked the Volvo, and Checkers and I went in. The place was as homey as a welfare office. It was obviously a neighborhood watering hole, but most of the neighbors had retired for the night. The bartender and an elderly patron were at the bar watching a late-night movie on television. From what I glimpsed of it, the story concerned itself with a humanoid variety of cactus, shooting its nuclear-tipped spines thither and yon, threatening to terminate civilization as we know it, which made me wonder if the cacti were the heroes of the piece.

Checkers and I got drinks from the bar and retreated to a far table. He took a pull at his drink and said, "I've been thinking. An old fart with as much money as Medford probably's got people around him with their eyes on the bread, making sure they don't come up with the short end of the stick when he dies."

"So?"

"So Bennett blows into town saying he represents the old man's granddaughter, who's alive and well and living in Seattle. Says he's got proof. Maybe even flashes it to somebody who's got his own plans for Medford's money. And then, right outa the blue, Bennett gets stuck with a shiv by someone tossing his room. How's that grab you for coincidence?"

"It could happen."

"Horseshit," he rumbled.

I wasn't surprised. Checkers didn't believe in a lot of things. He had a list that stretched from here to home plate. And near the top of it was his contempt for fortuity, happenstance, the fluke. But I didn't buy his supposition that someone close to Medford had killed Bennett. For one thing, April being Medford's granddaughter didn't mean a damn thing as far as the old man's money was concerned. If she wasn't in his will—and she probably wasn't—the best she could do was wait until it was offered for probate and contest it.

"I know that," Checkers said impatiently.

"And for another," I continued, "April says the old man's money doesn't matter."

He looked at me, dumbfounded. "You *believe* that?"

"It's possible."

He lifted supplicating eyes to heaven and muttered, "God help us."

I didn't want an argument. It would've been futile. Checkers held a black belt in cynicism. So I conceded that April also said she wouldn't turn down any Medford money.

"You're damn right she wouldn't." He finished his drink and went to the bar for two more, came back, and sat down, almost polishing his off without coming up for air. "Look, you ain't gonna convince me Bennett's murder didn't have something to do with April and her granddaddy. And if I'm right . . . if somebody around Medford's afraid she'll screw up their plans . . . then they did only half the job when they took Bennett out. They gotta deal with her, too."

"I still don't buy it," I said.

"Why not?"

"If there're people around Medford who have their hands in the till, they're smart operators who know what they're doing. The kind who'd do everything legally. Or make it look so legal no one could tell the difference. I don't think they'd panic because Bennett showed up. They'd cool it. Jolly him along. Or play hardball. Thumb their noses at him. Laugh at him. Tell him to get lost. But I don't think they'd kill him. Or have him killed. That's pretty damn crude."

"Maybe they're not as slick as you think. And that's all I'm saying—that it's *possible*. That they *could* panic. Now you gotta admit that."

I said anything was possible.

"Then ain't it smart to play it safe?"

"How?"

"Keep April under wraps. See what homicide comes up with."

"And what if she doesn't want to stay under wraps?"

"Talk to her. Explain it. Tell her it could be her ass if she ain't careful."

He was reaching for it and, knowing Checkers, I knew why. He had his eyes on all that Medford money and the possibility, however remote, that down the line April might come in for a big slice of it. And if he could keep a hook in her, he might walk off with a thick chunk of that slice. And I told him so.

He looked ingenuous. "What's wrong with that?"

"I don't like it. If you think she's in any danger, she should go to the police and tell them what she knows—"

"But she don't know nothin'," he interjected.

"—and let the police protect her."

"You think they would? Christ Almighty, didn't you learn *anything* in ten years in the department?"

"I guess I don't think she needs protection," I told him, "and if you want to play games with this situation, okay. But I don't. I'm pulling out."

Checkers studied me for a long moment with a look that held none of the guile that was as much a part of him as his right arm. I expected an argument. Or a demonstration of his unquestioned power of persuasion. I got neither.

He sighed and finally said, "Okay, we'll do it your way."

I eyed him warily. It was completely out of character for him to give in so easily. Or give in at all, for that matter. He tossed off the rest of his drink and moved to the bar, ordering a refill, then went into the men's room. I sipped my drink and wondered what I'd do about April now that Checkers'd handed me the ball. But all I accomplished before he came out of the john, picked up his glass at the bar, and returned to the table was to finish my drink.

"Want another?" he asked.

I said I didn't, and he sat down.

"So how do you wanna play it?" he asked.

I winged it. "Just let her do what she wants to do. Go to the police in the morning, if that's it."

"You got it."

"Don't try to shit me."

"I'm not," he protested with wide-eyed innocence.

"If I stick around, it's *my* case. You start fucking with it and I walk."

"You got it."

He looked as sincere as Easter morning. But I didn't trust him. Not for a minute. I told him it was time to go. He nodded, gulped his drink, and we moved to the door. The bartender and his customer paid no attention to us, enrapt as they were in the TV movie. I glanced at the tube. The Cactus Men still had the world hanging by its fingernails.

I was betting on them.

The freeways, those serpentine monsters by day, can be just as brutal at night. A tractor-trailer had tipped over on the transition from the Ventura Freeway to the San Diego, dumping its cargo of fifty-gallon drums of vegetable oil. It took me a half-hour to creepy-crawl through the backed-up traffic.

The apartment was dark, and the door to the bedroom was closed. I debated whether or not to wake April and tell her about the meeting with Checkers. I decided I should and rapped on the bedroom door. No answer. I called her name. Still no answer. I opened the door a crack. The glow from a living-room lamp threw a ribbon of light into the darkened room and across the unoccupied bed. I went into the room, making a mystified turn of it. The vial of Amytal was on the bedside table. I looked in the closet. The space I'd made for April to hang her clothes was unused. And her luggage, a vanity bag and small suitcase I'd put on a bench under a window, was missing. I had a sense of deja vu. I'd been here before. Well, not here exactly. But at the Pacific View Motel that afternoon. April was gone.

Again.

I went into the kitchen, poured myself a tot of Jameson, and took it to the den, sprawling in the recliner. Where the hell had she gone this time? To the police? Back to Seattle? Those were the only possibilities I could come up with. I speculated that she had friends in the Los Angeles area and had gone to them. But that came out with a minus sign beside it. If she had friends she could go to now, why hadn't she sought them out after she'd found Bennett dead? Why had she driven aimlessly around the city for hours? Why had she called me?

I considered calling Checkers, but that was as far as I got. I was tired, I had a headache, my knee was acting waspish. What I didn't need was another discussion about the inconstant Miss Tyson. I finished my drink and promptly went to sleep in the chair. Or at least I dozed. And I had a dream. I don't remember any of it but the very end. Someone was alternately ringing the bell and knocking on the door. They woke me up. The ringing doorbell and knocking had segued into the dream. The knocking and bell ringing continued. I looked at my watch. It was two-thirty. I trudged to the door blearily, opened it on the night chain. And batted rheumy eyes.

"Were you asleep?" April asked. It was a contrite whisper.

"What the hell's going on?" I demanded.

"May I come in?" Another whisper.

I opened the door and took her luggage from her as she entered. Her face was pallid, and there was fear behind her eyes. I demanded to know where she'd been.

"I—" She stopped. "I'm so tired . . ." Her voice drifted off.

"Would you like a drink?"

"I'd like some coffee."

"I can make some instant."

She nodded, and I went to the kitchen, put on the teakettle, and took two mugs from a cabinet. April followed, perching on a stool at the breakfast bar.

"I had a call from my grandfather," she announced. Just like that.

I almost dropped the mugs.

"That's who he said he was."

"How did he know you were here?"

"I don't know."

"What did he want?"

"He asked me to come see him."

"In the middle of the night?"

"He said he slept during the day."

I gaped at her. "And you *went*?"

"I started to."

"Why?!"

Her voice was apologetic as she explained she'd taken two more Amytal after I'd left and had gone to bed. She was very groggy, almost asleep when the phone rang. She was going to ignore it. But it kept ringing, so she answered it. She was dumbfounded when the caller identified himself as Price Medford, asking her to come to his home and bring any evidence establishing herself as his granddaughter. He also suggested she come prepared to stay with him if he accepted her proof of their relationship. Euphoric over the call, her mind muddled by the Amytal, certain she could convince Medford she was Julia's daughter, she dressed, packed her bags, and left immediately. She said she was going to leave me a note but decided instead to telephone after she'd talked to Medford. She'd driven as far as North Hollywood when it occurred to her to ask the question I'd asked—how could Medford have known where to call her? And the answer, clarion clear, was . . . there was no way. She had, she realized, through the Amytal-induced fog, been enticed from the apartment by someone who was planning something. And she shivered at the thought of what that *something* might have been. It didn't require much imagination. She'd turned around and come back to the marina.

"It couldn't have been my grandfather who called."

"Well, whoever it was, he found out you were here. The question is who and how."

"No one knew I was in Los Angeles except Paul."

"And his secretary. What's her name?"

"Marian Neff . . . But she didn't know where I went after I left the motel." April hesitated, clearly deciding something. "There was someone else," she said finally.

"Who?"

"A man named Duke Dekoven."

"Duke Dekoven?"

"You know him?"

"I know the name."

I knew it from spot announcements on television. Dekoven owned a chain of stores up and down the West Coast—the Import Bazaar, shlock houses selling gimcrack merchandise, from watches to waterbeds, imported from all over the world and sold at rock-bottom prices that were still several times more than the junk was worth. Dekoven starred in his own commercials. He was a tall, rawboned, boisterous pitchman dressed in checkered pants, an aloha shirt under a loud plaid jacket, looking as if he'd just made a miraculous escape from an explosion in a paint factory.

"How do you know Dekoven?" I asked.

"I met him once when he came to Paul's office. Paul was handling a case for him in Seattle."

"What kind of case?"

"A personal injury case."

"How does he know you're in Los Angeles?"

"I called him this morning. I thought maybe he'd seen Paul and would know where he was."

"And?"

"He said he'd had lunch with him day before yesterday, and Paul told him he was at the Airport Hotel. But if he wasn't there now, he didn't know where he was."

"You'd already hired Checkers. Did you tell him that?"

"Yes."

April looked drained, exhausted. I asked if she wanted more coffee. She didn't. All she wanted, she said, was to try to get some sleep, and I told her I thought that was a good idea. April slept.

I didn't.

I flopped on the couch in the den, my mind racing like a rat on a laboratory treadmill, accumulating a lot of miles to nowhere. But just in case sleep came, I set my alarm for seven o'clock to be sure I talked to Checkers before he left his hotel. I wasn't looking forward to the call, because I'd have to admit Checkers'd been right—someone, having dispatched Bennett, was now a threat to April. But even after reconciling myself to apologizing to Checkers, sleep eluded me. I kept flogging my brain for an answer to who and how someone found out that April had taken refuge in my apartment—a safe harbor no more.

Still wide-eyed at six o'clock, I gave up, put on the teakettle for more instant, then peeked in on April. She didn't stir. I returned to the den, tuning in on an all-news radio station while I dressed. There wasn't a story about Bennett's murder by the time the kettle whistled. I went to it, made a cup of coffee, and picked up the copy of the *Times* outside my door. A murder has to have some unusual elements to get much attention in a city and county that average over thirteen hundred murders a year, so the Valley Crown Motel slaying rated only a paragraph in the summary of local news. It contained two pieces of information I didn't already know. The first was that the police thought it was a burglary/homicide. That was no surprise. But the second jarred me.

"The victim," the story read, "was registered at the motel under the name of Philip Carpenter of San Francisco."

5

"Good morning."

I looked up sharply. April, in robe and slippers, was standing at the breakfast bar, looking appealingly drowsy. She sensed my surprise and asked if anything was the matter.

"Who's Philip Carpenter?"

She looked puzzled. "I don't know."

"You never heard of him?"

"No."

"You're sure?"

"Yes." Her voice had an edge of irritation. "Why?"

I handed her the newspaper, pointing to the story. She read it and looked up, appearing even more jolted than I'd been.

"Why would he register under an assumed name?"

She said she didn't know.

"Why did he leave the Airport Hotel?"

She shook her head.

"Why did he think the two of you should go back to Seattle?"

She shook her head again.

"Because he was running and hiding," I said.

"That's crazy."

"Then how do you explain it?"

She didn't answer the question. She made an announcement. "I'm going to the police."

"No."

"Yes!" The word cracked like a whip. She turned to go. I grabbed her arm.

"Listen to me, Goddamn it!"

She flinched as if I'd slapped her. I held her arm, pointing to a stool at the bar, telling her to sit down. Her eyes were defiant for a moment, then she complied, and I said I'd make her some coffee.

While I reheated the water, I recounted my meeting with Checkers and the reasons he'd given for keeping her under wraps, away from possible danger. I said I'd disagreed with him, but after the phone call she'd received, I had to give Checkers the benefit of the doubt. Her fear had apparently been eroded by sleep. She returned to the argument of the night before—that if she didn't go to the police, they'd think she was hiding something and might be implicated in Bennett's murder. But if she went now, she said, and identified Carpenter as Bennett, the police would be convinced she had nothing to conceal.

"They'll find out who he is without your help. His fingerprints must be on file somewhere."

She drank her coffee, her mind obviously churning like a Mixmaster. Mine, in contrast, was as active as a waterwheel in the Sahara. But as I watched her across the silent kitchen, a faint light, the embryo of an idea, flickered in my cerebral murkiness. Mentally, I sauntered around it, considering it from several angles, satisfying myself it might work.

"Maybe we can have it both ways," I said.

I went into the den and called Estevan O'Shea. I knew he was an early riser. He sounded brighter than the sun. I made an appointment for eleven.

Estevan's offices were in the Ortega Building on Spring Street. Felipe Ortega, a flamboyant figure in the chronicles of Los Angeles, had built the four story building, a gem of brownstone and decorative ironwork, a cenotaph to an era of buggies, boaters, bustles, Big Red cars, and the Angel's Flight trolley, which lifted the city's commercial and professional sachems to Victorian mansions, decorative as circus wagons, sitting atop Bunker Hill. Spring Street was once called—with habitual Angeleno hyperbole—the Wall Street of the West. If it had been, it was no more. It had fallen on hard times as the financial community migrated across downtown, erecting soaring boxes, creating a perpendicular wasteland.

But the Ortega Building still stood, a seawall against the riptides of change. Estevan O'Shea's grandfather, an iconoclastic lawyer in the burgeoning pueblo, had purchased the building from Ortega, then passed it along to his son, Estevan's father, who was also a lawyer and a thorn in the side of the establishment. Now Estevan was the owner, ensconced in the same suite of offices his grandfather and father had occupied, practicing law with the same nonconformist flair, taking delight in tweaking the noses of the city's panjandrums. No lawyer in Los Angeles had been involved in more pro bono cases than Estevan. He was, in particular, the bête noire of the law enforcement agencies.

Estevan used the Spanish first name out of respect

for his Mexican mother's ancestry. I'd met him when he represented the parents of a young Black man who had died after being beaten by a patrolman named Arbuckle—nicknamed Fatty Too, a fitting cognomen. I'd worked with Arbuckle briefly during my rookie years and had to restrain him once to stop him from beating a Latino senseless. Estevan learned of the incident and asked me to be a witness for the plaintiffs, my testimony to show a pattern of violent behavior by Arbuckle. I agreed, and the jury awarded the young man's parents one million dollars. Arbuckle was subsequently convicted of second-degree murder and sent to Folsom. And my relationship with Estevan developed into friendship.

In his forties, Estevan was tall and lean, face craggy, hair graying. An impressive man. April told her story, from her decision to let Bennett try to establish contact with her grandfather to finding Bennett's body and the mysterious phone call of the night before, ending with the fact that Bennett registered at the Valley Crown Motel under the name of Philip Carpenter.

When she finished, Estevan said, "You believe your life is in danger from someone associated with Price Medford."

April looked at me, back to Estevan, and then nodded.

Estevan moved to a leather chair near the couch on which April and I were seated. "What do you want me to do?"

April looked at me. I said, "She wants you to go to the district attorney and tell him Carpenter is Paul Bennett and your client knew him. Tell him that even though she doesn't know who killed him or why, she has reason to believe her life is in danger, too, and she won't risk going public until she sees how the investigation develops because she doesn't believe the police will give her proper protection."

Estevan leaned back in his chair, looking thoughtfully out a window.

"Can you make that stick as privileged communication?"

Estevan nodded and smiled. "Fuller'll probably scream." He looked at April. "Myron Fuller's the district attorney," he explained, "and there's no love lost between us. But that's another story." He smiled and went on: "If Price Medford or someone around him is even remotely connected with Bennett's murder, Fuller'll be happy to keep a lid on the case to be sure no one kicks over the wrong rocks. Medford money still greases a lot of political wheels. He wouldn't want to cut himself off at the pockets." He returned to his desk, made some notes, then looked up. "Anything else?"

"That's it," I said, and April and I got up to go. Estevan moved to the door with us, and I asked what he knew about the law firm of Woodman and Associates.

"Why?"

"I found their phone number in Bennett's pocket."

"That figures if he was trying to get to Medford. Woodman's Medford's attorney. He was a member of Charley Lenox's law firm. He bought the firm when Charley retired about eight years ago and kept most of Lenox's clients, including Medford. Charley represented Medford for years. I knew his son in law school. We became friends, and I got to know Charley. He sold out to Woodman because his son didn't want to take over. He's back in Washington with the Justice Department."

"You know Woodman?"

Estevan shook his head. "Not personally. All I know about him is what I've heard."

"And what's that?"

"That he believes corners were made to be cut." He eyed me narrowly. "Are you thinking of trying to see him?"

I said I was—after Bennett's identity was established.

"Why?"

I told him April had asked Bennett if he'd seen Medford's lawyer, and he told her he'd tell her about it when he saw her. "I want to know if Bennett *did* see him. And if he did, what came of it. Did he tell April's grandfather that she'd like to meet him? And if he hasn't, will he?"

He gave me a small, sardonic smile and said: "From what little I know about Woodman, if Price Medford's made up his mind not to see Miss Tyson, he's not a man to broach the subject, much less try to change Medford's mind . . . unless he had something to gain. And in this case, I don't see what it would be." He paused, turning something over in his mind. "Charley Lenox was close to Medford. Maybe he still sees him. I don't know. But you'd do better to try him than Woodman."

"How do I get to him?"

Estevan considered the question and said, "Let me see what I can do."

As we left the Ortega Building, I asked April if she'd like to have a look at her grandfather's house. She didn't seem enthusiastic. I told her that since there was a chance she might own it some day, she should see what she'd be getting. Besides, it was on the way to lunch.

I ransomed the Volvo from the parking lot and drove the Hollywood Freeway to Vermont Avenue, took it across Los Feliz Boulevard, then turned in Medford Lane, a short, winding road tunneling under towering eucalyptus trees. It was deep in shadow, and I thought about what might've been waiting for April if she'd traveled it in the dark of the night.

The lane ended at a formidable wrought-iron gate inset in a high brick wall. I stopped at the gate and we looked past it, up a stone driveway and across an immaculately groomed lawn and flower bed to the house. It was large, starkly white with a red tile roof, simple, sharp edged, unadorned. An architectural anomaly when it was built early in the century, its style was timeless. It radiated comfort and warmth and, I thought, deserved a better fate than being the cloister for a misanthropic old man hiding from the world.

"It's beautiful," April said.

"Did your mother ever talk about it?"

"A few times."

"What did she say?"

She eyed the house appraisingly for a long moment. "She wasn't happy there. And she didn't believe her mother was either. My grandfather was a very strict man. She told me once she felt it was more of a jail than a home. She hated her father."

"But after you were born and your father left her, she wrote him, asking him to forgive her."

"I think she did it only because of me."

I wondered. But I let it pass and was about to drive

away when two men emerged from the house. One was a mastodon who appeared to be in his middle thirties. His hair and close-cropped beard were rust colored, and he wore Levis, a plaid shirt, and Western boots. The other was tall, heavyset, but his size was depreciated next to Rusty. Yet he was clearly the dominant of the two. He was impeccably dressed and groomed, the flawless drape of his suit making Brooks Brothers look like a bargain basement. In his sixties, with an impressive mane of white hair, he moved with the sure strides of a man never uncertain about his destination in life. He was vaguely familiar. A chauffeur exited the stretch limousine standing in the parking area and opened a rear door.

"Be right back," I said to April, left the Volvo, and moved closer to the gate. The limo was parked facing the house. Without being noticed, I was able to get close enough to the gate to make out the personalized rear license plate. It read "SOG1," and I knew the guy in the fifteen-hundred-dollar suit was Nicholas Bell, son of the late Cornelius Bell and his father's successor as pastor-general of the Soldiers of God.

Nicholas Bell's ministry, as his father's had been, was one of unyielding fundamentalism that admitted no deviation from a literal interpretation of the Scriptures. He inherited a large congregation and increased it many fold. The new Soldiers of God Temple, built by Nicholas to accommodate his burgeoning flock, looked as if it had been constructed from a mammoth Erector set. It covered five acres in the San Fernando Valley in the middle of another twenty-five acres of parkland. The structure was topped by a glass dome through which the faithful could view the Great Beyond where they would one day ascend if they but followed the gospel according to Nicholas Bell. It was said that as many as fifteen thousand gathered on Sunday to get the True Word from the reverend, preaching from a circular pulpit that revolved slowly counterclockwise, raising the specter of hell and damnation, not only in the hearts and minds of those assembled in the temple but also to multitudes across the country over radio and television. And on another revolving stage, a choir of one hundred men and women, clad in a vaguely military style, belted out the hymns so dear to the hearts of old-time religionists.

But the Reverend Bell was more than an interpreter of inerrant scripture. He was a right-wing political power broker, both respected and feared. As pastor-general with an unquestioning army under his command and unlimited money at his disposal, he could deliver an impressive number of votes and an important amount of money to virtually assure the election of any candidate upon whom he turned his approbative gaze. On the turbulent sea of politics, Preacher Bell walked on water.

I returned to the Volvo. April gave me an inquiring look, which I ignored. We drove off and halfway between the house and Vermont Avenue, I stopped the car in the middle of Medford Lane, angling it so it couldn't be passed.

"Why're you stopping?"

I held up a hand for patience. In the rearview mirror, I saw Bell's limo move through the gates. I left the car, standing beside it. The limo stopped. I went to it. The window beside the chauffeur whispered down and he gave me a prefab smile.

"Car trouble?"

I shook my head. "I want to speak to Reverend Bell."

The chauffeur's face was born again into a suspicious slab of concrete. He opened his mouth to say something, but the lowering of a tinted rear window stopped him and the pastor-general's face appeared, wearing a toasty warm smile.

"What is it, Walter?" His voice was deep, rich, commanding, not unlike the one that, I imagined, Moses heard on the Mount.

I went to the window. "My name's Cage. I'm representing April Tyson."

"April Tyson?" It was a rhetorical question. He knew the name.

"Mr. Medford's granddaughter."

He nodded, his smile a mite fidgety. "I know," he said, his creamy tone showing a trace of skim milk.

"She's waiting in my car," I said. "Would you like to meet her?"

I didn't wait for an answer. I returned to the Volvo and told April to come say hello to Reverend Bell. The name meant nothing to her, and when she asked who he was, I told her he was her grandfather's vicar, took her arm, and escorted her back to the limo. Bell had left the car and was waiting for us, looking as if he'd asked for guidance from above, had been heard, and was his own warm self again, oozing clerical benignity. When I introduced April, he took her hands in his and expressed his delight at meeting her.

"I knew your mother," he said, appraising her goatishly.

April mumbled something, and Bell, getting to the

reason why he'd been intercepted in Medford Lane, asked what he could do for her.

April looked at me.

"She'd like to meet her grandfather."

Bell nodded charitably. "I'm sure she would—"

He broke off. He didn't have to add the "but." His clouding face said it for him. April and I waited. He had dropped her hands. Now he retrieved one of them. "You're aware of the breach between your mother and grandfather, of course."

April nodded.

Bell wagged his head dolorously. "So long ago." He mourned for a moment and went on. "Your grandfather and I've been friends for many years. I thought if there was anyone who could heal that breach, I could. But he wouldn't relent. And after your mother's death, I never again brought up the question. Price is an extremely strong-willed man. Once he's set his mind, it's impossible to change it."

I said, "But if he knew she was in Los Angeles, that you'd met her, and the only reason she wants to see him is that he's the only relative she has, isn't it possible he might agree to a visit from her?"

Bell thought about it, then nodded tentatively. "Yes, it might. Let me try." He capped April's hand with his free one. "I'll call you in a day or two, my dear. Where can I reach you?"

"At my number," I said, taking a card from my wallet and giving it to him.

He put it in a pocket without looking at it. April thanked him for anything he could do to persuade her grandfather to see her, and we returned to the Volvo and drove off.

* * *

We went to Musso's on Hollywood Boulevard. The restaurant's been doing business at the same location since World War I, a time as remote in Angeleno minds as the Punic Wars. Musso's saw Hollywood flourish and decay, remaining one of the few places of quality in what has become a rookery for every variety of bird of prey. There's been much hand wringing about the putrefaction of Hollywood. But considering the worth of most of the industry's product for the screen and tube, it seems an appropriately shoddy Mecca.

April and I had a leisurely lunch, and I managed, with some prodding, to get her to talk about herself. It was a sketchy report but I learned that her mother left Seattle shortly after Alex Tyson pulled stakes. April was raised on the move as her mother drifted through the West, pausing to work at an assortment of jobs in Reno, Las Vegas, Phoenix, Tucson, Albuquerque. And other towns and cities April remembered only dimly or not at all.

"We'd stay a few months in a town, then move to another. When I was old enough to know my father just ran off and left us, I thought maybe she was looking for him. But she wasn't. She was looking for something. Or someone, I think. But it wasn't my father." She toyed with the food on her plate for a moment, her mind back somewhere on the long trail that had been her life.

"We wound up in San Francisco and sort of settled down. It was the first time I ever went to the same school for more than a few months. I finished high school and went to San Francisco State College for a little while. Then three, almost four years ago, mother went back to Seattle. I stayed in San Francisco. When she died, I went to there to bury her and decided to stay. I don't know why." She sipped her coffee and managed a small smile. "Now you know all about me."

But I didn't, of course.

6

On the way back to the marina, April was moodily silent. I let her out at the ground-floor entrance and put the Volvo in the basement garage. When I reached the apartment, April was out on the balcony, staring vacantly at the boats moving in the main channel. I asked what was on her mind.

She took a moment to reply. "I think I should go back to Seattle."

I accepted the statement with an equanimity that surprised me. But I was curious enough to ask why.

"I just do."

"Without seeing your grandfather?"

"I don't think he'll see me."

"You never know. The Reverend Bell might talk him into it."

"I don't think he has any intention of trying, do you?"

"There's only one way to find out."

"Well, if he has to *talk* him into it, I don't think I'd want to see him."

She just looked at me, her eyes reflecting uncertainty, and I realized why, on first sight, I hadn't been able to decide whether she was strong or vulnerable.

It was because, I sensed now, she was both—a confused spectator of a tug-of-war between the emotions. Or maybe I didn't know my ass from my earlobe about what was nagging her. Perhaps, I thought, her vacillation was the result of Bennett's murder and the implications of the phone call she'd received the night before. Just a transient frame of mind.

I left her on the balcony and went into the den. The message light burned on my answering machine. I pushed the "play" button. Frances' voice came off the tape, asking me to call. I picked up the phone to dial and saw the slip of paper from Bennett's jacket and remembered I hadn't received an answer from one of the numbers I'd called the night before. I dialed it instead.

"Import Bazaar," a woman's voice announced.

"Import Bazaar?"

I was taken aback at having reached this emporium of gimcrackery. I didn't know what to say. I thought about it.

"You still there?" the lady on the phone asked.

"Yes."

"What can I do for you?"

I said, "I'm trying to reach Duke Dekoven."

"I'll ring."

I waited a few seconds, and another feminine voice came on the line. "Mr. Dekoven's office."

"Mr. Dekoven, please."

"Who's calling?"

"My name's Cage. Mr. Dekoven doesn't know me, but tell him I'm calling about Paul Bennett."

I waited again. It was more than a few seconds this time. It was a few minutes. I put the time to use by trying to figure out what I was going to say about

Bennett if Dekoven came on the line. And then he did.

"Who's this?" he demanded.

"Mr. Dekoven?"

"Yeah." His voice was crisp, imperative, the flipside of the one he used as the aw-shucks pitchman on his television commercials.

"My name's Cage. I'm a private investigator with Checkers and Associates."

"Checkers? You work for him?"

I didn't quibble with "work for," feeling it wasn't the time to clarify my informal arrangement with Checkers. I asked if he knew him.

He uttered what might loosely be interpreted as a chuckle and said, "Doesn't everybody?"

I said yes, knowing the question was only a slight exaggeration.

"What about Paul Bennett?" he asked, sounding concerned.

"I'd rather not discuss it on the phone," I responded. "I'd like to see you."

"When?"

"Any time."

"It's about three-thirty."

I looked at my watch. He was right.

"Can you make it in about an hour?"

I said I could.

The general offices of the Import Bazaar were on the floor above one of its outlets on Van Nuys Boulevard. The outer office was a half-acre jungle of mercantilism populated by natives frantically striving to bail out from under a monsoon of paper. Typewriters clattered, computers crunched, adding machines rasped. I asked a lady, typing furiously at a front desk, where I could find Dekoven. She paused long enough in her assault on her vintage Selectric to wave in the direction of a far corner of the room. I picked my way through the canebrake of commerce to a harried-looking brunette at a desk in front of a door with Dekoven's name on it. I gave her my name and was whisked into Duke's office without being announced.

The office was small, stark, ablaze with fluorescent light. Dekoven was entrenched behind a formidable pile of paper on his desk. There were more stacks of paper on a table, two filing cabinets, and the floor. The office could've been mistaken for a recycling depot. Duke, camera ready in his checked pants and an aloha shirt as bright as a kleig light, stood behind his desk. He offered his hand. I took it. It was a salesman's handshake, hale and hearty.

He gestured to the other man in the office, seated in a captain's chair, his feet barely touching the floor. "You know Max Polo." It wasn't a question.

I knew Max Polo.

We'd met during the trial of Bobby Vicari, who'd been charged with second-degree murder in the beating death of a shopworn Sunset Strip call girl. Bobby was the fun-loving son of Luigi (Lug Wrench) Vicari, a retired Mafia capo. Old now and arthritic, he sat on the front bench in the courtroom every day of Bobby's trial, glaring malevolently at judge, jury, prosecuting attorney, and witnesses for the state. A story making the rounds was that ol' Lug Wrench would have the heads of those who were trying to put his son behind the walls. Given Lug Wrench's reputation as an icy mob enforcer, no one laughed too heartily at the unverifiable threat. If his infirmities made it unlikely he personally could extract lethal retribution, he had younger men to do his bidding.

I was one of the witnesses, and Max Polo was Bobby's attorney. His trial ended in a hung jury. There were whispers of jury tampering, and I felt they had some substance when the charge was bargained down to involuntary manslaughter just before the gavel was to hit the fan for trial number two. Maybe it was just the goodness of the DA's heart or maybe it was because some witnesses suddenly became scarce, but Bobby ended up with a suspended sentence and was told to go and sin no more. He kept half the bargain.

He went.

Polo, known among the legal cognoscenti as a barrister with more angles than a geometry book, was a short, frail man with stainless steel eyes set in a face so dirge-like it could've won him a season pass to the best funerals in town.

"Max happened to stop by," Dekoven said, "so I asked him to stay."

That was bullshit, of course, but I was gracious enough not to say so.

Dekoven waved at a chair. "Sit down."

I sat down.

"So you're working for Checkers, huh?"

"Right."

"How is he?"

"Fine."

"Heard he'd opened a detective agency. I met him . . . oh, ten years ago or more when a good friend of mine, George Harris, was found murdered in his car up on Mulholland Drive. Maybe you remember it."

I said I didn't.

"Ask Checkers about it sometime," he admonished. "Interesting case. Never was solved. I had a suspicion about who killed George and why. Told Checkers but . . ." he gestured resignedly, "he couldn't nail it down." He sat behind his desk. "You said something about Paul Bennett?"

I nodded.

"What about him?"

A very good question. Much better than Dekoven knew. I wasn't sure what I wanted. I improvised. "Bennett's in trouble," I said, without knowing why I'd said it since his troubles were over.

Dekoven's face shadowed. "What kind of trouble?"

I wasn't about to tell him Bennett was dead. He'd have to find that out when, through the good offices of Estevan and the district attorney, the police established "Carpenter's" true identity. "He's afraid someone wants to kill him," I replied, still not knowing where the words were coming from.

Dekoven raised his eyebrows. Polo continued to look at me as if he'd just buried a dear friend. "Why's he think that?" Dekoven asked.

"I was hoping you might give me some idea."

He replied with a look of bafflement.

"He was doing some legal work for you in Seattle, wasn't he?" I asked.

"Yeah, but it wasn't anything. Personal injury case. An old lady slipped on a wet spot on the floor in one of my stores up there. Fell and broke her hip. Sued us. Paul negotiated a settlement with her."

Then Polo spoke for the first time. "Have you and Checkers been retained by Mr. Bennett?"

He had me on the bite of the line with the question. To wiggle off, I had to lie or equivocate. I juggled the options for a few seconds, gave Polo an abbreviated smile, and lied.

"Yes."

"If he thinks his life's in danger, why doesn't he go to the police?"

"Because he doesn't have any solid evidence, and he's enough of a lawyer to know that without it there's nothing the police could do." I looked back at Dekoven. "Did you know Bennett was in Los Angeles?"

"Yeah . . . yeah, he phoned me a couple of days ago, and we had lunch together."

"Did he tell you why he was in town?"

Duke and Polo eyed each other in silent consultation.

"Yeah," Dekoven answered, "he said something about his lady. I can't remember her name . . ."

"April Tyson."

"Yeah . . . Paul said she's related to some rich old guy named Medford. Said something about trying to leverage some money outa him."

"Leverage how?"

Dekoven shrugged. "He didn't say, and I didn't ask."

Polo leaned forward in the captain's chair. "What's the point of this, Cage?"

Fortunately, I didn't have to answer because Dekoven said, "It's okay, Max." He looked at me. "There's something else. This woman . . . Miss Tyson . . . called me yesterday. Said Paul checked outa his hotel and asked me if I knew where he was." He frowned, his face showing as many wrinkles as a cheap pair of pants. "If Paul's in trouble . . . or thinks he is . . . I want to help. Do you know where he is?"

I said I did. And that was no lie.

"Where?"

I went back to lying. "I'm not at liberty to tell you."

"For Christ's sake," Dekoven growled, his patience turning sour. "Why not? I'm a friend of his."

I gestured helplessly and said I was sorry.

Dekoven's face became as grim as an open grave. He came to his feet, barking: "Then get the hell outa here!"

I got to my feet.

"Just a minute," Polo said.

I sat down.

"This Miss Tyson . . . does she know where Bennett is?"

I nodded.

"I'm thinking she might be more cooperative."

"She might."

"How can we get in touch with her?"

"I'll tell her you want to talk to her and let her phone you . . . if she wants to."

"What is this?" Dekoven yelled. "Whaddya come here for? It's been a fuckin' waste of time!"

Sensing I'd worn out my welcome, I thanked Dekoven and Polo for their time and left. As I made another safari across the frenetic outer office, down the stairs to the parking lot, and got into the Volvo, I reflected on the interview. I was pleased with it. I hadn't expected to get a jot or tittle of worthwhile information. But I'd been wrong. Dekoven and Polo inadvertently told me they both knew something neither would openly admit. "He was doing some legal work for you in Seattle, wasn't he?" I'd asked, and got the personal injury story in return—instead of a "Why don't you ask him yourself?"

Oh, yes, they knew something, all right—that Paul Bennett was dead.

7

April's voice stopped me as I entered the apartment. The bedroom door was open, and I heard her say with some irritation: "All right, Ross . . . all right, I'll stay."

With that, she hung up the bedroom extension. I closed the door quietly as she came out of the bedroom, saw me and stopped short.

"I didn't hear you come in," she said, her voice wavy with surprise.

Our eyes held.

"I've decided to stay."

"I heard."

She moved into the room, going to her favorite spot—the glass door to the balcony—and stood with her back to me.

"Who's Ross?" I asked.

"He's a friend," she said, adding with an over-the-shoulder glance at me, "*Just* a friend."

"Where?"

"Seattle."

"And he talked you into staying here?"

She hesitated. "Yes."

"Does he have a last name?"

"Newkirk."

"What's his stake in this?"

She turned back to me. "He hasn't any. Except as a friend. I met him when he was going with Mona."

"Who's Mona?"

"Mona Crane . . . She lived in the apartment next to my mother's. When mother died I took over the apartment, and Mona and I became friends."

"Is this the first time you've talked to Newkirk since you got here?"

She averted her eyes. "No, I phoned him after I found Paul at the motel. And last night after you left to see Mr. Checkers."

"Why didn't you mention him when we were talking about the people who knew you were in Los Angeles?"

"I didn't think of it."

I looked at her, disbelief showing.

"And because he doesn't care why I'm here," she flared.

"If he doesn't care, why did you call him?"

"You don't believe me."

"You're not making it easy."

"To hell with you!"

I don't think the conversation would've gone anywhere after that even if we hadn't been interrupted by the telephone. I went to the den to answer it, and Checkers' voice came out of the receiver like rolling thunder.

"Hiya, fella! How's it goin'?"

"Where're you calling from?"

"Home," he replied. "The damndest thing happened. Wait'll you hear."

I said I was listening, and he told me the insurance

company received a tip that a lady juror had once been a live-in friend of Moffitt. Checkers investigated the information and nailed it down. She had, indeed. The judge declared a mistrial.

"The court calendars're so jammed, God knows when they'll get around to another trial."

I was as interested in the Moffitt trial as I was in the weather forecast for Punxsatawney, Pennsylvania.

"I want to see you," I said. "I'll be right over."

"How's our client? . . . still around?" He sounded surprisingly relaxed about her health and whereabouts.

"Yeah."

"Did she go to the police?"

"No."

"Talked her out of it, huh?"

"No."

"Then what changed her mind?"

"I'll tell you when I see you," I said and hung up.

I knocked on the bedroom door. April opened it. I told her Checkers was back in town, I was going to see him, and she was welcome to come along. She declined.

"Have you changed your mind about changing your mind about going back to Seattle?"

"You think I'm rather . . . erratic, don't you?"

I didn't comment.

"Look," I said, "if you're planning to stay, will you try not to answer the door or the telephone?"

She made a small noise. I didn't know what it meant.

I first noticed the car in the rearview mirror when I reached the Marina Freeway. It was about fifty feet behind me in light traffic. Under the freeway's mercury lamps I made it out to be a Mercedes. I wouldn't have paid any attention to it if one of its two foglights hadn't been out. But when it followed me through the transition to the San Diego Freeway and kept adjusting to my varying speed, I was convinced it was following me. It'd be easy enough to shake such a conspicuous tail, but that would've left me only to speculate about who belonged to the car. I considered ways I could get a look at its license plates and remembered a parking garage in Westwood I frequently used. My idea might work. It was, at least, worth a try.

I took the Wilshire offramp, and the Mercedes followed, moving up closer as I drove Wilshire to Gayley. I dug a five dollar bill from my money clip and made a left turn onto Gayley, but a red light hung up the Mercedes. I thought my plan had died aborning. I couldn't pull over and wait for it without its driver suspecting I knew he was there. But luck smiled. A line of cars was waiting to enter the parking structure. I joined it, and two more cars pulled up behind me before the Mercedes could make the turn and hook up with the garage-bound caravan.

I gained the entrance and took a claim check from an automatic dispenser. The arm rose, and I entered the garage, drove half its length, then made a left turn to the only exit ramp. I gave the cashier at the booth my claim check and the five dollars, told her to keep the change, made a right turn into Lindbrook Avenue, and drove into a gas station next to the garage, parked behind the service bay, and went back to the exit ramp, taking up a position from which I couldn't be seen but from which I'd be able to read the license number of the Mercedes.

It took time for it to appear. The driver hadn't seen

me exit and apparently cruised the structure's several levels in search of the Volvo. The Mercedes was dark green and in need of a bath. It had tinted windows. I couldn't see into it. But it didn't matter. I read the license plate and watched as the car turned into Lindbrook, made another right onto Westwood Boulevard, and disappeared in the direction of Wilshire. I went back to the gas station, used the pay phone, called Checkers, telling what had happened and giving him the license number.

He said he'd check it.

I moved through the Japanese garden behind Ito's, crossing the small arched bridge over an ornamental pool, alive with koi, and climbed the outside stairs to Checkers' apartment. As soon as he pulled the door open, he said he had the registration of the Mercedes. And he looked bemused.

"You won't believe it . . . It's registered to Bobby Vicari."

He was wrong. I believed it.

Checkers had a drink waiting for him on the curved bar separating the kitchen from the living room. Except for the bedroom and bath, the apartment was a large open space. Its decor had a tweedy feel that complemented Checkers' linsey-woolsey personality. While he poured me a drink, I told him about my meeting with Dekoven and that Max Polo was present.

"You think Polo got Vicari to follow you for Dekoven, thinking you might lead him to Bennett?"

"No," I replied, "because Dekoven and Polo know Bennett's dead."

Checkers' eyes widened. "How do you know?"

"I asked Dekoven questions he should've known I

wouldn't have had to ask if Bennett was alive and I was in contact with him."

Checkers smiled. "That was real smart of you."

I told him I hadn't planned any such entrapment. That I'd just happened to ask the right question. But in any case, it was clear if Dekoven and Polo knew Bennett was dead they also must've known that he'd checked into the motel under an assumed name.

Checkers wasn't smitten with my theory. If Bennett hadn't been killed because he posed a threat to those in Medford's coterie, Checkers' hope of eventually pocketing a wad of the recluse's money was out the window.

"Dekoven could've found out some other way that Bennett was dead," he argued.

"How?"

"Bennett could've told Dekoven where he was. Or Dekoven could've had him followed. Either way, he could've known Bennett was registered at that motel under the name of Carpenter."

"Why would Dekoven have him followed?"

"How the hell should I know? For a lotta reasons that'd have nothing to do with having him killed."

"Then why hasn't he gone to the police and told them Carpenter is really Bennett?"

"I dunno," Checkers fretted.

"And why was Vicari following me?"

He finished his drink without responding, looking as if it'd been mixed with wormwood.

"Do you want to know?" I asked.

He grunted.

"He was following April."

"She wasn't in the car."

"Vicari didn't know that. Or couldn't have been

sure of it. In case she was, he wanted to see where I took her. Or if she wasn't, where I was going to meet her."

Checkers mixed himself another drink, and I told him about the phone call that sent April on her aborted trip to see her grandfather. The information seemed to cheer him up, breathing hope into the possibility that Medford minions, not Dekoven and Vicari, were the real villains of the piece.

"Is the lady sure it wasn't Medford?"

I said she was sure. And so was I. "Medford or anybody around him couldn't have known she was staying with me."

"The same goes for Dekoven."

"Maybe not," I said and told him April called Dekoven when she couldn't find Bennett. "She told him she hired you, and it wouldn't have been much of a jump for him to go from you to me with a phone call to Jasmine."

Knowing Jasmine was about as discreet as the *National Enquirer*, he didn't argue. "If he got a line on you, it don't make any difference how he got it. But I don't think he did. Why would he go after the Tyson woman even if he did have Bennett killed? You said yourself you don't think she knows why Bennett was killed."

"That was last night."

"Changed your mind?"

"I'm not sure."

"What the hell's that mean?"

I said it meant April hadn't been as up front with her information as I'd like. I mentioned her oscillating attitude about returning to Seattle and finding out about a man named Ross Newkirk to whom she'd made several phone calls, including one right after she'd found Bennett's body. So I'd begun to wonder how much more information she might be holding back.

"Then maybe we oughta have a sit-down with the young lady and get all the cards on the table."

On the way to my apartment, I reported my meeting with Estevan and the encounter with Reverend Bell. Checkers made a sour face.

"I saw Bell on television once. Never saw a used car salesman I wouldn't trust before I would him. Be a cold day in the hell he's always preaching about before you hear from him."

I didn't say April had expressed the same opinion more kindly.

And succinctly.

As I drove into the underground garage, I caught a glimpse of the car, parked at the front entrance to the building. I couldn't be sure it was Vicari's Mercedes. But it looked like it. I parked the Volvo and asked Checkers what he thought the odds were, one way or the other.

"Only one way to find out," he replied as we stepped into the elevator and rode it up only as far as the lobby. Within seconds we'd exited the building, moved around behind the car, and come at it from either side. Teamwork: we jerked the front doors open simultaneously, and Checkers rammed his gun in the driver's ear.

He wasn't Vicari.

"Out," Checkers rasped, grabbing the driver by the arm. He resisted, clutching at the steering wheel.

"Who're you? Whaddya want?"

"Leggo that steering wheel, asshole," came the response, Checkers giving him a glimpse of the replica of the LAPD shield he'd got at his retirement party. He always carried it. And it wasn't the first time he'd used it. "Y' want trouble, I just got a fresh supply."

The driver showed us his palms. "Awright! . . . Just take your fuckin' hands off me."

Checkers released him, and the driver exited the car. He was in the neighborhood of thirty with a chunky body and a face that'd been shaved but didn't look it. He was, or had been, a boxer. Scar tissue around his nose and mouth advertised the fact. He wore cords, a brown leather jacket, Nikes, and had enough hair for a family of four. Checkers ordered him to put this hands on the car and spread his legs.

"Willya tell me what the shit—"

Checkers cut him off. "Do it!"

He did it.

While Checkers patted him down, I dug into the glove compartment, coming up with the registration slip. I took it to Checkers, who'd relieved the driver of his wallet and was looking at his driver's license. We exchanged the two. The man's name was Alfred Massi. He still had his hands on the car. I told him to relax, and he lowered his arms, turned, glaring at us.

"The car's registered to Robert Vicari," I said. "What're you doing with it?"

"I'm his cousin. Bobby loaned it to me."

Checkers made a disbelieving noise.

"Call his wife. She'll tell ya."

"Why his wife?" I asked. "Why not Vicari?"

"He's outa town."

"Where's outa town?" Checkers demanded.

"That's none of your Goddamn business."

Checkers took a handful of Massi's leather jacket. "Wanna answer now or after I break your legs?" He threw Massi back against the car. "Talk, you son of a bitch!"

Massi eyed us speculatively. I guessed he wasn't a stranger to the law and was smelling something amiss about our behavior.

"What the hell's goin' on?"

"Where's Vicari?" Checkers demanded again.

"Call his wife and—"

Checkers stopped him. "I don't wanna talk to his wife. I wanna talk to you."

Massi surveyed us again, apparently trying to decide whether to call our bluff. He would've, I thought, if he was convinced we really were police. He'd have told us to charge him or get lost. But having decided we weren't the police, he wasn't going to take a chance we'd have no inhibitions about working him over for some reason he couldn't fathom.

"He's in Seattle," he said finally.

Checkers and I exchanged a look.

I asked, "What's he doing in Seattle?"

"I dunno . . . and that's the fuckin' truth."

"Why were you following me?"

"You?"

"The green Volvo."

His suspicion was confirmed. "You ain't heat."

Checkers told him to answer the question, or he'd spend the rest of his life wishing we had been.

"Bobby asked me to when I drove him to the airport. He didn't say why. All he tol' me was where ya live and ya drove a beat-up green Volvo and to follow ya an' see where ya went."

"And *who* went with me? A young lady, right?"

He gave me a reluctant nod.

"All right," I told him, "get out of here."

Checkers started to object, but I short-circuited him, reminding him we'd agreed this was my case. He grunted unhappily, and Massi got into the Mercedes, brought it to life, giving us the finger as he drove off.

"What's the matter with you?" Checkers grumbled. "We mighta got something more outa him."

I started for the apartment building. Checkers went with me, shaking his head in disgust.

"Y' know, sometimes I wonder why you ever wanted to be a cop."

I didn't tell him I'd wondered the same thing.

Often.

Checkers was at his Dutch Uncle best with April. She had, he told her, come to him, to us, to find Paul Bennett. But when Bennett called her, she went to him without letting us know. She found him dead. She spent several hours driving around before she called me. Then it looked as if she were in trouble and she professed not to know why—except to endorse the possibility that someone in her grandfather's coterie might be worried that she could derail some scam they had going for them. If that was all, he went on, okay. But if she knew some reason why anyone would've wanted Bennett out of the way and was now a threat to her, we wanted to hear it. And if she didn't want to tell us, she could damn well pick up her marbles and go play games with someone else.

April sat, tight lipped, stiff as a steel girder, not interrupting, and I thought Checkers' massive dose of verbal cascara might be the purgative needed to dissolve any obstruction to the truth.

"I suppose I have seemed rather . . . secretive," she said, her eyes lowered, her voice soft and repentant, "but I've been truthful." She looked at me. "I really didn't think it was important to tell you about Ross. He has absolutely nothing to do with what's happened. He's just a friend, and I wanted his opinion."

"That's what you're payin' *us* for," Checkers replied.

"I know."

"Okay." Checkers stood up. "Now is there anything else you've forgotten to tell us?"

She took a moment, then shook her head.

"There's a guy named Bobby Vicari," Checkers said. "His ol' man was a capo in the Mafia. He started out as a hit man and Bobby's a chip off the same toilet bowl. He had Tug followed tonight, probably thinkin' you was with him. Got any notion why?"

April shook her head.

"Well, he knows you're here, so we better find someplace else for you to stay."

April asked where. Checkers didn't know. I remembered Ito Kurado owned an apartment building in Santa Monica and suggested he might have a vacancy April could occupy temporarily. Checkers wanted to stash her someplace more remote. I thought of Frances. She owned a house in Newport Beach that she used sporadically, and I knew she'd offer it in a good cause. But that was the drawback. I didn't want to tell her the cause. But I might get around that, so I excused myself, went into the den, and called her.

"Where've you been?" she asked.

"Busy," I said and lied: "I just came in and got your message." I looked at my watch. It was close to nine. "Have you had dinner?"

"Yes."

"Would you like a drink?"

"I've had a drink."

"I want to talk to you."

"Talk away."

"May I come there?"

"Sure."

"I'll see you in about a half-hour."

"Are you bringing your toothbrush?"

"Not tonight."

"Why not?"

"I have work to do."

"All right," she said, "you can use mine if you change your mind."

I went back to Checkers and April, told them about Frances and her house in Newport Beach. April had no objection, but Checkers expressed reservations about involving an outsider in the situation. I said I shared his reluctance and told him Frances didn't have to know the whole truth about why we wanted the use of her beach house.

"What'll you tell her?" he asked.

I said I'd think of something.

Frances Alden lived in a condo on Wilshire Boulevard. Not one of those sleek, elongated wickiups where apartments went of a million or so per copy—unless one of the penthouses tickled your fancy and you had four or five mil to lay out for a roof over your head. Frances occupied the top floor of an older building. One of the few left that wasn't just another variation on how high and in what shapes steel girders could be stacked and concrete could be poured.

Frances was tall, willowy, hair the color of sable, her eyes as flashy as a flamenco. We'd met a few months before on a rainy night in Benedict Canyon. I was driving through it, and near the summit I saw a car with hazard lights flashing and a woman waving for help. I stopped, and the stranded lady said her car had run out of gas. I offered to get her to a gas station. She accepted without hesitation. As we drove, I cautioned her about accepting rides from strangers. Male strangers in particular.

She laughed lightly. "If you tried to rape me now, you'd drown."

That was Frances—blunt, sardonic, irreverent, flippantly tough. But it was mostly surface. Underneath, kept in a place that was hard to reach, she was generous and compassionate, yet constantly on guard against being emotionally hurt. She'd been burned by two failed marriages. When she talked about them—to me, at least—she was skimpy on details. But what came through with abundant clarity was her determination not to be bit by the same dog thrice. I didn't realize it then, but I fell in love with her the night I rescued her in Benedict Canyon.

A free and determined spirit, she tried to break into television as a writer after her second marriage collapsed. She didn't make it. Not because she couldn't write, which she couldn't. But lack of talent, after all, is of little concern to the self-anointed geniuses who manufacture the material that fills the time between commercials. She failed because she didn't understand that television was a huge copy machine and a frantic exercise in finding the lowest common denominator.

When she became privy to that fact and made peace with it, her path was ever upward until she became vice-president in charge of new programs for Proscenium Films, an independent production company.

Frances had a steak sandwich and salad waiting for me, having deduced from my invitation to dinner that I hadn't eaten. I gobbled it up while she reported on the latest horror stories from her office, a few tragic, most humorous, and others a deplorable mixture of the two.

"You said you wanted to talk," Frances said after I'd finished eating.

"I've been talking," I responded, still not sure how to launch the subject of borrowing her beach house for April.

"*I've* been talking. You've been uh-huhing."

I took the plunge: "I've got a problem."

Her smile broadened. Frances liked other people's problems.

"There's this woman . . ."

Her smile went away.

"She's a client," I said hastily. "Or, rather, she's Checkers' client. But I got stuck with her when he had to go to San Diego. He's back now but—"

"But?"

"Now we're both stuck."

Frances was patient with me. Elaborately so. She examined her fingernails. She sensed I was in trouble. And I was. I hadn't rehearsed the story I was going to give her. Indeed, I hadn't even settled on a story, much less practiced it.

"Her name's April Tyson," I went on, feeling my way from word to word.

"What's her problem?"

"Well, it's like this," I said and stopped again.

"Like what?"

"Well, she wants to . . . to divorce her husband, but he won't stand still for it. Wants her to come back to him. Keeps pestering her. Not that he's potentially violent," I added quickly. "Nothing like that."

"He's just a pest."

"Right."

"What does she want you and Checkers to do about it?"

"Persuade him to leave her alone."

"I didn't know private detectives did that sort of work."

"Well . . . usually we don't. But she doesn't know where the guy is, and she wants us to find him."

"She wants you to find him to persuade him to stop pestering her?"

"Right."

"If he's disappeared, how can he be pestering her?"

She had me for a second. "By phone. He calls her at all hours, but he never says where he's calling from."

"Oh," Frances said, appearing—justifiably—a bit perplexed. "What do you want me to do? Look around the apartment and see if he's hiding here?"

I chuckled.

"Then what do you want? You *do* want something, don't you?"

I waggled my head. "Mrs. Tyson's in . . . well, in a hell of a state. She needs rest, quiet, and I thought maybe you might let her stay at your place in Newport for a little while. It wouldn't be for long."

"Well, of course," Frances said, looking delighted.

I sighed with relief.

"When does she want to go?" Frances asked.

"Would tomorrow be too soon?"

"Of course not."

I thanked her again and went to her, drawing her close to kiss her. She held back.

"Just one more question," she said. "Are you planning to stay with her?"

I looked properly shocked. "Of course not!"

"Good."

I kissed her.

"Can't you stay?"

I considered it, finally putting temptation behind me. "Checkers is waiting for me at my place."

She smiled at me. "Well, before you go, you sweet son of a bitch, tell me what kind of trouble this woman is *really* in."

8

With the traffic, it was a little over an hour's drive from the marina to Newport Beach the next morning. It seemed longer. April was in a taciturn mood. I made two or three attempts at casual conversation only to have them self-destruct on the launching pad. I'm not a loquacious man, and I respect anyone's right to silence. But April's muteness had a brooding quality that bothered me. I began to wonder if Checkers' homily of the evening before had purged her of her secretiveness after all.

The first thing you get a whiff of when driving into Newport Beach isn't the Pacific Ocean. It's the pervasive smell of money. It blankets the town from the harbor to the hills, its presence verified by sleek yachts, expensive homes, toney shops, and costly restaurants with indifferent cuisine. Though highly touted as a recreation area, I found my occasional visits there a debilitating experience, being afflicted as I am with a financial inferiority complex.

Frances' house, modest by Newport standards, was at the end of the Balboa Peninsula. Ramona, her part-time housekeeper, met us. And although her greeting was as warm as a crackling log in a fireplace, it did little to thaw April's icicle attitude. Miss Alden had telephoned, Ramona reported, to say she would be coming to Newport the next day to have dinner with April and spend the night. That eased my conscience about taking leave of April as quickly as possible. I told her to call me any time, day or night, if she needed to and decamped.

Back in Los Angeles, I went to Checkers' office and received my usual greeting from Jasmine—a look as dark as a stormy night. I went to the door of Checkers' office. "He's on the phone," she barked. I blew her a kiss and continued on.

Checkers was putting the phone down as I entered.

"Get our client settled okay?"

"Yeah."

He went to a cooler, drawing a paper cup of water. "I've been thinking." He took the cup back to his desk, sat down, sipping it thoughtfully.

I waited.

"About Bobby Vicari going to Seattle. That ain't no coincidence."

I agreed.

"I called that car lot of his. Gave a phoney name. Asked for him. Some guy said he was outa town. I asked where. He said he didn't know." He finished his water, crumpled the paper cup, and threw it into his wastebasket. "I'd sure as hell'd like to know what he's doing there."

I knew what was coming. So I beat him to the punch: "And you'd like me to go there and find out."

"Right."

"No."

"Tug—"

"No."

"Will you listen, for Chrissakes?" he demanded. "Just listen?"

That's when I made my first mistake.

I listened.

"Look, whatever went down here didn't start here. It started in Seattle. That's where April decided to let Bennett try to contact her granddaddy. And that's where Bennett was working for Dekoven, doing whatever he was doing. Right?"

I conceded it was. And that was my second mistake.

"Then if you'd go up there and do some nosing around—"

"Why don't *you* go?"

"You told me this is your case, didn't ya? And besides, I gotta go to Fresno."

"Why?"

"You know the lumber yard fire there about a month ago? I told you about it. The Fresno fire department says it wasn't arson. Seaboard still thinks it was. The yard was losing money. The owner may've had it torched. But if Seaboard can't prove it, it's gonna be out a million bucks. So I gotta go up there."

Need I go on?

I returned to the marina and made a reservation with Alaska Airlines, packed a bag, and called Frances' office at Burbank Studios.

She came on the line brightly. "Hi! I talked to my house guest in Newport. I'm going down there tomorrow."

"Ramona told us."

"Would you like to see a showing of a Movie of the Week we made for ABC?"

"When?"

"Tonight."

I told her I'd be in Seattle and why.

"You don't know what you'll be missing."

"Tell me."

"It's about an older man who sleeps with a young woman, not knowing she's his bastard daughter. But the girl knows he's her father and she tells him after he's screwed her. It's her way of getting even with him for deserting her mother twenty years ago. She knows he's a religious stiff-neck and—"

"He commits suicide."

Frances laughed. "That's my boy . . . always looking for a happy ending."

It was raining when I landed in Seattle that afternoon and rented a car. It was raining when I checked into the Bayside Inn and was given a room with a view of Elliott Bay with a backdrop of the snow-crowned mountains of the Olympic Peninsula. It was raining when I got Bennett's office address from the phone book and walked to the nearby building. But it'd dwindled to a gossamer veil, and I found it invigorating.

I'd been in Seattle nearly fifteen years before, and it had seemed to me to be a city that accommodated people rather than forcing people to adjust to it. Now it had changed. The mania of the architect and developer for the platitudinous tower had struck there, too, creating anthills of steel and glass, turning people into scrambling aliens in their own land.

Bennett's office was, however, in an older building of modest size. A woman with a soda straw figure was standing at a window when I entered the reception room. At the sound of the door opening, she turned, using a handkerchief to dab at tear-stained eyes.

"Yes?" Her voice had tears in it, too.

I asked if she was Marian Neff and she nodded. She looked as if she'd have to look over her shoulder to see forty again. Her face was as thin as her body. She wore her brown hair short, and her print dress was slightly too long to be fashionable. Or maybe not. Styles change too often for me to keep up. I introduced myself as a private investigator from Los Angeles, working for April Tyson.

"For April? Does it have anything to do with Mr. Bennett's murder?"

"You know then?"

"I heard about it on the radio a couple of hours ago. I called the police here, and they said they'd had word from the Los Angeles police. They told me he'd been killed day before yesterday but that he'd checked into a motel under an assumed name, and they didn't identify him until this morning."

"That's right."

"Does April know?"

"She knows."

"It's awful. It's just . . . just awful. I can't believe it."

There was a catch in her voice and she turned to the window, snuffling back more tears. But I had the feeling they were shed more from convention than sorrow.

"Have the Seattle police been here to talk to you?"

She shook her head. I looked at my watch. It was a few minutes before five. I suggested that if she drank, she could probably use one, and she turned back to me, agreeing. She asked if I'd give her a few moments to fix her face. Thin as it was, it was a pleasant face and in need of only minor repair. She took a key and went out the door to the corridor, and I made a turn of the reception room and what had been Bennett's private office. Both were prosaic, furnished with a cut-rate version of Swedish modern. Equally inexpensive drapes hung at the windows. Bennett's desk held only a desk set and a telephone. There was nothing on it to give it the personal stamp of the man who'd used it.

Marian Neff and I went to a nearby cocktail lounge, and she drank white wine while I had a Jameson and soda, sipping it slowly. She was composed and needed no prompting to talk. For an opener, she asked how April was. I said she was doing pretty well under the circumstances, and Marian said she was glad to hear it.

"I really don't know her very well," she continued. "But I like her. Mr. Bennett brought her in when my son Marty was sick. He's only ten. He almost died of pneumonia. When he came home from the hospital, I just had to spend more time with him. So Mr. Bennett had April come in. I guess they were already living together." She flushed, thinking she'd made a faux pas. "Do you know that?"

I said, yes, April had told me.

"People're so open about it these days. I really don't think it's right. Being so open, I mean. I couldn't be. But then I don't think I could live with a man without being married to him. But if I did, I'd certainly would be more—" She stopped, searching for the word.

"Discreet," I said, thinking her dress wasn't the only thing about her that was dated.

"Yes."

She tasted her wine, eyeing me questioningly, finally asking me why I was in Seattle, and I said I had reason to believe April's life was in danger.

Marian sucked in a sharp breath. "Why?"

"We're not sure. Neither is April. It's somehow connected with Bennett's death but we're not sure how. So I came here to see if I could find a reason."

"Could it have anything to do with her being the granddaughter of that man down there . . . what's his name?"

"Price Medford . . . You know about that?"

"April told me."

"It might have," I said and asked if she knew Duke Dekoven.

"I know the name. Mr. Bennett handled a personal injury suit against the Import Bazaar."

"Did he do any other work for Dekoven?"

"Not while I worked for him."

"How long did you work for Bennett?"

"About eighteen months."

She finished her wine, and I ordered another round. Marian stared vacantly across the lounge, her mind clearly stirring some sort of brew. We didn't speak until the waitress returned with our drinks. She tasted hers and stole another moment of thought before she spoke.

"Do you know a lawyer in Los Angeles named Robert Vickers?"

I shuffled through my memory. I didn't find the name of Vickers. But from somewhere deep, where the subconscious remembers, I recalled that old Lug Wrench had used the AKA of Vickers when in the company of governors, mayors, senators, and other such VIPs, including an aging singer who apparently thought he'd been declared a national monument.

"Why?" I asked.

"He was in the office before I found out about Mr. Bennett. He said he was a lawyer from Los Angeles and was replacing Mr. Bennett as Mr. Dekoven's attorney. He wanted me to give him all our files relating to Mr. Dekoven, including a tape cassette of a conference Mr. Dekoven and Mr. Bennett'd had in Los Angeles. I said I didn't know about any cassette, and I couldn't release the files without Mr. Bennett's or Mr. Dekoven's permission. He told me to call Mr. Dekoven's office. I did. Mr. Dekoven came on the line and confirmed that Mr. Vickers was representing him."

"Did you give them to him?"

"No," she replied. "I said it'd take a day or two to get them together. But that wasn't the real reason. I had the feeling there was something wrong. April called the day before, worried about why Mr. Bennett had checked out of his hotel. Then he called, asking to speak to April. I told him she was in Los Angeles and where he could reach her. Then after Mr. Vickers came in this morning, I tried to phone Mr. Bennett, but the motel said he wasn't registered."

My estimation of Marian Neff jumped several notches for her caution. Her thin head still held an ample supply of brains. To be perfectly sure about what I was already perfectly sure about, I asked her to describe Lawyer Vickers. She said he was medium height, heavy set, black hair, somewhere in his thirties, and had a scar running from the left side of his mouth to the point of his chin. She asked if I recognized him. I said I did and told her who and what he was. She looked horrified. "What in the world does he have to do with Mr. Dekoven?"

"I don't know . . . Do you know if he's still in town?"

She shook her head. "I asked how I could get in touch with him. But he said he'd telephone me in the morning."

"And you don't know anything about a tape cassette?"

She shook her head.

"What's in Bennett's files on Dekoven other than the personal injury case?"

"Nothing."

"Then why would he go to the trouble of sending Vicari to get them?"

Marian thought about it. "After what you've told me, I have a feeling the story about the files was just an excuse."

"For what?"

"To find out where April is."

"Oh?"

"He asked if I knew how to get in touch with her. He said he'd met her with Mr. Bennett when he was in Seattle a couple of months ago. I told him she was in Los Angeles, but I didn't know where she was staying."

"And that was it?"

"Except he asked if I heard from her, he'd appreciate it if I'd let him know when he called back about the files. I asked if there was any message. Could I give her any idea what he wanted? He just kind of smiled and said no, and I thought he wanted to ask her for a date, go out with her. That he . . . you know."

I said I knew. I also said I hadn't eaten all day and would she have dinner with me. She gave it some wary consideration, perhaps speculating about *my* intentions but finally giving me the benefit of the doubt, going to the trouble of explaining she lived with her mother and there was no need to rush home to her son. That left me in doubt about the whereabouts of her husband, if any, and a little uneasy about *her* expectations for the evening.

We left the lounge. The rain had stopped, and on Marian's suggestion we walked to a nearby seafood restaurant that was short on ambiance and long on good food. I had Dungeness crab from Puget Sound, the King of the Crustaceans, in my opinion. Marian toyed with a filet of sole, leaving most of it, answering any question I had about why she appeared in an advanced stage of anorexia.

As we ate, I inquired where Bennett and April had lived, and she said he had a house in the Montlake district. When I asked if she knew how I could get a look inside the house without breaking in, she said Bennett had given her a key to use in case of an emergency when he and April were away.

"Where?"

"Reno, mostly. Sometimes they'd go to Las Vegas."

I asked if she thought Bennett's murder and the threat to April constituted an emergency. She looked hesitant.

"The police'll probably take a look at the house," I said, "and I'd like to beat them to it."

"Why?"

"Because they won't be looking for the same thing I will."

"What?"

"Something that might give me a hint of why

April's in danger. The Seattle police don't know she is, and they might overlook that something . . . if it's there."

She considered that. "Do you want to go tonight?"

"Will you lend me your key?"

"I'll go with you," she said.

I didn't argue.

The rain returned when we left the restaurant, so we took a cab back to the Bayside Inn. I picked up my rental car, and we drove to the Montlake district. On the way, I asked her to tell me what she knew about Bennett.

She gave me an apologetic smile. "I really don't know anything about him outside the office."

"What about his friends? Other lawyers? Anyone he knew?"

She shrugged.

"How about Ross Newkirk?"

She brightened. She knew him. Slightly. He'd been in the office a few times to talk to Bennett and April.

"April *and* Bennett?"

"Yes."

"Do you have any idea what they talked about?"

She said she didn't. But she knew Bennett wasn't representing Newkirk. If it had been a legal matter, she'd have known it. I asked her if she knew how to contact Newkirk, and she said she didn't unless his name was in April's address book on her desk in the office.

"Are you going to be there tomorrow?"

"I hadn't thought about it." Now she did. "Yes, I suppose I will. I don't know what's going to happen. I don't know who to talk to. Mr. Bennett had a sister in San Jose. Do you think she knows what's happened?"

I said I didn't.

"I wish I could talk to April. How can I telephone her?"

I hesitated. I didn't want to risk compromising April's refuge. I told Marian I'd call April and have her phone the office the next day. Then I reminded her that Vicari/Vickers said he was going to phone about Dekoven's file and I'd appreciate it if she'd be there to take the call.

"I don't know what to say to him."

I gave the problem brief consideration and replied, "Tell him he can pick up the files around three o'clock. And tell him you found the cassette he may have wanted."

She looked puzzled, disturbed. "But I can't give him the files if he isn't entitled to them. And besides, the police—"

"You won't have to give them to him," I interrupted.

"But he might—"

"I'll be in the office when he gets there," I said, adding, "if he shows up."

Bennett's house was on a dead-end street near the Arboretum. It stood dark, trying to imitate a Queen Anne cottage and giving a poor performance. I parked at the end of the street, two houses beyond Bennett's humbug cottage and turned off the headlights. The inkiness of the Arboretum loomed ahead. I asked Marian for the key. She dug into her purse and came up with it.

"You stay here."

I left the car and moved back toward Bennett's house, staying in the shadows of the huge maple trees lining the parkway, their branches almost touching those of their own kind across the street. The rain continued to fall. The Bennett house showed no light. I moved to a box elder, scanning the front of it from there, receiving nothing but tenebrous silence. I went to the small porch and carefully tried the door. It was locked. Using the key, I went inside, moving slowly, closing the door soundlessly behind me.

I waited inside the door until my eyes accommodated the darkness, then moved from the entry hall into the living room. I stood listening, hearing nothing. The room was large, meagerly furnished, dark and musty. An orphaned place. I crossed it to the dining room, which looked as if it'd never seen a square meal, and started for the swinging door to the kitchen but was stopped by a faint noise I couldn't identify. I returned to the living room and again stood listening. And again heard nothing. I went to a door on one side of a red brick fireplace. But I got no more than a quick glimpse of the room beyond before the half-opened door slammed against me, the force propelling me back into the living room. I hit a refectory table and grabbed it to keep from falling, tipping it, sending a vase crashing to the floor. Then the figure of a man appeared in the doorway. I heard a click and the blade of a switch knife snapped into place.

He was dressed in dark trousers, deck shoes, turtleneck sweater, and wore a watch cap. An improvised mask fashioned from what looked like a man's scarf covered his face from below the eyes. He was part of the darkness as he came toward me slowly, his knife poised, a bulky man moving on crepe-soled shoes. I backed away, circling the room, my eyes searching for something I could use to defend myself. He moved with me. We were two silhouettes on a slow, silent carousel. I saw what I wanted. A poker leaning against the fireplace. And he saw that I saw it.

"Uh-uh," he said, springing toward me. I twisted, sidestepped, and dived for the poker, snatching it up with an " 'uh-uh' my ass" just as he lunged again. I swung, catching him on the arm just above his knife hand. He dropped the weapon with a gutteral rasp of pain. I whipped the poker again, missed. He scooped up the knife and bolted for the entry hall. I scrambled after him, yelling something traditionally intelligent like "come back here, you sonofabitch," but he fled through the door into the night and the rain. I followed as far as the porch, breathing audibly and wiping the spit from my lips with the back of my hand and watched until he was lost from sight, a shadow swallowed by shadows. A moment later I heard the motor of an unseen car come to life.

I went back into the house, found light switches and snapped them, crossing to the room from which the man had emerged. It could've passed under any of several names—den, study, office, studio, rec room—and all of them a misnomer. It held a desk, a swivel chair, a ping-pong table pushed into a corner, two nondescript arm chairs, and stereo equipment with a few records and tapes. The shelf of records was undisturbed, but the one holding the tapes was in disarray, each cassette apparently having been examined. I looked them over. The labels indicated they held rock music of one persuasion or another.

I returned to the living room, going to the fireplace. The mantel held photographs of April and Bennett. I opened and closed the drawers of two side tables. Both were empty. I made a turn of the rest of the house. The kitchen, too, had obviously been searched, as had the two bedrooms, their closets, bedside table, and large chest. The drawers in the latter had been dumped, and clothing—a man's and woman's—had been thrown on the bed. But there was no clue to what the knifer'd been after—except for the scattered cassettes. And the house showed no sign of forced entry. The knifer had entered with a key.

Bennett's key?

I left the house and went back to the car. Marian was unaware of what had gone on inside, and I left it that way, telling her only I'd found nothing useful. I drove her home, an apartment building in the University district, waited until the apartment house door closed behind her, then drove off.

It was still raining.

Back at the Bayside Lodge, I called Newport Beach and was taken aback when Frances answered.

"What're you doing there?"

"Talking to you."

"What about the film you invited me to see?"

"We postponed the running. The network is as bad as you are. It wants a happy ending, too."

"How do you get a happy ending to a picture about incest and illegitimacy?"

"The network thinks the father goes off to a monastery, and the daughter gets an abortion."

"An abortion? Her father got her *pregnant*?"

"Sure. At the end, when she's mocking him, she says she isn't going to have a son or daughter but an uncle or aunt. Didn't I tell you?"

"Thankfully, no."

"Well, we'll come up with something. We always do. How's the weather up there?"

I told her it was raining and it was a welcome change from all the California sunshine and she said it was raining there, too. I said she was a damn liar and she laughed again and said she and April were sitting on the patio watching the boats passing in the channel, drinking B&B and getting acquainted.

"How's her frame of mind?" I asked.

"Subdued," she reported tactfully. "Want to talk to her?"

"Do you think I called to talk to you?"

"Of course not," she replied. "You didn't reverse the charges."

"Call April."

"Ape-RILLL!" she bellowed and told me to give her love to my web-footed friends, then April came on the phone.

"What're you doing in Seattle?" She said it with the same tone she might've used if she'd caught me in her bedroom inspecting her lingerie.

I told her I was trying to find out what Bobby Vicari was up to and that he'd appeared in Bennett's office using a phony name and posing as a lawyer representing Dekoven, asking Marian for Bennett's files on Dekoven.

"Did she give them to him?" Her voice was indifferent.

I said no, and she asked if Marian knew about Bennett. I said she did.

"Did you tell her?"

"She heard it on the radio."

"How'd she take it?"

"With a respectable amount of tears. But she's up in the air about what to do about the office and wants to talk to you."

"What makes her think I know what to do about it?"

I ignored the question. "I told her I'd call and ask you to get in touch with her. You take it from there."

"Anything else?"

"Yeah . . . Someone searched Bennett's house. Do you have any idea what he was looking for?"

"No."

"The only thing I could see that he might've been interested in was the cassettes in the den."

"Cassettes?"

"Tape cassettes."

"Why would he be interested in them?"

"Vicari told Marian he wanted one Bennett'd made of a conversation with Dekoven in Seattle. Do you know anything about it?"

"No."

"Well, another thing Vicari wants is a line on your whereabouts. So keep your ass covered."

She didn't respond, so I said good night and went down to the hotel bar. When the bartender asked what I was drinking, I ordered a Scotch and water, then changed my mind.

"Make it a B&B."

9

The next morning the sun was out, and the air was as crisp as a just-ripe melon. I walked to Pioneer Square for breakfast. The square was once Seattle's skidrow, home to the city's wine-soaked, whiskey-warped drifters. It was a moving—or staggering—target for developers until the city stepped in to start restoring the area, saving its nineteenth-century buildings. One slice of Seattle's heritage had been rescued from the wrecking-ball, wielded—as always—in the name of progress.

After a leisurely breakfast, I used a pay phone to call Bennett's office. Marian reported that the answering service had no messages from Vicari/Vickers. She'd checked April's address book and told me where I could find Ross Newkirk.

The address was a houseboat moorage on Lake Union. Newkirk's was one of two boats at the end of the dock. I went aboard, but my knock brought no response. I started back toward the street. A man was coming toward me. He was somewhere in his thirties, a rugged looking guy wearing faded blue jeans, deck shoes with a lot of miles on them, a heavy plaid work shirt, and a Greek captain's hat that'd aged with his footwear.

"Who're you looking for?" he asked as we came abreast on the walkway.

"Ross Newkirk."

"You got him."

I started to introduce myself, but it wasn't necessary.

"You're Cage."

"April called you."

"Last night. Said you might be coming around." His face clouded. "Is she in the trouble she says she is?"

"What kind of trouble did she say she's in?"

An elderly, gray-haired woman exited the houseboat opposite Newkirk's carrying a sprinkling can, exchanged pleasant hellos with him, and started watering flowers in boxes on the deck railings. Newkirk gestured to me, and I followed him into his house. His living room was a vague replica of a captain's cabin on an old freighter. It was surprisingly neat. Newkirk apparently was a place-for-everything-and-everything-in-its-place sort of fellow. The trait of a seaman. He asked me if I'd like a beer. I accepted and followed him into the kitchen. He took bottles from the refrigerator, uncapped them, led the way back into the living room, and waved at a cracked and peeling leather couch. He sat in a chair, facing me.

"She called me night before last," Newkirk said, "and told me Paul Bennett'd been murdered and later someone pretending to be her grandfather called her and asked her to come see him. She said she was on her way when she realized it couldn't have been Medford, so it must've been somebody wanting to get her out in the open."

"And what did you tell her?"

He drank some beer and said, "I didn't say much of anything." He shrugged. "What could I say? I just told her to take it easy. Be careful. She'd called me earlier in the day to tell me she couldn't find Paul and she'd hired a private detective named Checkers. And when she called night before last, she said you worked for the guy and she was staying in your apartment."

"She's been running up quite a phone bill talking to you."

He grinned and drank more beer.

"She called you yesterday evening, too."

"Right."

"And said she wanted to come back to Seattle."

"Right."

"But you talked her out of it."

"Right."

"Why?"

"Why not?" He finished his beer with another gulp. "I figure if someone is after her for some reason, she'd be better off with you and your boss protecting her than she'd be back here." He got up and went back to the kitchen and kept on talking from there. "And I have to tell you, I don't think she's in as much trouble as she thinks she is. Or that you and your boss believe she is. That call from Medford could've been legit." He came out of the kitchen with a fresh bottle of beer. "Sure, April says he didn't know where to call her. But a guy with the kind of money Medford's got has ways of finding out things." He eyed me curiously. "What're you doing in town, Cage? You didn't come here just to talk to me."

"Didn't April tell you?"

"Tell me what?"

"That Bennett's murder might've had nothing to do with April trying to put the arm on Medford."

"Aw, come on, that's not fair."

"What isn't fair?"

"Putting it like that. Saying April wants to put the arm on the old guy."

I said she'd admitted she wouldn't turn down any Medford money if it was offered to her.

"That's a helluva lot different from you saying she's trying to shake him down."

"All right," I conceded, "but that's beside the point."

"Then what're you getting at?"

"Bennett was representing a man named Dekoven."

"Paul told me."

"Did he tell you Dekoven's kind of tight with the mob in Los Angeles?"

"No."

"Well, he is. I don't know how tight, but he's close enough to have a thug named Bobby Vicari come to Seattle to find out if April came back here. Or if she didn't, where she is."

"Why the hell would Dekoven care about April?"

"I was hoping you could tell me."

"Why don't you ask April?"

"I have."

"And?"

"And she says she doesn't know. But I have a feeling she isn't telling the truth."

Newkirk had been as cool as a meat locker and I'd wondered if it was his personality or if he'd been putting on a front. I got an answer. He came to his feet, body tensing, expression hardening.

"Who the fuck're you working for?" he demanded.

I stood up. "April."

"You sure as shit don't sound like it." He took a couple of steps toward me. "I'm gonna to tell you something. April's a great girl. An honest girl. She's a friend. A damn good friend. And nobody's coming in here and dumping on her, understand?"

"I understand," I said, "but there's one thing you should get clear."

"You'd better go."

I counted on his belligerence being as much of a facade as his composure had been and continued. "Checkers and I can't do a damn thing for her unless she's frank with us. And I . . ."

"I said you'd better—"

". . . don't think she is. Now she's told me she respects your opinion. If she does, call her and tell her she isn't doing herself any good by not telling us everything she knows."

He took another step toward me, making fists of his hands. "Get out! I'm telling you for the last time!"

"I hope so," I said.

I drove to Bennett's office, weighing the implications of Newkirk's abrupt change of attitude. He didn't impress me as one given to such an explosive display of gallantry in defense of a friend's veracity. I wondered if his relationship with April was closer than either admitted. If so, why was April living with Bennett rather than Newkirk? The question prompted a review of what she'd told me about how she met each man. Newkirk had been a friend of Mona Crane. As for Bennett, she said she'd met him eighteen months ago but hadn't said how or where. But chronologically, she knew Newkirk before she did Bennett. I wondered if there was any significance in that when an unbidden question, coming from nowhere, crossed my mind. Could Newkirk have been in Los Angeles when Bennett was killed?

April said she'd telephoned him after she found Bennett dead. Did she say that against the possibility that Newkirk, somewhere along the line, might need an alibi for his whereabouts when Bennett was murdered? Except for being troubled by April's evasiveness and a suspicion there was more to her relationship to Newkirk than she'd admitted, I had no reason to believe she was covering for him, so I dropped the idea. But there was a problem with that.

It bounced.

It was noon when I got to Bennett's office. Marian had heard nothing from Vicari/Vickers. She was at her desk, picking at a salad from the building coffee shop. She asked if she could order me something. I said no thanks and went into Bennett's office and punched up an outside line to call Jasmine and try to wrestle a Fresno telephone number for Checkers out of her. Doc Hooper answered, coughing and wheezing.

"Hello, Doc."

"Who's this?"

He'd got into the sauce a little early today. "Tug," I said.

"Tug?"

"Tug Cage."

"Oh."

"Is Jasmine there?"

"Jasmine?"

"Is she there?"

"Why?"

"I wanted to get Checkers' phone number in Fresno."

"Fresno?"

"Yeah."

"I'll ask him."

A moment later, Checkers' voice thundered. "Hallo, Tug!"

"You made short work of that Fresno arson case," I said.

"Arson case?" he asked, then remembered and stammered around for a moment. "Oh, that fell out. Seaboard changed its mind. Decided to pay off the claim."

He was lying, of course. He'd invented the story to con me into coming to Seattle. But I wasn't surprised. The tactic was vintage Checkers.

"Where you calling from?"

I told him.

"What're you doing there?"

I said I was probably wasting my time waiting for Bobby Vicari to show up.

"If he knows Bennett's been identified, he won't show. My guess is he's back in L.A. by now. Maybe you oughta come on home."

"I just got here," I replied and told him about the knifer I'd encountered in Bennett's house.

"Whaddya suppose he was doing there?"

Before I could answer, the office door opened, and Marian looked in.

"He's on the phone," she whispered.

I told Checkers I'd call him back.

"Do you still want me to tell him he can pick up the files?"

"And the tape cassette."

"But I haven't found any cassette."

I smiled. "So lie a little."

I followed her into the reception room.

"Mr. Vickers?" she said into the phone. "I'll have the file ready in about an hour. And I found a tape cassette in Mr. Bennett's desk. I don't know what's on it, but it might be the one you mentioned . . . yes . . . yes, that'll be fine." She put the phone down. "He'll be here about one." She was more than a little nervous.

I went to her. "Why don't you leave now?"

She looked startled by the suggestion. "Oh, I couldn't."

"I think you should."

"If you're expecting trouble . . ." Her voice drifted off.

"I'm not," I said, not knowing what I expected. But given Bobby Vicari's pyrotechnic disposition, I was sure he wouldn't take kindly to having been suckered. "I just think it'd be better if you weren't here."

She hesitated, then agreed. "Will you call me when he's left?"

I said I would, and she gathered up a raincoat, umbrella, and her purse and went to the door. "Be careful," she said.

"Sure."

"And you *will* call?"

I said I would.

She left. I made a turn of the office, stopping at a lineup of steel filing cabinets along a wall, located the Ds and opened the drawer, found Dekoven's file, and sat at Marian's desk, looking through it.

There were a number of letters from Bennett to

Dekoven, all routine correspondence about the personal injury suit. Marian was right. The file contained nothing Dekoven wouldn't have already known. It seemed more likely that the file was just a smoke screen and what Vicari was really after was the whereabouts of April. And if Dekoven was so desperate to find her, April must know why. It just wasn't credible that she wouldn't.

And yet there had to be more to Vicari's visit to Seattle than locating April. There was some connection between the guy in Bennett's house and Vicari. What had he been looking for? He'd asked Marian about a cassette of a conversation between Dekoven and Bennett. And I'd interrupted the knife wielder—Vicari? —as he was examining the cassettes in Bennett's house. What was so important about the Dekoven-Bennett conversation? And why the urgency about finding April?

I replaced the file and made an idle turn of the office, stopping at the other desk in the reception room. It was April's. There was a loose-leaf address book on it, showing age and wear. It contained surprisingly few names, addresses, and telephone numbers, all in the Seattle area, and most of them were of commercial establishments—a beauty salon, an auto repair shop, a bank, the gas, light, and telephone companies. Under the Cs, there was only one listing. It was the name of Mona Crane, the ladyfriend of Ross Newkirk. There was no address. Only a phone number. With nothing better to do at the moment, I dialed it.

A man's voice answered. "The Jury Box."

It was a bar. I could hear voices, laughter, music —a jukebox playing a melancholy ballad from the Fifties. I asked for Mona Crane.

For a long moment there was nothing but the background music and hubbub. Then the man at the other end of the line said, "Mona?" His voice was a croak of surprise. And something more. Guarded.

"Is she there?"

"Who is this?"

I started to give my name, but something—I had no idea what it was—stopped me. Instead, I said, "A friend of hers from out of town. If she isn't there, could you tell me where I can reach her?"

The man took another time-out. I heard some more music and laughter punctuated by a voice calling someone named Larry, asking for another round. It was Larry who was on the phone with me. I heard him call "Coming!" to the customer, then he said to me: "Gimme your name and number, and I'll have her call." He sounded urgent, challenging.

"I'll call back."

"Wait!" Larry said quickly.

I waited.

"She'll be in about six."

I said thanks, hung up, and left the desk, wandering into the private office, thinking about Larry. My call had upset him. I looked up the Jury Box in the phone directory. It wasn't listed. I tried information. It said it had no listing, and I remembered a short story I'd once read—a haunting tale about a man who'd made an innocent phone call and was connected with the past, hearing the rumble of Manhattan's Sixth Avenue elevated, which had been demolished years before, and speaking to a friend long dead. The feeling of unreality I was experiencing was broken by the sound of the door in the reception room opening and closing. It was twelve-thirty.

Vicari was early.

Only it wasn't Vicari. It was a kid in his early twenties, with an acne-marked face. He wore an old leather jacket, old dungarees, old motorcycle boots, and a new baseball cap. I asked what I could do for him, and he said he was from the Dispatch Messenger Service to pick up an envelope for a Robert Vickers. I gaped at him, mentally kicking myself for not considering the possibility that Vicari, whether he suspected anything or not, would send for the file rather than appear in person after Bennett's real identity had been made public.

"I don't know anything about it," I said. "The secretary's left for the day. If you'll wait a minute, I'll see if I can find it."

" 'Kay," the messenger replied.

Stalling for time, I went back into the private office. I looked through the desk drawers and found a handful of blank paper and some large manila envelopes. I stuck the paper into an envelope, wrote the name of Robert Vickers on it, sealed it and went back to the messenger. He was looking through a magazine called *Jurisprudence*, undoubtedly puzzled by the absence of a centerfold.

"Found it," I announced.

" 'Kay." He took the envelope and started for the door.

"Just a minute."

He looked back.

"Where're you delivering to Mr. Vickers?"

He extracted an order pad from a pocket, consulted it, and said, "Madison House."

"What room number?"

"Suite six-oh-six."

I held out a ten-dollar bill. "You take this. I'll deliver the envelope."

"Can't do that."

"Why not?"

He thought about it. " 'Cause I can't. Got this order. Mr. Vickers gotta sign for it."

"What if you hadn't found anybody here to give you the envelope? What would you have done?"

He thought about that, too. "Gone back to the office and tol' 'em."

"Mr. Vickers is a friend of mine. I want to play a little joke on him." I waved the ten. "How about it?"

He deliberated—if that's the word for what was going on in his gummy mind—for a moment, then shrugged.

" 'Kay."

The Madison House had already qualified as an historic landmark, yet it was still one of the city's most distinguished hotels, succeeding in incorporating modern amenities without sacrificing its Edwardian ambience. I crossed the large, opulent lobby to one of its birdcage elevators, now operated by an elderly, white-haired man who pushed buttons instead of moving a lever. On the sixth floor, I walked along a corridor wide enough to accommodate a Greyhound bus and pulled a bell cord. Chimes sounded in 606, and a man's voice came through the door, asking who was there.

"Messenger service," I called.

The door opened to reveal Bobby Vicari. He wore a silk robe and was in his bare feet. And under the robe, bare everything else as far as I could determine. He recognized me.

"What the shit?"

I asked if I could come in.

"What the fuck're you doing here? What d'you want?"

"I want to talk to you."

He started to close the door. I put a hand against it.

"It won't take long."

He glared at me, then relented, stepped back.

An ambrosial blonde, as well endowed as the Ford Foundation, was standing by a divan in the sitting room. She, too, had on a silk robe and, quite obviously, was wearing nothing more than a professional smile. Vicari told her to leave us alone, and she went into the bedroom, closing the door behind her, a slow, undulating exit as subtle as a thumb in your eye. When she was gone, Vicari turned to me. It'd been seven years since I'd last seen him. His hair, the color of coal, now had a few strands of gray in it, and a small circle of it on the top of his head had disappeared completely. His youthful muscles were rapidly turning into middle-age flab. His face was bloated and his nose, which was too big for him to begin with, appeared to have put on weight. And so had his large mouth with thick lips. Only the scar on his chin hadn't changed. Seeing him, my mind darted back to Bennett's inky living room the night before. In broad outline, Vicari and the knife wielder were of a pattern.

"Been a long time," Vicari said, sounding as if forever would've still been too soon.

"I didn't think you'd remember me, Bobby."

"How could I forget a lying bastard like you?"

Need I say he was being provocative? I smiled, not rising to the bait.

"Well, whaddya want to talk about?"

"April Tyson."

He managed, just barely, to look blank. "Who?"

"Come on, Bobby, let's cut the bullshit. Paul Bennett's girlfriend."

"Who's Paul Bennett?"

"He was Duke Dekoven's attorney until he was murdered."

"So?"

"And he was the guy whose house was searched last night by someone packing a knife. I've been wondering if it was the same man who stuck Bennett."

His gaze didn't waver. "You're not making any sense at all, y' know." He picked out a cigar from a box on a table and shucked the wrapper. "What's this got to do with me?"

"You *do* know Dekoven, don't you?"

"I've seen him on TV is all."

"Max Polo's his lawyer, too."

"That so?" He put the flame from a gold lighter to the cigar and laid down a smoke screen that stunk up the room, big as it was. "I ain't seen Max lately." Something that might've been taken for a smile touched his meaty lips. "He sure made an asshole outa you at my trial, didn't he?"

"Since he kept you out of prison, I guess you could say he did." I lighted a cigarette as a defense against the mephitic cigar fumes. I thought about asking about the tape cassette and why he wanted it if both Bennett and Dekoven were strangers. But I knew it would do no good. So instead I said, "I met a cousin of yours night before last in Los Angeles."

"Yeah?"

"Alfred Massi."

Vicari's eyes went on the defensive.

"He'd been following me in your car. He said you'd told him to tail me."

"Why the hell'd I want him to follow you?"

"That brings us back to April Tyson. Massi said you wanted to know if she was with me and if she was, where I took her. Or if she wasn't, where I met her."

"That's a pile of shit and I've heard enough of your crap. Get the fuck out."

I was hearing variations on that theme a lot lately. From Dekoven, then Newkirk, now Vicari. But I wasn't ready to leave. I said, "You're looking for April Tyson. And I know it has something to do with Bennett's murder. I don't know what. And I don't much give a damn. But I'm telling you . . . knock it off. Leave April Tyson alone, or I'll personally burn your ass and love every minute of it."

Big talk. Tough talk.

Vicari's face had turned as red as a traffic light. He dropped his cigar into an ashtray and came at me, grabbing a fistful of my jacket, yelling: "Get outa here, or I'll break your fuckin' neck."

I thought of using my knee—my good one—on his crotch but opted for my cigarette instead. I jammed it against his hand, grinding it in. He howled and released my jacket. I backed off. He lunged at me. I tipped over a straight-back chair, Vicari got tangled up in it, lost his balance, sprawled on the floor, and the blonde came out of the bedroom wearing nothing but black panties.

"What's going on?"

"Get back in there!" Vicari roared at her, and she

retreated. Still on the floor, he fixed raging eyes on me, cradling his hand, wincing in pain as he climbed to his feet.

"Out!"

Back at the hotel, I had a drink at the bar, feeling ambivalent about the confrontation with Vicari. I tried to tell myself it wasn't a complete waste of time. Letting him know I was aware he was after April might make him back off. I didn't find myself particularly persuasive.

I ordered another drink and asked the bartender if he knew where the Jury Box was located. He did, telling me I could find it across James Street from the county courthouse, and I was relieved to hear it wasn't in another dimension.

The Jury Box was out of the Fifties, faded but mellow. Walls of photographs of resolute-looking men in judicial garb and of yellowed clips of newspaper headlines and reports of criminal trials tried to justify its name. The lunch hour was waning. The jukebox was silent. I went to the bar. There were two men behind it. I ordered a beer from the younger of them and asked if he was Larry. He jerked a thumb toward his partner. I took my beer to him. He looked to be in his fifties. A solemn face showed boredom and, I imagined, the sadness of past hurts. Or unfulfilled longings.

"Larry?"

He looked up.

"I called earlier about Mona Crane."

He stiffened, eyes narrowing.

I looked around the lounge. "Is she here?"

"You don't see her, do you?"

I smiled apologetically. "I wouldn't know her if I did."

"Then why—"

He broke off as a man came to the bar and sat one stool away from me. Larry told his colleague he was taking a break, came from behind the bar, motioned at an isolated table, and I followed him to it. He lit a cigarette, inhaled deeply, and said, "If you don't know her, why'd you call?"

"April Tyson mentioned her name. She said they'd been neighbors. I wanted to talk to her about Ross Newkirk. I understand they went together."

"Yeah."

"Did you know April Tyson?"

Larry nodded. "Didn't she tell you what happened to Mona?"

"No," I answered. "What happened?"

He stubbed out his cigarette and stared at the butt, bitterly thoughtful. "She disappeared. Been three months now. Just vanished. Took some of her clothes and was gone. Not a word to anyone."

"April didn't tell me," I said. And thought: among other things.

He didn't hear me. He was somewhere else. "But I don't believe it. I think she's dead."

"Why?"

"I don't know. I just do." He looked at me. "When you called, I thought maybe you might be some kook and it was your way of getting it off." He lit another cigarette. "I even thought maybe you could be the guy who killed her."

"You think she was murdered?"

"I said I don't know. Nobody does for sure. But I think so."

"And what if you thought I'd been the guy who did it?"

"I would've played you along and called the cops." He took in a lungful of smoke, blew it toward the ceiling, then put his eyes back on me. "Who the hell are you?"

I told him I was a private investigator from Los Angeles and why I was in Seattle, holding nothing back, then asked, "Did you talk to April after Mona took off?"

"She didn't take off," Larry insisted.

"Did you talk to April?"

A shake of his head. "I called her a couple of times. Left messages. But she didn't call back."

"How about Ross Newkirk?"

"He was in two, three times after Mona disappeared. He was pretty shook up, but he said he didn't think anything had happened to her, that she'd sometimes talked about leaving Seattle. About going to Los Angeles, mostly."

"Did she ever talk to you about leaving Seattle?"

"No."

"Then why was Newkirk so shaken?"

"He said he'd asked her to marry him and she said she would. They were going to tie the knot after he got back from a trip to Alaska."

"Had Mona ever said anything about getting married?"

"No." He put out the second cigarette, giving me a long, assessing look. Maybe he read the question in my eyes. "You're wondering why I should give a damn about Mona. You're thinking I was in love with her. That maybe she *did* tell me she was going to marry Newkirk and I—"

He stopped with a bitter smile and a shake of his head.

I sipped my beer.

"I liked Mona. I own half of this place. Mona was good for business. Maybe that's why I liked her. Or maybe because she reminded me a little bit of Ginny. My daughter. She was killed in an automobile accident about five years ago. She'd've been about Mona's age."

"Did the police investigate her disappearance?"

"They went through some motions and finally told me there wasn't anything to investigate. Said people pick up and leave all the time without saying goodbye, kiss my ass, or anything."

We sat in silence, Larry's mind foraging around somewhere in the past. I finished my beer, and Larry asked if I wanted another. I said I did. He motioned to a waitress, and I asked if I could buy him something and he said he didn't drink.

"Maybe I'm wrong about what happened to Mona," he said after my beer came. "But I can't get over the feeling I have. There's so damn many loonies running around nowadays, raping and killing. Just the other day they found a woman's skeleton across the lake near Kirkland. Her head'd been bashed in, and all her teeth'd been knocked out. Police say it was to keep her from being identified from dental charts. I've been wondering if it was Mona."

He fired up another smoke and got to his feet, saying he had to get back to work. I thanked him for talking to me, he went back behind the bar, and I left the Jury Box.

And my beer.

* * *

I strolled Pioneer Square with my mind full of Vicari, Newkirk, and Larry Simmons. And Mona Crane and the fact that April hadn't mentioned her disappearance. I went back to the hotel and had an early dinner, sitting at a window table, looking out at the bay and the long twilight.

After dinner, I went to the desk and asked if there were any messages. There was one. From Marian. I called her from my room, and her phone rang just once before she picked it up. Her voice was raspy, febrile.

"I have to see you!"

"What's the matter?"

"Please! Right away!" She sounded on the edge of hysteria.

I told her I was on my way, and a half hour later I rang her doorbell and she asked who it was from behind the closed door. I told her, a lock snapped, and she opened the door on the night chain before admitting me. Her thin face was ashy. She was trembling. She closed the door behind me, snapping the dead bolt. The living room was tastelessly furnished, everything in it old. Faded, threadbare. She sank down on the edge of a sofa and looked at me with flat, listless eyes.

"What is it?" I asked.

She shivered. "I had a phone call right after I got home. It was a man. He asked me about April. About where she was. I told him I didn't know. He said I was lying and if I didn't tell him, something would happen to Marty. He said he might start to school some morning and never come home. That I'd . . . I'd never see him again. Never know what happened to him. He told me to think it over. That he'd call back. He did. About ten minutes later."

Tears came to the surface, overflowed, and she buried her face in her hands. I went to the couch and sat beside her, putting an arm around her skimpy waist, urging her to go on. She raised her head, wiping away tears with the back of a hand, staring at the wall across the room. She swallowed hard and groaned.

"I told him."

"Told him what?"

"Where April is."

My stomach knotted. "How do you know where she is?"

"She called me this afternoon. She told me to close the office and have all the furniture and files put into storage. And she asked me to call Mr. Bennett's sister in San Jose and ask her to claim Mr. Bennett's body. Then she told me she was staying in Newport Beach with a woman named Frances Alden."

"Oh, shit!"

"I'm sorry," Marian cried.

"It's not your fault."

"I was so frightened. And he said if I was lying to him, that Marty'd be—" She broke off and buried her face in her hands again.

I looked around the room, spotted the telephone, went to it, and dialed Frances' Newport number. The phone rang and rang and rang. But no answer. I broke the connection and dialed Checkers. He answered.

"How are ya, fella?"

"Not so good," I said and told him why.

"Jesus Christ!" he grumbled. "Look, I'll keep calling Newport until I get hold of her."

"Screw that," I told him. "You get down there and get April and Frances away."

"Now wait a minute. I don't think—"

"I don't give a damn what you think!"

"Okay, okay."

"Then get going!"

I hung up and spent fifteen minutes trying to reassure Marian that everything would be all right. I didn't succeed. That wasn't surprising. I hadn't convinced myself, either.

When I got back in the hotel, I phoned Newport Beach and Frances' condo in Westwood again, coming up empty. I slumped into a chair, watching the ferryboats as they moved across Elliott Bay, thinking of Vicari —the kinds of thoughts that made Heinrich Himmler the man he was. After a millennium or two, the phone rang. It was Checkers.

"You in Newport?"

"Yeah."

No, it wasn't Checkers. Not the blustery, bombastic Checkers I knew. His voice was just a few rungs above a whisper. I knew something was wrong. I said, "Something's wrong."

"Yeah."

"Was April—"

He cut me off. "No. I don't know where she is. She's missing."

"Missing? What the hell's going on there?"

"Your girl friend—"

He stopped.

"What about her?"

"She was hit by a car."

"What?"

"Hit and run. The son of a bitch tried to get both April and Frances when they crossed a street to a restaurant. Must've been following 'em. He missed April and hit Frances."

I didn't say anything. I couldn't.

"She's dead, Tug," Checkers said and the world imploded, collapsing in on itself.

10

The next week was an incorporeal time. I can't recall it in much detail. It's mostly impressions. But there's one thing I remember doing after Checkers announced Frances' death. I went looking for Vicari. I went to suite 606 in the Madison House and hammered on the door. When no one answered, I tried to kick it down. House security grabbed me and threatened to make a citizen's arrest if I didn't leave quietly. I met them halfway. I left. On the way out, I was told "Mr. Vickers" had checked out. I knew it was a lie.

Until I found out it wasn't.

I went back to the Bayside and spent the rest of the night getting drunk. Full of guilt, remorse, and eighty-proof sauce, I returned to Los Angeles the next day. Checkers met me at LAX. And driving to the Marina, he—I vaguely recall—reported that the Newport Beach Police were at Frances' house when he arrived there. They were treating her death as a hit-and-run accident and were disinterested in the identity of her companion. In fact, from the confused reports they'd received at the scene, they weren't sure there was another woman with Frances. Checkers told them he was an acquaintance of Miss Alden, had been driving through town, and decided to stop by her house and say hello. And to further protect April from police attention, he'd managed to spirit her luggage from the house.

At the marina, Checkers invited himself into the apartment and launched into a monologue, speculating that it was Vicari who'd threatened Marian and then relayed the information she gave them to someone in Los Angeles in time for the driver of the car to locate Frances' house, see April and Frances leave, follow them to the restaurant, and—since he probably didn't know which woman he was after—tried to kill them both as they were crossing the street.

Checkers finished his drink and poured another. "But that sounds like a lot to have happen in five, six hours, don't it?"

Even in my sottish condition, I knew he was getting back to his favorite scenario that the people around Price Medford represented as much of a threat to April as did Dekoven and Vicari. Indeed, more of a threat. I was sick of the subject. I exploded.

"Jesus Christ! Frances is dead and all you're worried about is keeping April hidden so you can be there with your wallet open if she gets any Medford money."

I poured myself a drink from a bottle of Jameson on the coffee table. "April's gone. And I don't give a damn. I don't want to see her again. She's all yours . . . if she comes back."

"She'll be back."

"You think so?"

"I *know* it," Checkers said confidently. "She wants her shot at Grandpappy's bucks." He looked museful.

Then: "You might be right, though. Maybe Medford's crew ain't done nothing but sit tight. Maybe Bennett was killed for some other reason. But I'll tell you something. The police ain't gonna bust their balls finding who killed him. If they happen to stumble across something, fine. If they don't, fuck it."

"I don't give a shit about Bennett," I snarled. "I don't want any more to do with this goddamn business."

"What about Frances? If you think Vicari was after April when Frances was killed, wouldn't you like to get some evidence on the bastard that'd bury him?"

I just looked at him. He was as out of focus as a cut-rate camera. He finished his drink, got to his feet, told me to get some sleep and think about it. He left. I didn't think about it. And I didn't sleep.

I passed out.

I came to halfway through the morning, hanging like a wet flag. My head felt as if it had spent the night inside a foundry. I needed some hair of the dog. But the dog was gone, taking his hair with him. I considered having a steaming cup of coffee instead, but the thought of it made my stomach rise and fall like the tide. The phone rang, and every nerve in my body jangled with it. It was Checkers. He'd obviously done some more drinking after he'd left me. He sounded in as bad shape as I.

"Got any booze?" he whispered plaintively.

I told him I was about to embark on an errand of mercy, and he said he'd be right over. I went into the bathroom and looked at myself in the mirror. It wasn't an inspiring sight. My face had the color of old vomit. I needed a shave. I needed a shower. My shirt was rumpled. My jacket and slacks looked as if they'd spent a month stuffed in a cigar box. But I wasn't up to undertaking a personal reclamation project of such magnitude. My favorite spirits merchant would have to accept me as I was.

I bought a fifth of Jameson for Checkers and one for myself, went to my car in the parking lot, broke open my bottle, and surreptitiously administered first aid. And after I'd driven into the underground garage and parked, I partook of more sustenance from the brown bag survival kit. I felt better. I even dared to predict that I was going to live—a mood soon shattered.

The first I knew of the man was while I was waiting for the elevator, clutching the bag holding the two bottles of Jameson. I felt something hard jam into my back, and a voice commanded:

"Don't move."

I didn't move.

The elevator arrived and the doors opened as a car entered the garage. The man with the gun gave it a quick glance while admonishing me to keep quiet. But feeling I had a constitutional right to know who he was and what he wanted, I asked.

"Shut up," he replied, shoving me into the elevator. He jabbed the button for my floor. I wondered melodramatically if the elevator was taking me for my last ride.

He was dressed in a black suit and probably had said goodbye to fifty two or three years before. His mousy hair had long ago started to desert him. His face was as distinguished as a dollar bill. The revolver in his hand was the most personable thing about him. Without it, he could have lost himself in a phone booth. With it, he commanded my qualmish, undivided attention.

"Where is she?"

"Where's who?"

"You know who I'm talking about."

"Remind me."

The elevator reached my floor, the doors parted, and we went down the hallway to my apartment. I'd forgotten to lock the door. We went inside, Mr. Cypher—as I now thought of him—closed the door behind us and ordered me to sit down. I went to the divan, perching on the edge of it, putting the bagged bottles of Jameson beside me.

"April Tyson," he said.

I forced a smile. "Now that wasn't hard, was it?"

He still didn't like my little jokes. His face clouded and took on a hint of personality. "Where is she?"

"Why do you want to know? You a friend of hers?"

He crossed the room, standing over me. "I asked a question."

So did I: "Who're you working for? Bobby Vicari?"

He didn't bat an eye. But what he did was, he brought the .32 a few inches closer to my head, causing me to recall an old aphorism that there's no herb to cure death. I asked hopefully: "Putting a bullet in my head isn't going to get you an answer, is it?"

He shook his head slightly in a way that wasn't entirely reassuring.

"I don't know where she is," I said.

"I think you're lying."

"That's your problem."

"You're wrong," he said. And with that, his gun collided with the side of my head.

The pain exploded with the force of several megatons. I heard bells, chimes, and sundry other noises that I couldn't identify. Mr. Cypher, I saw blearily, raised his hand to strike again. I knew I had to do something to avoid another blow. But I couldn't. The pain was a straight jacket. Even my hangover hurt. I think I managed to raise a feeble arm. I'm not sure. But I do remember the front door banging open and a voice, sounding as if it came from somewhere in the vicinity of Pismo Beach, ordering:

"Don't do it."

Mr. Cypher spun and froze. I looked past him with watery eyes to see Checkers in the doorway, his leviathanesque revolver ready to put a period to Mr. Cypher's breathing.

Checkers indicated a chair. "Throw the gun on it."

Mr. Cypher was no one's fool. He threw the gun on it.

Checkers closed the door and moved into the living room, circling around to me.

"You okay?"

I must've wagged my head affirmatively because he handed me a handkerchief and asked if I was well enough to stop bleeding to death. While I staunched the flow of blood, Checkers ordered my visitor to hand over his wallet. He did.

Checkers said, "Now get the hell outa here."

Mr. Cypher looked appropriately baffled. I was just as stunned. I struggled to my feet, yelling at Checkers:

"What the hell're you doing?"

Checkers ignored me, growling at Mr. Cypher: "G'wan! Beat it!"

The man went to the door in reverse, apparently skittish about getting a bullet in the back. I took a couple of uncertain steps to try to stop him, but Checkers blocked my path and Mr. Cypher bolted from the room. Checkers went to the door and watched him disappear.

"Why'd you let him go?!" I roared.

Checkers closed the door and stuck his revolver under his waistband and told me I'd better sit down before I fell down.

"Why?" I demanded again. "He's after April! He may've been driving that car last night! He might've killed Frances!"

Checkers came to me, taking my arm. "Sit down."

I jerked my arm away, stumbled, and managed to catch myself in time to drop into a chair.

"Goddamn you and your Goddamn games. I'm fed up with—"

I didn't finish because Checkers'd left the room. He reappeared a moment later with a towel and damp wash cloth. He came to me, carefully mopped away the blood, and inspected the cut on the side of my head.

"Ain't as bad as I thought," he said, "but maybe we'd better have a doctor look at it."

"I don't need a doctor. I need a drink."

He didn't quarrel with that. He took the brown bag into the kitchen and came back with two tumblers of Jameson on the rocks. We drank, then I asked how he knew to come roaring into the apartment with his gun in hand.

"I saw you with that bastard at the elevator when

I drove into the garage. Didn't smell right. So I took the gun from the glove compartment . . ." he patted the artillery under his belt ". . . just in case and come to see what was going down."

I raised my glass. "Here's to coincidence."

He chuckled and drank.

But I wasn't mollified. I again demanded to know why he'd let the son of a bitch go.

He took Mr. Cypher's wallet out of a pocket, gave it to me, and watched me examine its contents. They included three hundred dollars in cash, a driver's license, and several credit cards. The name on them was Harry Lassen. The license bore a Laurel Canyon address.

"Harry Lassen, right?" Checkers asked.

"You know him?"

"I recognized him."

"He didn't seem to recognize you."

"No reason why he should. We never met. I saw him a coupla times, once in the lobby of the Roosevelt Hotel. The guy I was with pointed him out to me. Told me about him. Then I saw him again about a year later at Santa Anita." He had more of his drink. "That was a long time ago."

"Who is he and what is he?" I asked.

"A mechanic. No ties to anybody. Strictly freelance."

"Hired killers use guns, not cars."

Checkers shrugged. "No law says they can't use a car if it's handy." The shadow of a smile crossed his face. "Maybe he isn't working for Dekoven and Vicari."

"We'd have found out if you hadn't let him walk out of here."

Checkers looked at me disgustedly. "You know, if I didn't know you weren't as stupid as you sound sometimes, I wouldn't walk across the room to spit on you if you was on fire. Look, Harry Lassen's been around for ten, maybe fifteen years. Christ only knows how many people he's snuffed. But nobody's laid a glove on him. So what if we turned him over to the cops? You know what he's gonna do? Call in some smart lawyer, have him arrange bail, and be back on the street in time for supper."

"He's back on the street now," I said, "so what did we gain by letting him walk away? If the cops'd had a run at him, maybe they'd have got something out of him."

He looked at me with profound disgust. "How many times do I have to tell you? People don't pay us to yell for the police. They could do that themselves. The cops're competition. Why give away our business? It's like the old saying . . . Macey's don't tell Gimbel's.

"And if you wanna know what we gained, I'll tell you." He held up a forefinger that looked as if it'd be helped by a month at a fat farm. "One, if he was driving the car, whoever he's working for knows he blew it. April got away, right? So now he braces you, thinking he can make you tell him where she is, and if he gets arrested, his client knows he messed up again. Now that doesn't do his reputation one bit of good. The word's gonna get out that Harry Lassen's a fuckup. That he ain't got it any more. But this way, he can tell his client he couldn't find you, but he'll catch up with you and make you talk. So he's still got the contract on April."

His corpulent middle finger stood up. "And that brings us to two. Lassen's walking around as free as the stink from a garbage dump, and we tail him and maybe he takes us to Dekoven. Or to someone who's snuggled up to Medford." He finished off his Jameson. "Think about it."

I did. It made some sort of shifty eyed sense. But I had one objection to his scheme. I asked who was going to tail Lassen. Since he knew us, he might spot us.

Checkers had an answer for that, too. We'd use Wilbur Stump. "Shit, the kid ain't doin' nothing else. The closest he's come to a courtroom was when he hadda pay a parking ticket. Besides, I've had to lend him the money to pay his share of the rent and Jasmine's salary the last coupla months. He owes me. And the fresh air'll do him good."

In my opinion, Wilbur couldn't follow the Rose Parade. But I didn't say anything. It didn't matter. I didn't care.

Or so I thought.

After failing to talk me into having more drinks and some lunch at Ito's, Checkers left. The anesthetic effect of the Jameson had relieved the throbbing in my head. I had a bump behind my right ear from Lassen's blow, but the small cut had stopped bleeding. I was sobering up. I wasn't sure I wanted to because I couldn't keep Frances out of my mind, visualizing the car—with Lassen at the wheel—bearing down on her, hitting her, killing her. I poured myself more Jameson, but I didn't drink it, a wave of guilt and disgust cresting over me. I took what was left in the glass and the fifth into the kitchen and dumped it down the drain. Then I showered, shaved, and put on fresh clothes and called the Checkers-Stuckey-Hooper office. Jasmine answered, of course.

"This is Tug."

"Checkers isn't in."

"I want to talk to Wilbur."

"Wilbur?" She sounded incredulous. "Wilbur Stuckey?"

"How many other Wilbur's have you got there?"

"But why?"

"It's none of your damn business!" I yelled. "Put him on!"

She did and I asked him if Checkers had been in touch with him.

"What about?"

"Doing some surveillance work."

"Surveillance work?" he asked bewilderedly. "Why would he ask me to do—"

"Never mind why," I interrupted. "When he does, tell him I said I'd do it myself."

The address on Lassen's driver's license was a house on the back side of Laurel Canyon. The front of it clung to the brink of a steep ravine. The rest of the house was cantilevered over it, suspended a couple hundred feet or more in the air. It looked like a great place to live if you were contemplating suicide. I drove past it. There was a dowdy looking Buick in the carport. I parked a short distance from the house and settled down to wait. I turned on the radio and listened to the rest of the world's troubles for about a half hour before Lassen came out of his airborne abode carrying a leather tote bag and drove off in the Buick. I followed him to Laurel Canyon Boulevard, into the Valley, then to a restaurant called the Beefeater on Riverside Drive. He left his car with a parking attendant and went inside. I parked on the street and debated whether or not to risk following him in. I flipped an imaginary coin to decide.

I lost.

The Beefeater was one of those restaurants whose monthly electric bill probably nudged all of two figures. I groped my way across the foyer and stood behind a huge cactus plant while my eyes adjusted to the darkness. I finally saw Lassen sitting in a booth with a woman. She sat facing me, a handsome woman who, I judged, was on the far side of thirty. She was smiling. It was a nice smile, and their conversation seemed easy, casual. There were empty booths on both sides of them, but there was no way I could get into one without being seen.

I went back outside, climbed into the Volvo, turned on the radio, and listened to a talk show hosted by a lady psychiatrist who diagnosed—and solved—the emotional problems of ten callers in the forty-five minutes before Lassen and the lady came out. They talked, holding hands, until her car—a middle-aged Chevy—was delivered. I couldn't see the license number from where I was parked. Lassen took her in his arms, kissed her, and they parted reluctantly.

When Lassen redeemed the Buick, I followed. He took the Ventura Freeway to the interchange with the San Diego Freeway, moved through the cloverleaf, and headed south. There was an optimum amount of traffic. Not enough for Lassen to get lost in it. Not too little that I couldn't be part of the pack. He turned off at Century Boulevard, drove toward the airport, and put his car in a satellite parking lot, taking a shuttle bus to terminal. Checkers had been wrong. Lassen wasn't going to lead us to anybody.

He was gone.

The telephone was ringing when I entered my apartment. It was Jasmine.

"Mr. Cage?"

"He isn't in."

But before I could hang up, Checkers came on the line. "Where the hell you been?"

"Didn't Wilbur give you my message?"

"That's why I'm calling."

I told him what had happened, and we shared thirty seconds of silence.

"You think he took off?"

I said I didn't think he'd carried his lunch to LAX in a tote bag to spend the day watching the planes take off and land.

"Guess he took off because he wasn't sure we wouldn't sic the dogs on him," Checkers said mopishly.

I let another few seconds of dead air reply to that.

"Whaddya think?"

"It's after five," I answered. "I'm through thinking for the day."

The next two days were no better than the last two had been. With one difference. I went through them sober. I had a call from Frances' secretary. She said Frances' brother from Connecticut had arranged for his sister's body to be flown to Hartford for burial. She also told me Frances' friends and co-workers at Proscenium Productions were holding a memorial service the following evening. Would I come? I said I would. But it was a lie. I'd already said goodbye to Frances, oafishly self-pitying though my farewell had been.

I gave little thought to April. Or where she had gone. To Seattle, maybe. And, I was sure, Checkers and I would never see her again. It was one of my less depressing thoughts.

It was mid-morning the next day when Estevan O'Shea's secretary called me. She said Estevan was out of town and had asked her to give me a message to call Charles Lenox. She gave me the number. I dialed it and the voice that responded was weak, thready.

"Mr. Lenox?" I asked.

"Yes."

I told him who I was.

"Estevan O'Shea's friend? The private detective?"

I confirmed that and asked if I could see him.

It was a moment before he said, "Could you make it this afternoon?"

I said I could and he gave me his address.

The Lenox home in Pasadena was a low-slung, deceptively spacious house of wood construction, a gem of craftsmanship still admirable more than a half-century after being built. It hunkered down in a small forest of trees, Monterey pines predominant. I parked in a circular driveway, went up on the porch, and rang the bell. The door was opened by a Latino woman somewhere in her fifties. She was pleasant looking and squeaky neat in a starched, white uniform. She smiled as she asked if I was Mr. Cage.

I confessed.

"Mr. Lenox is expecting you," she said, standing aside so I could enter. She closed the door and I followed her along a large entrance hall and across an airy, contented living room to double doors. She rapped once and opened them.

"Mr. Cage," she announced softly.

I entered, and Lenox came to the door to greet me, extending a thin, mottled hand.

"Come in, Mr. Cage."

Lenox was somewhere over seventy, a tall, thin man with porcelain-like skin, his long face topped by a lean crop of white hair. His eyes, quick and darting, sized me up over half-glasses perched precariously on the end of his nose. He wore an elderly cardigan over baggy khaki pants, and his feet were stuffed into carpet slippers. He gestured at a leather chair and invited me to sit down. I sank into the chair, its leather soft as velvet. The room was large and consolatory, one grown restfully mellow with years of quiet, peaceful living. Three walls held shelves of books climbing to the raftered ceiling. Lenox sat in a matching chair, facing me across a low table cluttered with books, magazines, and papers, coming right to the point:

"What do you want from me, Mr. Cage?"

"How much did Estevan tell you?"

His hands kneaded the arms of his chair. "He said he was representing an April Tyson and had seen documents confirming she is Price Medford's granddaughter. He also said the lawyer who'd been representing her had been found murdered in a motel at which he'd registered under an assumed name. And someone purporting to be Price had telephoned Miss Tyson, asking her to come see him in an apparent attempt to lure her from your apartment. I told Estevan the idea that Price'd made that call was absurd."

Lenox pushed his glasses up to the bridge of his nose with a forefinger and stared at me challengingly as though waiting for me to argue. I didn't. Instead, I inquired if Estevan had asked if he could persuade Mr. Medford to see his granddaughter.

"Yes."

"Can you?"

"No."

I shifted in my chair, not knowing where to go from there except to apologize for bothering him and take my leave. Lenox sensed my discomfiture and put me at ease by asking if I'd care for a drink.

I didn't, but I said I would.

He rose and went to a small bar. I went with him. He asked me what I wanted, I told him, and he poured me a Scotch and water.

"I haven't seen Price since I retired eight years ago," he said, pouring himself a sherry. "Or spoken to him by telephone in the last six or more. Before that, our relationship was quite close, that of friends as well as lawyer and client."

We went back to our chairs. Lenox peered pensively into his sherry before sipping it and then for another moment after he did. "Price was always a reclusive man. He had few friends. And none of the friendships lasted . . . except that with Nicholas Bell." A flash of dislike crossed his face. "You know who he is, I assume."

I nodded, saying nothing about my brief meeting with him.

"Before I became his lawyer, Price named Bell the

trustee of his estate, giving him complete authority over the management of his financial interests. I always dealt with Bell. Seldom with Price. And when I did, he was totally disinterested. He always behaved as if the wealth he'd inherited was a cross to bear."

"How did you get along with Bell?"

He was noncommittal. "As Price's attorney, I had to deal with him, and I did. It was only late in our relationship that—"

He stopped for a moment of reflection. "I probably shouldn't be talking to you, Mr. Cage. Even though I'm no longer active as a lawyer, I'm still a member of the bar, and feel bound by its code of confidentiality."

"Then why *are* you talking to me?"

He took the question under advisement. Then: "The answer requires some history," he said. "After Lora Medford was killed and Price went into complete seclusion, he changed his will, leaving everything to the Soldiers of God Foundation. I was opposed to that. I tried to convince him that Lora would've wanted him to leave a substantial amount of his estate to their daughter. I knew Lora had never forgiven Price for severing his relationship with Julia. But I got nowhere with him."

Lenox's glass was nearly empty. He got to his feet. "May I freshen yours?"

I shook my head.

Lenox went to the bar and poured more sherry for himself. "So Bell was both the trustee and, in actuality, the beneficiary of the Medford estate since he was the president of the SOG Foundation. And almost immediately, he started authorizing large grants to the Foundation. I argued with him. I said that although the grants were legal, I thought it unseemly. But he wouldn't listen, so I finally took it up with Price."

"Did Medford know about the grants?"

"Yes."

"And?"

"He was unconcerned. But unexpectedly, he listened to me for reasons which had nothing to do with Bell's use of his money." Lenox took a slow, reflective sip of the wine. "He'd obviously been doing some soul searching. Although he was never demonstrative about it, Price loved his wife deeply, and her death was a terrible blow to him. He knew she bitterly disapproved of his intransigent attitude toward Julia's marriage. In fact, I've always suspected Lora was leaving Price—even after forty years of marriage—when she died in that plane crash and Price knew it and had been brooding about it for years. He told me he wanted to change his will, leaving his entire estate to Julia or, if she was dead, her descendants, if any."

"Did he actually change it or just talk about it?"

"He changed it."

"Then isn't April—"

"No."

I looked puzzled.

"Let me explain," Lenox continued. "It was changed, signed by Price, and witnessed by the Telners . . . Hans and Cora Telner, who worked for Price at the time . . . without Bell's knowledge. But Bell must've found out. That's my assumption, anyway. I never asked, and he never said." He took a bitter nip of his sherry. "At any rate, a few months later Price said he was transferring his legal work to Woodman."

"What reason did he give?"

"I'd had a heart attack. Rather severe. It occurred

shortly after the death of my wife. I was out of action for several months. Price said he thought I was carrying too heavy a work load." His lips twisted with a tight, acerbic smile. "I was sure Bell and Woodman had given him the idea. But it really didn't matter. I was thinking of retiring. At any rate, one day . . . three or four years ago now . . . I got a phone call from Woodman. Ostensibly, it was a social call, but during it he let drop that Price had changed his will again, reinstating the one making Bell the trustee of the estate and leaving everything to the SOG Foundation."

"Did he say why?"

Lenox nodded. "He said that at Price's insistence, he and Bell had hired a private detective to try to locate Julia. He said the man had been conducting a search for the past year and had finally found out Julia had died."

"In Seattle?"

"He didn't say where," Lenox replied. "But he did say the private investigator also reported that Julia had no descendants."

"Did you do anything to try to confirm the report?"

"I had no reason to."

"Who was the investigator?"

He frowned. "A man name Mason. Something like that."

"Could it've been Matson? Jack Matson?" I asked.

"Yes . . . yes, I believe that was the name. Do you know him?"

"Only by reputation," I replied.

Lenox eyed me quizzically. "I gather from your tone of voice it wasn't of the best."

"That's right. I understand he's no longer in Los

Angeles." I moved to the edge of my chair. "Everything you've told me suggests Medford may have acted under duress."

Lenox considered that, then shook his head. "I don't believe Bell has *forced* him to do anything. He doesn't have to. He's Price's only contact with the outside world except for the Riddells . . . Cliff and Edna Riddell, who replaced the Telners . . . but they're just retainers, so to speak. Price trusts Bell completely."

"And Woodman?" I asked.

"I'd assume so."

"And you don't think Bell and Woodman have anything to fear from April? That she'd have any legal grounds to contest her grandfather's will when he dies?"

"Not if Woodman was telling the truth when he said Price had it reinstated, restoring the SOG Foundation as the beneficiary."

"And if he wasn't telling you the truth? If he and Bell had reinstated the will leaving his estate to the SOG without Medford's knowledge?"

He looked at me, his eyes mere slits. "Are you saying. . . ?"

He left it suspended there and I said, "That's what I'm saying. Someone tried to lure April to the Medford house. You're right. It wasn't Medford. Could it have been Bell?"

"To try to kill her?"

"Or have her killed."

"I couldn't believe that about Bell."

"Woodman?"

He gave it a moment's consideration, then shook his head.

"Someone tried to kill her in Newport Beach last

Thursday," I said and told him what had happened, watching as his face paled and his expression tightened.

"You're certain it wasn't an accident?"

"Yes."

He moved to the large stone fireplace, cold and barren now, and stared into it broodingly. "Do you know where Miss Tyson could've gone?"

"Back to Seattle. But that's just a guess."

He turned to me. "I'll make a call to Price and ask if he'll see me. I doubt he will. Or even talk on the phone. But if he won't, then I'll talk to Bell or Woodman. I'll be in touch with you if I learn anything I think you should know." He rose and went to a desk and asked how he could reach me. I told him and hoisted myself from the butter-soft chair, thanked him, and left.

11

I drove the Foothill Freeway to the Ventura. Lenox's story of Price Medford's pendulating behavior about his will rekindled my interest in April's whereabouts. That, in turn, led me to wonder about Harry Lassen —where he'd gone and if he'd returned. I left the Ventura at Laurel Canyon Boulevard and climbed into the hills, driving by Lassen's precarious perch to see if his Buick was in the driveway. It wasn't. But the Chevy belonging to the lady I'd seen him with at the Beefeater was. I parked, considered a cover story, and went to the door, ringing the bell.

A Judas window in the door opened, and the lady looked out. She was smiling.

"Yes?"

"Excuse me," I said. "I'm looking for Harry Lassen."

"I'm sorry, but he isn't here."

I showed disappointment and said, "I should've phoned. I'm a friend of his from out of town. I was in Studio City and decided to stop by and say hello."

"Just a moment."

She closed the Judas window, opened the door, invited me in, and I entered a large living room. It was being dismantled. Packing boxes sat on the floor. Several paintings and prints had been taken from the walls and were propped against furniture. The bookcases were bare, their contents in boxes or stacked on a table.

"I'm Ruth Zenakes."

I manufactured a name. "Stan Roberts."

She offered her hand. I took it. It was firm. She was tall, her figure was lithe, her titian hair was streaked with silver, and she was dressed in slacks and an embroidered blouse. She eyed me for a moment, her head cocked, wearing a small, perplexed frown and then laughed lightly.

"You'll have to forgive me. I have a terrible time with names. They go in one ear and out the other. Harry's probably spoken of you but—"

She broke off with a helpless gesture.

"No offense," I told her. "Harry may not've mentioned me. Actually, I'm more of a business acquaintance than a friend."

"Are you in real estate, too?"

The question could have been a trap. But I thought not.

"That's right."

She glanced around the room, smiling apologetically. "Excuse the looks of the place. I'm helping Harry pack."

"He's moving?"

"*We're* moving," she replied. "As soon as Harry gets back, we're going to be married."

"Congratulations."

"Thank you." Her face radiated happiness.

"Where are you going?"

"To Idaho. Harry has a ranch there. That's what

he calls it, anyway. It's not much. Only forty acres. And way out in the boonies. Near a little town called Willow River. Harry wants to raise some sheep and have an organic truck garden and raise vegetables that taste like they're supposed to taste. It'll be fun."

"I'm sure it will," I said, though I didn't believe it, being a man for whom the rustic life had as much appeal as a stroll on a bed of hot coals.

"Where did Harry go?" I asked casually.

"Seattle."

I pretended more surprise than I felt. "Seattle? . . . That's a coincidence. I'm planning to be there in the next day or two. What's he doing in Seattle?"

"Some last business thing he had to do. He tried to explain what it was, but I didn't understand." She laughed softly again. "I'm as bad about business as I am about names."

"How long's he going to be there?"

"A few days. He wasn't sure when he left."

"Well, maybe I can get in touch with him if he's still there. Where's he staying?"

"The Cascade Hotel."

"I'll give him a ring."

"Why don't you?"

She gave me her hand and said it was nice to have met me. I returned the compliment, wished her luck with the sheep and organic vegetables in Idaho, and left, feeling a sorrow for the woman, knowing the man she was going to marry was a stranger to her, knowing there'd be no wedding, no Idaho, no garden with vegetables tasting the way vegetables should taste. And, unaccountably, I felt a twinge of sadness for Lassen, too.

I didn't like that.

* * *

Back in my apartment, there were two messages on the answering machine. One was from Checkers. The other from Marian Neff. Her voice on the tape was tremulous. I was reaching for the phone when it rang. It was Marian, sounding full of portent. She said she'd heard on a radio news broadcast that the body of a man found floating in Lake Union had been identified.

It was Ross Newkirk.

I telephoned Checkers at his office. There was no answer. I called his apartment. The line was busy and no "call waiting." At times, Checkers could be as long-winded as a three-day Santa Ana. I decided not to wait for him to get off the phone, and fifteen minutes later I arrived at his apartment. He greeted me in his sock feet and with a drink in hand. He could read me. He knew I came bearing news.

"What's up?"

I told him about the call from Marian. His reaction was one of mild surprise and placid interest until I told him I'd decided to go back to Seattle.

"What the hell for?" he demanded. "So this Newkirk drowned." He shrugged. "It could've been an accident."

I shafted him with: "Just a coincidence, right?"

He gave me a reproving look. I ignored it and said April could be in Seattle.

"You told me you didn't give a damn about her, remember?"

"I remember."

"So what changed your mind?"

"Newkirk drowning," I replied, and added, "And the fact that Lassen went to Seattle."

"Yeah? . . . How do you know?"

I told him of my short visit with Ruth Zenakes.

His eyes became skeptical slits. "You sure the lady wasn't stringing you along?"

"Positive," I said. "And there's another thing. I had a talk with Charles Lenox this afternoon."

That commanded his full attention, and I reported what Lenox had said.

"Well, now that's very interesting." He took a sip of his drink, looking pleased. "So Medford had a will that would've left everything to April."

"Until he reinstated the one making the Soldiers of God his beneficiary."

"But Lenox's only got Woodman's word that Medford knew about the change, right?"

I nodded.

"I'll give all the odds you want Medford doesn't know. And when the old guy dies and the will goes to probate, April could—"

I cut him off with: "*If* she's around."

Checkers nodded, staring thoughtfully into his drink before he spoke. "Okay," he said, "go to Seattle. Find her if she's there. Find her wherever the hell she is. But stay away from the cops up there. And don't waste your time on Newkirk. I don't give a damn if he jumped, fell, or was pushed into that fucking lake."

He finished his drink, the prospect of April inheriting her grandfather's fortune kindled anew.

It was drizzling the next morning when I left Los Angeles, but the sun beamed in a cloudless sky when I landed in Seattle. Mount Rainier looked close enough to pat on the head. I drove to the Cascade Hotel and used the house phone in the lobby, asking for Harry

Lassen. The operator said there was no one registered by that name. I talked to the room clerk. He told me Mr. Lassen had checked out the day before. I wondered if Ruth Zenakes had talked to Lassen and told him about "Stan Roberts," revealed that he was at the Cascade, and Lassen had decided it would be prudent to find other lodgings. I also considered that, with Newkirk dead, Lassen's business was completed and he'd returned to Los Angeles en route to Idaho.

After checking in again at the Bayside Inn, I went to the Public Safety Building. Detective Sergeant James Farnum of homicide was the man I saw. He was a rotund, corn-fed looking man, and I decided he had to be someone's favorite uncle. I also concluded that behind his bland exterior there could lurk a bear-trap mind. I showed him the plastic card that identified me as a licensed private investigator in California. It was the first time I'd had it out of my wallet in over a year. Farnum wasn't impressed. He asked what brought me to Seattle.

"The drowning of Ross Newkirk."

"What about it?"

"He was the friend of a Seattle attorney, Paul Bennett, who was murdered in—"

Farnum cut me off. "We know about Bennett. Los Angeles asked us to investigate his background for a possible motive. But we didn't come up with anything. Bennett seemed pretty much a loner. The only person we got any information out of was his secretary. She told us about a woman named April Tyson who lived with Bennett. She said Miss Tyson was in Los Angeles. You know about her?"

"She's my client."

"She hire you to find out who killed Bennett?"

"It turned out that way."

Farnum shifted impatiently in his chair. "Los Angeles said Bennett was probably killed by someone burglarizing his motel room."

"I know what they say."

Farnum eyed me narrowly, hearing the edge of dubiety in my voice. "You don't agree?"

"No."

"Why?"

I equivocated. "Just a hunch."

A small, derisive smile crossed Farnum's lips.

I went on: "And with Newkirk's drowning, my hunch is stronger than ever."

"Why?"

"Bennett being stabbed and Newkirk drowning within a few days of each other and their deaths not being connected is a little hard to swallow."

Farnum gave me another barely visible smile of disdain. "I imagine both of 'em knew a lot of other people who're still alive and well."

I agreed.

Farnum took a pipe from a pocket and filled it from an oilskin pouch. "The Harbor Police say there's no evidence Newkirk's death wasn't an accident."

"What makes them think it *was*?"

He put a match to the pipe and puffed heavily to get it burning, raising enough smoke to fog the whole of Puget Sound. With the tobacco on fire, he settled back in his chair.

"The Harbor boys knew Newkirk pretty well. He owned a skiff, tippy little thing, with an outboard motor. About all he used it for was to cross the lake to a place called Nelson's. Did a lot of drinking there. Sometimes when he got in his boat to go home, he was so boiled he didn't know whether he was on Lake Union or the Gulf of Alaska, and Harbor had to tow him to his houseboat. He was in Nelson's the other night and was carrying quite a load when he left. Coroner's report confirms that from blood alcohol tests. And it was foggy. Harbor figures Newkirk got confused, stood up to try to get his bearings, fell into the water, and was too drunk to get back in the skiff. His body was found floating near the Aurora Bridge, and the boat was picked up bobbing around off Gasworks Park. That's about it.'' He spread his hands.

I didn't comment. As long as there was a plausible reason for believing Newkirk drowned accidentally, Farnum wasn't going to put himself to any more trouble than necessary. He had, judging from the stacks of paper on his desk, more urgent homicides to worry about.

He looked at his watch, stood up, extended his hand, and thanked me for coming in.

"A phone call might've done as well," I said.

"Might've," he agreed.

Nelson's and its clientele were on the rough-hewn side. The barroom was busy and beerily boisterous. I surmised the noontime patrons were from the boatyard on the one side and the moorage on the other. I found an opening at the end of the bar and ordered a bottle of beer from a lady bartender named Lily with a build a logger would envy. She brought it, took my money, and started away without a word.

"Too bad about Ross," I said.

She turned back and sized me up with an armslength look, one that said she'd never seen me before and didn't give a damn if she ever saw me again.

"Yeah."

"May I talk to you for a minute?"

"Who're you?"

I told her I was a private investigator who'd been hired by a friend of Newkirk's to check out the circumstances of his death.

"I didn't think anybody gave a damn," Lily said.

"She does."

"She who?"

"April Tyson."

"Oh, yeah. I know her. She was in a few times with Ross. I was hoping he'd dump Mona for her."

"What was the matter with Mona?"

"Did you know her?"

"No."

"Well, she was kind of a pain in the ass as far as I was concerned. Kinda looked down on this place, you know. So I was just as happy when she took off like she did. Hard on Ross. But he got over it." She inspected me more closely. "You're not from around here."

I admitted I wasn't.

"Where you from?"

"Los Angeles."

"Oh," Lily said, looking as if she'd discovered where the bad odor was coming from.

"Is April living there now?"

"Temporarily."

"Why's she interested in what happened to Ross?"

I said I was just doing a job, and what April's reasons for wanting it done were her business. "Do you think it was accidental?"

"What happened to Ross?"

"Yeah."

She shrugged.

"I hear he wasn't feeling any pain when he left here."

A couple of lake-faring men down the bar yelled at Lily to fetch more drinks. She did and answered other demands for service, then returned and I repeated my question.

"Ross'd been taking it easy with the booze for a coupla weeks until the other night. It was kinda slow. Then this guy came in. I'd never seen him before. He sits down right next to Ross, and the two of 'em get to talking."

"What did they talk about?"

"I dunno. Just bullshitting, I guess. The guy was doing the buying, and Ross got pretty loaded."

"What did the guy look like?"

She thought about it. "He was, oh, around fifty, maybe." She frowned and shrugged. "I dunno. What can I tell you? He was just a guy, you know. I mean, you see guys like him all the time. Not in here. On the street. A dime a dozen, you know."

I knew. One of the men who might fit the description was Harry Lassen.

"What happened?"

"Nothing," she said. "They just drank and talked, then the guy left. I noticed he was sorta nursing his drinks while Ross was really putting 'em away, you know."

"Loaded, hm?"

"Like a freight car."

"What happened after the man left?"

"Ross bought himself another coupla drinks, then took off."

"His skiff was tied up at the dock out there?"

"Yeah."

"Did you see him shove off?"

She shook her head. "Just heard the motor start."

"Did you talk to the police?"

"Yeah, the Harbor guys came around. I told them what I've told you." She shrugged. "That's it." She looked pensive for a moment. "Yeah, I think it was an accident. What else could it've been?"

She didn't wait for an answer.

I drove around the lake and parked across the street from Newkirk's moorage, thinking of a way to enter his houseboat without trying to break in and being seen by one of the tenants of the other houseboats on the dock. I thought of a story I could give the moorage manager if I could find him. Or her.

The elderly woman I'd seen when I'd visited Newkirk was at the mail boxes at the head of the dock.

"Aren't you the gentleman who was here to see Ross a week or so ago?" she asked.

I said I was. She introduced herself as Mrs. Anderson. I gave her my name, and she asked if I was a friend of Ross.

"I'm his brother," I lied. "His half-brother."

"Oh, dear," Mrs. Anderson exclaimed. "Then of course you know what happened."

"Yes," I said, trying to appear as if I was manfully suppressing grief.

I walked along the dock with her.

"Ross never mentioned a brother."

"I live in Los Angeles, and Ross and I weren't close. But we were the only ones left in our family."

"It was a terrible thing," Mrs. Anderson said, her eyes watery. "I'm so sorry."

I gestured appreciatively.

"If there's anything I can do . . ."

"As a matter of fact, I was going to find the manager of the moorage to ask if he had a key to Ross' boat and would let me in to see what needs to be done to close it."

"Oh, I can let you in. Ross left a key with me so I could put his mail inside when he was away. Just a moment."

We'd reached her houseboat, and she hurried inside and returned with a key. I thanked her and asked if Miss Tyson had been around.

"April Tyson?" She shook her head. "I've never met her. But Ross mentioned her name a few times. He said she was a friend of Mona Crane's." She sighed sadly. "That was another awful thing."

I said I knew about it and left her lamenting Mona and Newkirk, letting myself into the houseboat. I went to a desk and started to work, wishing I had some idea of what I was looking for so I would know it when I found it.

The top of the desk held a generous pile of magazines. There were several copies of catalogs from mail-order houses hustling everything from hand tools to vitamins. It also held a portable typewriter that looked old enough to be a collector's item. I inspected the drawers. One contained an impressive number of unpaid bills. I could see why Newkirk would've been anxious for April to establish her bona fides with her grandfather and he could maybe pocket some of the old gentleman's money. His creditors, if they knew, must certainly have been cheering him on. I went on to another drawer, and it was there— among other correspondence—that I found a note from Mona Crane. It was in a plain envelope without a return address. I made out the postmark to be Los Angeles, but the date was unreadable. The note was handwritten.

Dear Ross,

Perhaps I should have told you I was leaving Seattle but I couldn't find the courage. I was afraid you'd again persuade me to stay with you. I couldn't do that. I won't go into all the reasons. You know them as well as I do. Suffice it to say that as much as we love each other, we weren't meant for each other. Sad but true. I had to leave in order to find my own happiness. I hope you find yours.

Mona

I thought of Larry at the Jury Box and pocketed the note to take to him, hoping it'd reassure him that Mona Crane, although missing, was alive and well.

I went into the bedroom. It was small and furnished with a single bed, a table beside it holding a phone, a note pad, and a pencil. The table had one drawer. It contained a telephone directory. I picked up the telephone and received a dial tone. Newkirk had kept abreast of one creditor at least. I opened the door to a closet. It wasn't large. It didn't have to be. There was a glen plaid suit and a pair of dress shoes, and the rest of the apparel was work clothes—Levis and cord pants, wool shirts, and jackets for all seasons and weather. I thrust my hand into as many pockets as I could find. All I found were several matchbooks until I dug into a windbreaker and came up with a slip of paper—a receipt for the rental of a post office box, number 611, issued two months before for a term of one year. It came from the Lake Union substation. On it, written in pencil, was the notation, "E 1. full trn to J & r. to D." Clearly, it was the box's combination. Why did he have a post office box when, from what Mrs. Anderson said, his mail was delivered to the houseboat address?

It was Saturday, and although the substation's windows were closed for business, the boxes were accessible. I went to number 611, followed the combination penciled on the receipt, and the small door opened. The box was jammed with the ubiquitous crab grass of modern postal communication, most of it addressed to "boxholder." I disposed of it and found a small, flat package addressed to Newkirk buried under all the debris I'd extracted from the box. The return address, without a name, was that of his houseboat. But the faint postmark said the package had been mailed from Los Angeles. The date was illegible. I tore off the wrapping paper to reveal a tape cassette. There was nothing on it to indicate what, if anything, had been transcribed on the tape. I was remembering the cassettes in Bennett's house and Vicari's asking Marian if there was one in Bennett's office when I felt something hard jamming into my back and heard a man's voice quietly tell me:

"I'll take that, Cage."

I knew the something hard was a gun. And that the voice belonged to Harry Lassen—a replay of our encounter at the garage elevator. I started to turn but a nudge of the gun stopped me.

"Give it to me."

I handed him the cassette over my shoulder.

"Now just stay where you are."

As silently as he'd arrived, he started to leave, backing away. I glanced around. A woman had entered the lobby and was coming toward us. I yelled, "Look out!"

Lassen whirled. The woman saw his gun and stiffened with fright. I moved. Lassen heard me coming. As he turned, I grabbed his gun hand. The revolver exploded, the slug hit the floor, the sound reverberating off the marble walls. The woman screamed and ran. I hung onto Lassen and sank my teeth into his hand. He gasped and dropped the gun. I kicked it out of reach. He took a swing at me, missed, hesitated for a second, then ran from the building. I snatched up the gun and went after him with my flat-wheeled run, exiting the building as Lassen reached his car. The frightened woman was gone. The parking lot was deserted. I yelled at Lassen to freeze. He did, slowly turning toward me.

As I moved to him, the captured gun leveled at him, something happened to him. Nothing physical. Nothing I could see. But I sensed it. A tangle of emotions invaded him. Weariness and resignation. And, perhaps, dread. A dormant fear now come to life. I demanded the cassette and, almost docilely, he handed it over.

"What's on it?"

"I don't know."

He saw my disbelief.

"All I know is that it's something important to Dekoven and Vicari."

I didn't push the point. I'd find out when I played it. I moved around him to the car, pulling open the door on the driver's side.

"Get in."

He got behind the wheel, and I climbed into the back seat.

"Let's go," I said.

"Where?"

"Just drive."

He drove.

"How did you know where to find me?"

He didn't answer.

I leaned forward and put the revolver to the side of his head. "There's something you'd better understand, Lassen. The woman you killed in Newport Beach was a special friend of mine. *Very* special. And it wouldn't trouble me one damn bit to put a bullet in your head."

I knew I didn't mean it. And I couldn't tell if Lassen knew I didn't. But it was a tantalizing idea—forcing him to drive to some isolated spot and kill him. It'd be his gun, his bullet, his head. A clear case of suicide.

"I was waiting to see if the Tyson woman showed up."

"So you could kill her, too."

"I didn't kill your lady friend."

I saw his eyes in the rearview mirror. Flat, desolate eyes. I felt he was telling the truth. "Then who did?"

He took a minute or more to answer. "I wouldn't know."

"Take a guess."

"There's a guy named Al Massi. He's—"

"Vicari's cousin. We've met."

I thought about it being Massi. It played. A little

off key, maybe. Would Vicari and Dekoven trust him with such an assignment? Why not? Vicari had to move fast after finding out where April was. Massi might've been the only one available on short notice. Then, suddenly, the name of the driver of the car didn't seem important. Whoever he was, he got his orders from Vicari. And Dekoven. They were the ones I wanted.

Lassen drove an aimless course that took us into Volunteer Park and the Seattle Art Museum. The museum was closed, its parking lot nearly deserted. I told him to park.

"What's the connection between Dekoven and Vicari?"

"I don't know."

"Who hired you?"

"Vicari."

"To kill Bennett?"

"No."

I leaned forward with the gun.

"That's the truth," Lassen said.

"When did he hire you?"

"The morning I came to your apartment. After he found out that the wrong woman bought it in Newport Beach. He wanted me to find her."

"And kill her."

He didn't answer. He didn't have to.

"And that's why you're here, right?"

His answer was a small sigh and nod.

"And Newkirk . . . You killed him."

He didn't respond. I waited. Four young boys ran past the car, carefree, aimless, laughing and shouting at nothing at all for no reason at all. Lassen stared vacantly out the windshield at the same nothingness, his attention on something inside himself. The kids disappeared around a corner of the museum. The tide of a bottomless sea of quiet rose inside the car. I waited.

Finally, Lassen said, "What do you want from me, Cage?"

"I want to know why Dekoven and Vicari wanted Newkirk dead."

"I don't know."

"I want to know why they want April Tyson dead."

"I don't know that either."

"I want Dekoven and Vicari."

He didn't say anything.

"And *you* want Ruth Zenakes . . ."

His head jerked around.

". . . and those sheep and vegetables in Idaho."

"How did—?"

He didn't finish and I told him about my visit with his bride-to-be. After that lightning bolt, we were silent for a moment. It was as heavy as an anvil. I tried to decide how helpful Lassen could be to me. He was a killer. But I could overlook that if I could use him to nail Vicari and Dekoven for Frances' murder. I knew my chances of trusting him were slim to none, but I decided to risk it.

"I've been told you're not wanted for anything."

"No." It was a husky whisper.

"But if Ruth found out what you really are . . . ?"

I left it at that. I knew I didn't have to say more. From the look on Lassen's face, the answer hung over his head like a noose.

"What're you getting at?" he asked, his voice still scratchy.

"Cooperation."

"A minute ago you said you could kill me." He glanced around. "Now you're talking a deal. How do I know I can trust you?"

"You don't. And I meant it when I said I could kill you. But I'm willing to deal with you only because Vicari and Dekoven are more important to me."

"What do you want me to do?"

"I want the truth out of you." He opened his mouth to protest. I stopped him. "But first I want to listen to this tape. Then we'll take it from there."

He looked away, thought about it, then said, "All right."

"You'd better mean it. And when I say I want the truth, that's exactly what I want. If I find out you're lying to me . . . or even *suspect* you're lying . . . I pay Ruth another visit . . . Understand?"

He didn't respond.

"Look at me, Lassen."

He glanced around.

"I mean a good look."

He squirmed around in the front seat and looked. And his eyes said he understood.

I emptied the shells from Lassen's gun, put them and his revolver into a pocket, and climbed into the front seat. I had to know if Lassen was conning me, and I concluded I might as well find it out upfront. I told him to drive back to the post office so I could pick up my rental. He looked surprised.

"What then?" he asked.

"Where you staying now?"

"The Colfax."

"Go there and wait for me. And if you're not there when I want you, Ruth'll get a phone call."

* * *

I still had the key to Bennett's house. I drove there. I made a turn of the rooms, starting with the living room, the dining room, the so-called rec room. All looked in the same state of glum neglect as they had when I'd seen them before. I entered the kitchen. That was a different story. The sink contained a cup and saucer, and a small coffee pot still held a brew of recent vintage. I went back through the dining room, living room, and down the short hall to the bedroom. One of the twin beds had been slept in. On top of the other was an open suitcase packed with women's clothes. April's clothes. She'd been here. And the suitcase said she'd be back.

I returned to the rec room, found a battery-powered tape player, and inserted Newkirk's cassette. There was nothing but a whine and static, then I heard the sound of a door open. The quality of the tape improved. But only slightly. It still crackled and popped.

"How're you, Duke?"

"You tell me."

"Hi, Bobby."

Bobby replied with a grunt.

The door closed. "Paul" asked "Duke" and "Bobby" if they wanted a drink. Both declined. The voices were subdued, tense, preoccupied—the voices of men with a big worry.

"Let's have it," Duke said.

"You've got a problem." This sounded like Paul.

"You told us that on the phone," Bobby said impatiently.

Paul: "I talked to Vince just before I left Seattle. Spent a couple hours with him. He still wants to make a deal with the government. He said if I won't go along, he'll get a lawyer who will."

Bobby muttered: "The cocksucker."

Paul: "You've got to look at it from his standpoint. He—"

Duke cut in: "Fuck his standpoint. If he talks, it's my ass, Bobby's ass, and the asses of a lot of other people."

Paul: "I know, Duke." He was insistent. "But he doesn't give a damn about that. The narcs got him cold. The government's going to hang him out to dry. He doesn't have a prayer, and he knows it."

Bobby: "It wasn't *our* shit he was nailed with!"

Paul: "That doesn't make any difference to Vince. Your operation's the biggest. His hole card. If he can give you guys to the government, he'll get immunity and enter the government witness program. He doesn't like the idea but—"

Duke chopped him off: "Then why's he gonna do it?!"

Paul: "You should see the guy. He's a basket case worrying about what'll happen to Teresa and the kids while he's in prison. Vince's broke. Flat on his ass."

Bobby: "What the fuck does he do with his dough?"

Paul: "Ask him. I don't know."

Duke: "Tell him we'll take care of Teresa."

There was a pause.

Paul: "I told him that, but he doesn't believe me."

Duke: "Get him on the phone. I'll tell him."

There was another pause.

Bobby: "Somethin' wrong?"

Paul: "I don't think he'd believe you either unless . . ." Paul paused ". . . unless you make a down payment. Say a couple hundred thousand."

Duke: "Tell him he's got it."

Bobby: "Wait a minute, wait a minute." He was hot. "Where the fuck did that figure come from?"

Paul: "What do you mean?"

Bobby: "From you or from Condotti?"

Paul (indignant-like): "What're you trying to say?"

Whatever Bobby was getting at, he backed away from it. Reluctantly. "Nothin', nothin'."

Paul (challenging): "Go on, say it."

Duke: "Drop it, Paul."

Paul: "No!"

Bobby: "Okay . . . I know you've got big problems in Reno and Vegas. I'm wonderin' how much of that two hundred thousand you'd use to bail yourself out."

Paul: "Now wait a minute—"

Bobby didn't wait. "And I'll tellya another thing . . . I don't trust Vince. I'm askin' myself . . . what's to stop him from taking the money and dumpin' on us anyway?"

Paul: "That'd be pretty stupid."

Bobby: "Vince never struck me as bein' a Rhodes Scholar."

Paul: You're forgetting something. You and Duke asked me to represent Vince and keep you posted. And that's what I've done, and you have to take it from here because when I get back to Seattle I'm going to tell Vince if he wants to roll over for the government, he'll have to find himself another lawyer."

Bobby: "That's up to you. But when you're talkin' to Vince, tell him if he goes on actin' like he is, we're gonna have to do something about it."

Paul: "Like what?"

Bobby: "He'll know."

Paul: "Is that how you feel, Duke?"

Duke (uneasy): "Yeah. If he's gonna to play rough, we gotta play it the same way."

Paul: "Well, you two're gonna have to deliver your own threats."

Bobby: "That's fine with us."

The tape transmitted a moment of tense silence, then Duke said he and Bobby had to leave. A door again opened and closed, and there was a click and the taping stopped.

I sat for a few moments eyeing the cassette player. Clearly the "Paul" on the tape was Bennett. "Bobby" was Vicari. And the "Duke" was Dekoven. Bennett had been wired for sound. The taping started when Dekoven and Vicari entered the room and stopped when they left.

But why had Bennett wanted this tape? It revealed that Dekoven and Vicari were dealing in narcotics in one way or another. I guessed they were running it into the country through merchandise destined for the Import Bazaar. And Dekoven's chain of cut-rate stores, doing a big cash business, would provide an excellent way to launder illegal profits. But if so, Bennett already knew that. And as a lawyer, he would've known the tape was useless as evidence, that it would never be admissible in a court of law—unless he'd been turned over by local or federal narcs who had a warrant for the bugging. I doubted that. Something told me this was a personal effort on Bennett's part. It smacked of blackmail. Of Bennett needing money. Vicari had mentioned "big problems" for Bennett in Las Vegas and Reno. That could only mean gambling debts. Then there was Vicari's remark about what would happen to Vince Condotti if he became a prosecution witness. The meaning was unmistakable.

Whoever he was, Condotti wouldn't live long enough to testify. And if blackmail was Bennett's motive for the taping, he'd have had to play the tape for Dekoven and Vicari at some point. That would've been dangerous, and he'd have had to protect himself. Did he tell them that the tape—or a copy of it—would surface if anything happened to him?

April lied when she said she knew of no reason why Dekoven and Vicari were looking for her. It would be a logical assumption on their part that Bennett had given his lady friend a copy of the cassette. So they had to find her and kill her whether or not the original had been found in Bennett's motel room after he was murdered. But Newkirk was a different story. Dekoven and Vicari wouldn't immediately suspect him of having a copy. Had he decided to carry on the blackmail even in the face of what had happened to Bennett? It was hard to believe he'd be so stupid. Unless, like Bennett, he was desperate enough—or greedy enough—for money. Frantic men are seldom sagacious men.

I turned my attention to Vince Condotti. Who was he? Where was he? Since Bennett had represented him, Marian would know. I called her apartment. We went through the obligatory prologue. She was surprised I was back in Seattle and asked why. She was shocked that I suspected Newkirk had been murdered. When she wanted to know how April was, I said she was all right and left it at that. She didn't know about Frances, and I had no intention of telling her and risk sending her on another guilt trip. We eventually got around to why I was calling.

"Yes, I remember Mr. Condotti," she said. "He was arrested for possession of narcotics. Ten kilos of cocaine. He was released on a hundred-thousand-dollar bond. I remember he came to the office one day, and he and Mr. Bennett had an argument. Mr. Condotti was so loud I could hear him through the door."

"What were they arguing about?"

"Mr. Condotti wanted Mr. Bennett to make some sort of deal with the government in return for a plea of guilty. Mr. Bennett refused, and Mr. Condotti finally stomped out."

"What happened then?"

She was silent for a moment, then said, "He committed suicide."

"Suicide?"

"About a week after the argument with Mr. Bennett."

"How'd he kill himself?"

"With an overdose of heroin."

Frances killed in a hit-and-run "accident." Newkirk "drowned." Condotti a "suicide."

"Why're you interested in Mr. Condotti?" Marian asked. "Do you think it had anything to do with Mr. Bennett's murder?"

"It's possible," I replied, and said I'd heard Condotti had a wife and family.

"Yes, there was his wife and two young children."

"Where's Mrs. Condotti live?"

"The Condottis lived in Bellevue. But after Mr. Condotti killed himself, Mrs. Condotti sold the house and moved back East. I don't know where."

It didn't matter. Either Mrs. Condotti believed her husband had committed suicide, or if she knew he'd been murdered, she'd kept quiet in return for an annuity from Dekoven and Vicari. Either way, she would have been no help to me.

* * *

It was time to see Lassen—if he was still at the Colfax. He was, and I wasn't surprised.

He'd bolstered his morale with the help of a bottle of Bushmills, which sat on an end table. He wasn't drunk. But he wasn't sober either. Mostly he was numb. After opening the door for me, he went back to his chair and reached for the bottle. I got there first.

"Later."

I sat on the edge of the bed and put the Bushmills beside me. He looked at me, his eyes full of profanities.

"Have you called Ruth?"

He nodded.

"What did you tell her?"

"That something'd come up. I might not get back as soon as I thought I would."

"I like her," I said. "What does she do?"

"She's an illustrator. Children's books. And she paints. Water colors, mostly. I met her at a gallery on La Cienega that was exhibiting some of her work." His eyes grew gentle with remembrance.

"Met her and fell in love with her."

"Not that it's any of your business, Cage, but she's the best thing that's ever happened to me. That's why I've been sitting here waiting for you. I don't want to risk losing her."

"Why did you risk it by taking the contract on Newkirk?"

"The price was right, and I needed the money. It was going to be my last job."

"It still is."

Lassen got up and came to the bed, picking up the

Bushmills. I didn't try to stop him. He went back to his chair, poured a drink, downed it.

"Do you know Dekoven?"

"I met him once."

"But Vicari gave you the contract on Newkirk, right?"

"Yeah."

"Why did Vicari send you? Why didn't he handle it?"

"I don't know."

"Why did he want Newkirk taken out?"

"Vicari said the guy was trying to shake him down. Him and Dekoven."

"Tell me about it."

"What's there to tell?"

"Why did you make it look like a drowning?"

"Vicari said he wanted it to look like an accident if I could manage it. I was watching Newkirk's houseboat. I saw him get in his skiff and watched him go across the lake. I knew it was Nelson's from the big sign on the place. I went there and sat down at a table with him. I told him Vicari and Dekoven sent me to find out what he wanted."

"What did he want?"

"A hundred and fifty thousand dollars."

"For the cassette?"

Lassen nodded. "I bought drinks, pretending to dicker, and when he was pretty well cooked, I said okay, I'd talk to Vicari and Dekoven and get back to him. Then I left and waited outside for him and said I'd better help him across the lake. I was steering the outboard. He was in the bow, showing me where to go. It was foggy. He stood up. I swerved the boat and he went into the water. I circled him until he went under."

Lassen shrugged and poured another drink. He'd narrated the killing as if it were as commonplace as taking out the garbage. He didn't have blood in his veins. Or ice water. He had Freon.

"What do you want from me, Cage?"

"You're going to call Vicari. Or Dekoven. Either one. Tell him you saw me come out of Newkirk's houseboat and followed me to the post office. You saw me open a post office box, take out a small package, and open it. You saw it was a tape cassette, but you couldn't do anything about getting it away from me. There were too many people around. You followed me to Bennett's house. I met April Tyson there, and we drove to the airport and took a plane back to L.A."

He looked at me with astonishment. "Do you know what you're doing to yourself?"

"Make the call."

He shrugged and picked up the phone and dialed direct. Then: "This is Harry Lassen . . . Let me talk to Bobby." We waited. "Bobby . . . Harry . . . Got something you should know."

Lassen sounded credible. There wasn't an extension in the room, so I couldn't hear what Vicari said. But it didn't take long. Lassen said okay, hung up, and told me Vicari'd call back.

"You're going back to L.A. in the morning," I said. "I want you to stay close to Vicari. If he plans some kind of move to get that cassette from me, find out what it is."

Lassen didn't like any of this. Not for a minute. "What if they want me to take a contract on you?"

"Would you?"
"No."
"Why not? It'd solve your problem with Ruth."

He gave me something that was somewhere between a cynical smile and a sneer. "You'd have someone primed to visit Ruth."

"Good thinking."

Lassen had time for another drink before the phone rang. The call took less than ten seconds. All Lassen said was two okays.

"Well?"

"He said he'd handle it from there," Lassen replied. He gave me a foreboding look. "You know what he means."

I knew.

12

The Jury Box was only a couple of blocks from the Colfax. The dinner hour had past. Larry was in a booth, a cup of coffee in front of him, talking to an impressive looking man, white haired and stern. I tabbed him for a judge from the nearby county courthouse. If he wasn't, he should've been. Larry saw me, excused himself, and met me as I moved to the bar. He didn't seem any less lugubrious than he had on my previous visit.

"You still in town?" he asked.

"Not still," I replied. "Back."

"Have anything to do with what happened to Ross Newkirk?"

I said it did, and he asked what he could do for me and I told him I'd brought him a message of glad tidings. I handed him Mona's letter. He read it once, twice, bounced a quick glance off of me, then stared at the note some more. Then he asked, "Do you believe it?"

"The note? . . . I don't have any reason not to," I replied. "Don't you?"

"Mona wrote it. I recognize her handwriting."

"So what's wrong?"

He shooked his head. "I'm not sure," he said, then turned, gesturing for me to follow.

He led me past the bar and along a short corridor to a small office. Its furnishings were old and sparse, consisting of a roll-top desk, an ancient swivel chair, and an equally elderly Naugahyde couch as big as a gunboat. The walls were covered with sepia photographs of Seattle, a pictorial history of the city dating from the days of the Klondike. Larry sat at the desk, his eyes again fixed on Mona's note. He finally looked up.

"Maybe I'm a nut on the subject," he said.

"What subject?"

"Mona disappearing without saying a word to anybody."

I waited while he perused the note for another moment.

"You notice it isn't dated," he said, handing the note back to me. He was right. It wasn't dated.

"So?" I asked.

"So it could've been written before she disappeared."

"Before?"

"Say it was. I'm just thinking out loud. But say it was. Say Mona wrote it, planning to leave it for Newkirk. Or mail it after she left. Say Newkirk found it. They had an argument. A fight. And he killed her. Did something with her body and—"

I stopped him: "What're you talking about?"

"I just—"

"You're reaching for it. Reaching for something that isn't there."

His head went up and down desperately. "That's

what I have to know. I've got to know if she's alive or . . . dead."

He stood up. His face was damp with perspiration. He mopped it with a hand. "I told you what Newkirk said once. That Mona'd talked about going to Los Angeles. Well, you're from there. Maybe you could find out."

I opened my mouth to refuse, but he didn't give me a chance.

"I'll pay you."

He pulled a drawer open, took a large, flat checkbook, and sat at the desk again. "How about a thousand up front and a thousand every month 'til you tell me there's nothing more you can do?"

"I'm pretty busy right now," I said. "I'm not sure I have the time to—"

"Do what you can when you can." He pressed fingers against his eyes. Maybe it was to force back tears. Maybe not. "Please try . . . please."

"You *were* in love with her, weren't you?"

He looked as if he were going to deny it. But then he took a deep breath, letting it escape slowly. His voice was barely audible. "I never told her. She never knew."

I believed he'd never told her. I wondered if she never knew.

"Look," he continued, "if you find her, you don't have to tell me where she is. All I want to know is if she's all right. I'll take your word for it."

"You're being pretty trusting. You don't know me. I could take your money and tell you anything."

He looked at me flatly. "I don't think you would, would you?"

"No," I replied.

He wrote the check, and I spent twenty minutes asking questions. She'd been born and raised in Los Angeles, Mona'd told him. Her parents were dead, but she had a younger brother. From what she said about him, they weren't close. The last she heard, he was attending the University of California at Santa Barbara. When I left the Jury Box, I took Larry's check and Mona's note from my pocket. I glanced at the note and put it away and looked at the check for a long moment, standing at the curb. Then I tore it into confetti.

And dropped it in a trash basket.

I drove past Bennett's house and parked at the end of the cul de sac where the street surrendered to the Arboretum. The sun had gone to brighten the day of the other side of the planet, and the moon was hiding somewhere. The house stood lightless, lifeless, appearing as if it had given up caring.

I entered, locked the door behind me, and wandered through the rooms. April hadn't been there while I'd been gone. The bedroom with the open suitcase on the bed was just as I'd last seen it. So was the kitchen. It'd been a long day. I'd greeted it at five in the morning to catch a six-thirty flight out of LAX. My eyelids drooped like a pair of baggy sox. I kept hoisting them up but finally grew tired of being tired and was ready to tell sleep to come get me when the reflection of headlights swept across the closed draperies.

I went to the window and peeped out to see a taxi pull into the driveway at the side of the house, moving out of my line of sight. I heard a car door close. The taxi stayed in the driveway. I turned from the window. There was the sound of a key in the lock, the door opened, and April stepped into the entry hall. She snapped a switch beside the door. A lamp glowed dimly, creating the atmosphere of a time-worn mortuary's slumber room. April turned, saw me, stiffened briefly, then seemed to go limp as though accepting an unpleasant inevitability.

I smiled, trying to keep it light. "Hi."

"What're you doing here?"

"Waiting for you."

She entered the living room, putting her purse on a table, staring at it, looking exhausted, limply resigned. "I'm sorry, Tug." She looked at me. "You blame me for what happened, don't you?"

"I blame both of us. Me for getting Frances involved and you for telling Marian Neff where you were."

"I didn't think there was any harm in giving her Frances' name and phone number."

"Now you know."

She just stared at me, retreating into herself, then turned abruptly and went toward the kitchen. I followed her. She snapped on a light, extracted ice from the freezer compartment, dumped a couple of cubes into a glass, and filled it from a bottle of vodka from a cabinet. I waited while she took a long drink and then asked her to tell me what happened after the "accident." She had more vodka before she replied.

After running from the scene of the accident, she wandered around Newport Beach, her only thought being to get away as fast and as far as she could. She had some money with her. Enough to buy a bus ticket to Seattle. She rode it as far as San Jose. She debated with herself whether or not she wanted to come to Seattle. She decided she didn't.

"Why not?"

"Because of Ross. Because I knew what he'd say when I told him that after what'd happened I wanted to forget trying to see my grandfather. That all I wanted was to go where no one knew me. Where I'd be safe. But I knew Ross wouldn't understand. That he'd keep pressuring me."

"You know he's dead?"

She nodded, giving no indication of remorse, and went on: "When the bus got to San Jose, I called Paul's sister. She invited me to stay with her."

"When did you get back here?"

"Night before last."

"Did you see Newkirk?"

"Yes, that same night. I told him what'd happened and to hell with my grandfather."

"And what'd he say to that?"

"I expected he'd argue with me, but he didn't. He said it was my decision. He told me not to worry about him."

"Why did he think you'd worry about him?"

"He needed money. But he said he was going to get some soon."

"How?"

"He didn't say."

"Is that the only reason you came back? To talk to Newkirk?"

"That and to get my clothes and some money I had in a savings account."

"And then?"

"I'm going to Hawaii."

"Before you leave, there's something I want you to hear."

She followed me into the rec room. I started the cassette. She listened for a moment, then went to the player, and turned it off.

"You knew about it," I said.

"Paul played it for me before he went to Los Angeles," she said. "Where did you get it?"

I told her and asked, "What was Newkirk doing with it?"

She finished her drink and replied: "Paul must've sent it to him."

"After he played it for Dekoven and Vicari to let them know what he had, he mailed it to a post office box Ross rented for safe keeping in case they came after him, right?"

"Yes."

"Is this the only copy, or did Bennett make dupes of it?"

"Paul said it was the only copy."

"Well, Dekoven and Vicari wouldn't count on that. They'd suspect you had the original. Or a copy of it. And they found out Newkirk had one when he tried to take up where Bennett left off, and they had him killed."

"It wasn't an accident?"

"Did you really think it was?"

"No."

She stared into her empty glass, clearly weighing a decision, and was apparently trying to find advice left behind by the vodka. I don't know whether she did or not, but she finally said:

"There's something I haven't told you."

"I know."

She stiffened.

"Let me tell you . . . You knew the tape was why Bennett was murdered."

"Yes."

"And it was why Dekoven and Vicari were after you."

She nodded weakly.

I blew. "Goddamn it, why'd you lie?!"

She flinched. "I was so . . . afraid."

"Of Dekoven and Vicari or Checkers and me?"

She put the glass aside and turned away.

"Why was Bennett trying to blackmail Dekoven and Vicari?"

"Paul was a compulsive gambler. He lost thousands of dollars in Reno and Las Vegas. A couple of casinos carried him for a while but then started demanding he pay them. He couldn't. He couldn't come close. He was desperate, so he went to Dekoven and asked to borrow fifty thousand dollars. Dekoven said he'd let him have it for six months. I don't know what interest he charged him, but by the time the loan was due, Paul owed him over a hundred thousand."

"When did he get the loan?"

"Last September."

"So it was due in March."

"Yes."

"And Bennett couldn't pay."

"He asked Dekoven for more time and got another thirty days. And then another. When he went to Los Angeles this last time, he thought Dekoven would give him some more time if he told him I was Price Medford's granddaughter and he was sure he'd get some money for me and I'd give him enough to pay him back. But Dekoven turned him down."

"So Bennett played the cassette, threatening him with it."

"Yes."

"What was he going to do with it? Give it to the narcs?"

"I don't know."

"Did he let you know he told Dekoven he'd given the cassette to a friend and that it would surface if anything happened to him?"

"He told me he'd sent it to Ross."

"He wouldn't have mentioned any names to Dekoven and Vicari," I said, "and they wouldn't have known about Newkirk then, so they'd probably think you had it."

"Yes."

"And they still do."

Bennett's game had been a fool's gambit. He hadn't divined until it was too late that Dekoven and Vicari would have his head if he threatened to take the tape to the authorities. Even though it had no legal value, it would attract the attention of the narcs to their drug trafficking, forcing them—if nothing else—to declare a long moratorium in their operation. Their losses could've run into big bucks.

I asked her if she'd been staying in the house.

"No, I just came back for some clothes."

"Why didn't you take them?"

"I saw a car parked across the street. There was a man in it. I thought he might be watching the house. So I left the suitcase and went out the back way."

"His name was Lassen and you were lucky he didn't know you were here."

"How do you know who it was?"

I said never mind how I knew and asked when she was leaving for Hawaii.

"I have a reservation for a ten-fifteen flight in the morning."

"Are you all packed?"

She said she was.

"Then let's get out of here. You can take a room at the Bayview and get some sleep."

She agreed and I went out and paid off the cab.

The room the hotel gave April adjoined mine with a connecting door. When we got to it, she said she wanted a nightcap. I went into my room and ordered her a vodka and tonic from room service while she changed into pajamas and robe. After the drink arrived, she came in and sat in a chair sipping the drink. I told her about my meeting with Lenox and what he'd told me about Price Medford having written a will leaving his estate to April's mother.

"Then I'm—"

"No . . . According to Lenox, your grandfather's previous will left everything to the Soldiers of God and made Nicholas Bell the trustee. Bell and Woodman had a private detective try to find your mother. He found out she'd died and reported he couldn't find any children she might've had. So your grandfather allegedly reinstated the will favoring Bell and his foundation."

"What do you mean . . . allegedly?"

"Lenox has only Woodman's word that your grandfather knows the will favoring Bell was reinstated. Just as he has only Woodman's word that the private detective couldn't find you."

"You think . . ."

"Woodman was lying. But we'll never know unless we try. Unless *you* try. And that means you'd have to go back to Los Angeles."

She left the chair and wandered the room, trying to decide. I waited. It seemed like a couple of hours, but it was an hour and fifty-five minutes less than that before she shook her head.

"No, I'm not going. I didn't want to get into this in the first place, and I just want to get out."

The vodka hadn't had any revivifying effect on April. Her face was still taut with fatigue. She eyed me as if she expected an argument. I didn't say anything. I didn't know what to say except she'd better get some sleep.

Her eyes held mine for a moment, and she said softly: "Come with me."

I thought of Frances, only five days dead. It was too soon. Too soon. I said, "Maybe some other time."

She winced. "I'm sorry. I shouldn't've said that."

"It never hurts to ask."

"That depends on the answer," she said.

And went into her room.

13

I put on pajamas, turned out the lights, and climbed into bed. My body was ready for sleep, but my mind wasn't. It caromed around like a cue ball, going from April to Bennett to Newkirk to Lassen, settling on the latter. Doubt about whether I could trust him crowded in. I tossed, twisted, turned, punching pillows and finally uncoupled Lassen and remembered Frances for the spring breeze of a woman she'd been, recalling the times—too few, too brief—we'd had together. Once more I found myself trying to accept the unacceptable—that she was gone, snatched away by a needless, senseless death. I wrenched my mind from it and sleep slowly rescued me from more mental anguish.

The ringing telephone on the bedside stand woke me up. With torpid eyes, I looked at the window. The dark beyond had surrendered to steely daylight washed by rain. I picked up the phone and heard, "I thought you was gonna keep in touch."

"The phone works both ways," I replied.

"What's happening?" Checkers demanded.

I told him to hold, went into the bathroom, splashed

cold water on my face, returned to the room, lit a cigarette, and picked up an extension beside the bed.

"You still there?"

Checkers growled, and I reported finding the tape Newkirk had hidden in the post office box, my encounter with Lassen, and that he denied he'd killed Frances or Bennett but admitted doing Newkirk in with the help of Lake Union's murky waters.

"Where's Lassen now?"

"Back in L.A. Or on his way."

"Huh?"

I explained the deal I'd made with him and the phone call he'd made to Vicari. Checkers was somewhat less than enchanted.

"Why'd you set yourself up like that?"

"To take the heat off April and maybe smoke them out."

"You're taking a big chance. And it ain't worth it."

"There's nothing I can do about it now."

"Shit," he said and changed the subject. "Get any line on April?"

I told him she was in the next room.

"You found her?" That, at least, seemed to please him.

"Temporarily."

"What's that mean?"

I broke the bad news that she had given up trying to become reconciled with her grandfather and was going to Hawaii.

"The hell she is!" he roared. "Lemme talk to that dame!"

"I think she's still asleep."

"I don't give a damn if she's dead! Wake her up!"

"Hang on," I said, went to the connecting door, knocked, and April called for me to come in. She was hoisting herself up in the bed, still more asleep than awake.

"What is it?" she asked.

"Checkers is on the phone in my room and wants to talk to you."

"What about?"

"I'm sure he'll tell you," I replied and went back into my room.

April appeared a moment later, shrugging into a robe. She went to the phone by a chair. I sat on the bed and picked up the extension.

"Hello."

"What the hell's this Hawaii shit?" April recoiled, holding the receiver away from her ear, stunned. She could've still heard him if she'd thrown the phone out the window. "Now you listen to me. Me and Tug've been damn patient with you. Tug especially. You disappear and show up and disappear again."

"I just want to forget this whole thing. I don't care—"

"Listen to me!" Checkers bellowed. And April listened. "I don't know what's goin' on in that head of yours. But you're sure as hell one mixed-up young lady. Maybe that's because you're scared. And I can't blame you for that. But you started something, you and Bennett, and if you don't see it through, you're gonna be scared the rest of your life because someone's trying real hard to put you away, and they ain't likely to stop until they do."

April tried to speak. She didn't make it. It was as futile as trying to hold back a high wind with a screen door.

"And then there's the matter of our money arrangement. I said I was willing to gamble on you getting something outa your granddaddy. That didn't mean you could throw in your chips any time you felt like it."

"I'll pay you what I owe you when I get a job and—"

"You couldn't make enough to pay Tug and me if you lived forever. Now you get back here, understand?"

"Yes."

"You coming back?"

She gave me a pleading look. I gestured that it was her decision. She took a deep breath and said, "Yes."

"Now?"

"Yes."

April and I had breakfast at the hotel before going to the airport. She was in a sullen mood from the telephonic blasting she'd received from Checkers. By way of making conversation more than anything else, I told her about Larry Simmons wanting to hire me to find Mona.

April looked impatient. "I guess he's a nice man, but he's a little crazy on the subject of Mona leaving Seattle."

"He admitted he's in love with her. He said he never told her but—"

"She knew. She told me. And that made it uncomfortable working for him. I think that's one reason she left town."

"Was Newkirk another?"

She thought about it. "Yes, it could've been. They

weren't getting along. Nothing specific. A lot of little things that kept building up."

"You believe she's alive?"

She fumbled for an answer for a few seconds. "I know she is."

"How do you know? You haven't heard from her, have you?"

"No."

"Then?"

"I just *know*." Her voice was peevish.

I left it at that.

We arrived at the marina four and a half hours later. I felt as if we were closing some lopsided, senseless circle. After I wrestled the luggage into the apartment and April went to unpack, I checked the messages on the answering machine, and Charles Lenox's uncertain voice responded on the tape, asking me to call. I did.

"Oh, yes, Mr. Cage," he said. "I called you yesterday evening."

"I was out of town."

"I tried to reach Price following our visit. I was told he was sleeping and couldn't be disturbed. I asked to have him call me. I said it was urgent. He didn't return my call, but that didn't surprise me. But Don Woodman phoned yesterday afternoon, asking if there was anything he could do. Have you heard from him?"

"No . . . Was I supposed to?"

"He said he'd call you after our conversation."

"And what did you tell him?"

"I was frank with him. I told him about your visit. That you were employed by Price's granddaughter and that she wished to see her grandfather. Understandably, he asked why Miss Tyson had employed a private investigator."

"Did you tell him?"

"I said you'd told me there had been an attempt on her life."

"And what was his reaction?"

Lenox took a moment. "Constrained, I'd say. He asked how he could get in touch with Miss Tyson. I said I didn't know. Then he said he'd contact you. If you haven't heard from him by tomorrow, let me know. I'll call him again."

I hung up and called Lew Jaffe.

I'd worked with Lew in Hollywood Division narcotics. He was still a narc but was now a lieutenant with an office in Parker Center. We'd seen each other intermittently since the fast food shoot-out put me on the shelf. He was a tall, graceful man with a fine-spun face crowned by prematurely white hair. The story was that he had attended Los Angeles' Hebrew University, bent on becoming a rabbi. How and why he was detoured into being a cop, I never knew. Nor, to my knowledge, did anyone else. Including, perhaps, Lew.

Not having seen each other for several months, we briefly updated our lives, and then I said I wanted to see him.

"When?"

"As soon as possible."

"Is an hour possible enough?"

"I'll be there."

I put the Bennett tape in one jacket pocket, a small cassette player in the other, and called through the bedroom door to April that I was going out.

* * *

I told Lew I had something for his ears only at the moment, and we went into his office, closed the door, and I brought out the tape and player.

"What's this all about?" Lew asked.

"Listen."

I identified the voices of Bennett, Dekoven, and Vicari as they came off the tape. Lew listened, never taking his eyes off me, showing no surprise, no excitement. He'd long since past those career milestones. When the tape finished, he asked me how I got it. I gave him the history, omitting Lassen's name and the deal I'd made with him.

"Look," I continued, "I know the value of this is only informational. But we might use it to nail Dekoven and Vicari, assuming you're interested."

He smiled. "That's a safe assumption . . . But what do you mean by *we*?"

"Dekoven and Vicari know I have this cassette."

"How do they know?"

"Let me pass on that, Lew."

"Why?"

"Just buy what I'm going to tell you, okay?"

"That's asking a lot."

"Will you or won't you?"

"Go on."

"They know I have it, and they want it. Now what if I could set up a meeting with Dekoven or Vicari or both? Tell them I'm willing to give it to them for a price and—"

Lew anticipated me. "You were wired."

I nodded. "And you had a court order to be on the other end of the wire."

Lew thought about it. "It might work . . . if they'd agree to meet you."

"All they can do is say no."

"True."

"How about it?"

"I don't know what the district attorney's office'll say about it. Or a judge, if the DA tries for a warrant. But we'll need the tape to show probable cause, and we might have to name you as the informant."

"That can be kept confidential."

Jaffe nodded. "But you've got to assume Dekoven has connections of one sort or another. It might leak."

"I know."

"You're living a little dangerously, Tug."

"Yeah," I answered with a small smile.

It was forced.

Back at the apartment, a woman's voice, as sultry as a rain forest, was on the answering machine saying Mr. Donald Woodman's office was calling regarding Miss Tyson and would I get back to Mr. Woodman at my convenience.

April appeared in the doorway of the den, and I asked her for the originals of the documents establishing her relationship to Medford. She asked why I wanted them. I played the message from Woodman's secretary and said I might need them if I could arrange a meeting with Woodman.

She looked puzzled. "You don't want me to go with you?"

I said I didn't. I told her about the deal I'd made with Lassen, and that one objective was to replace her as Dekoven and Vicari's target.

"But it might not work," I said. "Maybe all I did

was to make both of us targets. We're going to have to find somewhere else for you to perch."

"We've already been through that," she said with more than a dollop of Lysol in her voice.

"Yes," I replied, "and we both know why it didn't work, don't we?"

Checkers was dictating a letter to Jasmine when I entered his office. She glared at me, objecting when Checkers said they could finish the letter later.

"This is important," Jasmine said.

"Yeah."

"It has to go out today."

"Okay."

"If you don't finish it now, you won't finish it at all," Jasmine insisted. "Tug can wait." She riveted me again. "You *can* wait . . ." she gave me her most intimidating stare . . . can't you?"

I said no, and she got up and grumped out of the office. I sat in the chair she'd vacated and reported the message from Woodman's office. Checkers smiled, and his eyes sparkled, happy as Christmas tree lights.

"Whaddya suppose he wants?"

I shrugged.

Checkers pushed the telephone toward me. "Let's find out." He left his desk and went to a couch to listen in on an extension.

I dialed the number and asked for Woodman. His secretary, the downy voiced lady who'd left the message, answered and said Woodman wasn't in. However, he'd said if I returned his call to ask me if I could see him in his office at three o'clock that afternoon. I said I could.

"We," Checkers hissed, covering his phone's mouthpiece. *"We."*

"Mr. Checkers will be with me," I told the secretary.

"Mr. Checkers?"

"He's working with me."

"I see," she said, and—click—she was gone.

Checkers moved back to his desk, sat down, and leaned across it, squinting censoriously. "You know, that deal you made with Lassen was a real Hoosier move."

"It's done," I replied. I didn't want to discuss it. And knowing how he'd yowl if he knew I'd seen Lew Jaffe—joined hands with our "competition"—I kept silent about the meeting.

"You should've talked to me about it before you did it."

"You're forgetting something."

"What?"

"You agreed this was my case. That I called the shots."

"You called the shots all right," he said. "Right at you. Have you thought about how you're gonna dodge 'em while you're trapping whoever's pulling the trigger?"

"I'm still thinking about it."

"I'll put that on your tombstone."

The twentieth floor Century City offices of Woodman and Lenox looked across Little and Big Santa Monica boulevards to the fairways of the Los Angeles Country Club, a watering hole for the city's movers and shakers—an impelling view. The decor of the office was as modern as the day after tomorrow, white on white accented by touches of Chinese red. That included the carpeting, the pile standing tall. We waded through it to the reception room where we were greeted by Woodman's secretary, the lady with the pillowy voice. It was incongruous, that voice. She was in her upper forties, short, overweight, wearing a dress that had all the flair of a surgical gown. Her eyes bulged behind lenses as thick as bulletproof glass.

And her name was Nessie.

Woodman's private office was different from the rest of the suite. There was even more of the bloodless atmosphere. And it seemed out of keeping with Woodman himself. He was a tall, muscular-looking man with a rugged face, pleasantly lined and fashionably tanned. He wore a tan cashmere jacket and dark brown slacks. His hair was also dark brown, rumpled, and showed some evidence of gray. His eyes were clear, quick, searching. His smile, when he greeted us, was warm, his handshake firm. He gestured to chairs in front of his desk. We took them, and he sat on a white leather throne behind it and frowned inquiringly.

"I thought Miss Tyson would be with you."

"We think it's better if she stays out of sight . . . under the circumstances," I said.

Woodman nodded. "Mr. Lenox said you told him there had been an attempt on her life. Something about a hit-and-run accident in which a friend of yours who was with Miss Tyson was killed."

"That's right," I replied.

"Do you believe the threat to Miss Tyson is somehow related to the fact that she's Mr. Medford's granddaughter?"

"We ain't sure," Checkers responded. "But there was a call she got from someone sayin' he was—"

Woodman cut him off. "Mr. Lenox told me that, too. I can assure you it wasn't Mr. Medford."

"That's the point," Checkers said. "So who was it? And why'd he make it . . . except to get April outa Cage's apartment? Then you gotta figure in Bennett's murder."

Woodman said, "The police seem to think—"

Checkers interrupted him. "We know what the police think. That Bennett walked in on a burglary. With the case load they carry, if they get a killing that looks open and shut, they shut it fast. Or put it on a back burner. Can't blame 'em."

"No, I suppose not," Woodman agreed, and stood up, asking, "Would you care for something to drink? Fruit juice, coffee, beer?"

I passed. Checkers said he'd have a beer. Woodman went to a paneled wall and opened doors, revealing a built-in bar. He took a beer and orange juice from a refrigerator and poured them in sparkling crystal glasses. He returned to his desk, handing Checkers his beer, and stood sipping his orange juice thoughtfully. To break the silence, I offered Woodman the manila envelope containing April's proof of relationship to Medford.

He gestured it away. "I've seen it. Bennett gave me photocopies."

"Then you saw Bennett."

He nodded. "Briefly." His expression lapidified. "I ordered him out of the office."

"Why?" Checkers asked.

"In return for a payment of two hundred fifty thousand dollars, he offered to tell Miss Tyson her grandfather flatly refused a reconciliation. I told him to get out."

"I'm sure Miss Tyson didn't know anything about it," I said.

"I'm not suggesting she did. This meeting wouldn't be taking place if I thought so."

"Look, why is it taking place? Why'd you call Tug?"

Woodman hooked a leg over the corner of his desk. "I want to clarify something." He looked at me. "Mr. Lenox said he told you Mr. Medford once drew a will naming his daughter and/or her descendants as the heirs to his estate."

I said, "He also told me Medford withdrew that will and reinstated one naming Nicholas Bell as trustee and the Soldiers of God Foundation as the beneficiary."

"That's true, Mr. Cage. He did it after a lengthy investigation produced the fact that Julia Medford Tyson had died and, to the best of our knowledge, had no offspring."

"Well," Checkers said, "he knows he's got a granddaughter now . . . Or does he?"

"He knows."

I said, "Bell said he'd try to—"

"He told me about the conversation with Miss Tyson and you," Woodman broke in.

"And?"

"He spoke to Mr. Medford, urging him to see her. He flatly refused."

Checkers started to say something. Woodman held up his hand, stopping him.

"Let me finish . . . Mr. Medford telephoned me yesterday. He said he'd reconsidered his decision. He wants to see Miss Tyson."

14

"When?" April asked.

"This evening," I said.

She rose from the couch and moved edgily around the room. Checkers and I watched.

"Something wrong?" Checkers asked.

She shook her head and stopped in front of the open door to the balcony. Although there was a wisp of a breeze across the bay, the day was exorbitantly hot.

"I don't know," she replied.

"There's nothing to worry about," Checkers told her. "Tug'll be with you."

"It's not that. It's just remembering all the things mother said about him. How much she hated him for the way he acted."

"That was your mother," I said. "That was then. This is now. This is you."

"I know. But still I grew up hating him. I can't change that."

Checkers lumbered to his feet impatiently. "What were you thinking when you told Bennett to take a run at getting some of granpappy's money?"

April flared. "I didn't say I wanted any of his money!"

"Maybe you didn't say it, but why'd you wanta snuggle up to him if you hated him? And don't gimme any of that sentimental crap about him being your only relative."

April didn't reply.

"You knew all Bennett was after was some of the old man's money, so don't be so damn touchy on the subject. Okay, so you hate him. That's got nothing to do with it. He kicked your mother's ass out the door. She hadda tough time because of it. So did you. You got something coming." He went to the door and looked back at her. "Like I said before . . . you're gonna need it when you get my bill."

April was thoughtful for a long moment, then she said she'd better change and went into the bedroom. Checkers shook his head, drew a deep breath, and exhaled, exasperated.

"Jesus," he said.

April's appointment with Medford was for eight o'clock. Floodlights illuminated the front of the house and the parking area. I used the intercom implanted in the gate post. A man's voice responded, and the gate swung open as soon as I identified myself. "Rusty"—whose name Lenox'd said was Cliff Riddell—was waiting for us, still wearing Levis, plaid shirt, and Western boots. He gave us an indifferent nod and escorted us across the entry hall.

The walls were stark white. Its few pieces of furniture, all of an Amish simplicity, glowed with the pride of fine craftsmanship from a time when pride mattered. Subdued tapestries clung to the wall above a staircase making a semicircular climb to the second floor. When the front door had closed behind us, I felt we'd entered a sound lock. A bathyal hush engulfed the house.

As Riddell led us to towering double doors, he announced that Reverend Bell was waiting in the living room. April and I were surprised. We hadn't been told he'd be present. Riddell opened the doors. Bell rose from a chair beside a large, empty fireplace and came to us wearing a benedictory smile.

"Miss Tyson." He took a hand. "How good to see you again." He turned to me. "And Mr. Cage." He turned back to April. "I can't tell you how delighted I am that your grandfather decided to see you. I told him he'd be making a dreadful mistake if he didn't." He indicated the divan facing the fireplace. We sat and he took a chair facing us, radiant with saving grace.

As with the foyer, the room was without pretense. The furnishings, befitting a recluse, were spare, austere, impersonal. The walls were white here, too, and the ceiling raftered. But it was Simon Medford rather than Price who dominated the room. A huge portrait of the old scamp hung over the fireplace. He looked as ironfisted as the boss of a chain gang.

"Your grandfather is a bit under the weather," Bell said to April. "Nothing serious. A slight cold. But at his age, he has to be careful, so his doctor instructed him to remain in bed. And, as I'm sure you appreciate, this will be a very emotional encounter for him as well as for you. I'd suggest you keep it as short as possible. Just long enough to break the ice, so to speak." He turned his eyes on me. "And I might propose that he see you alone."

"No," April replied quickly. "I want Tug to be there."

Bell spread his hands. "Very well."

We got to our feet, and Bell led us up the staircase and along a wide second-floor hallway to a door at the end of it. He rapped lightly, and a woman answered, slipping out of the room beyond, closing the door behind her. Bell introduced her as Edna Riddell. She was, I guessed, nudging thirty, a plain woman of medium height, wearing navy blue slacks and a white blouse, her straight black hair gathered into a pony tail. Her expression tilted toward the sullen. When Bell asked if we could go in, she merely nodded and strode, stiff-backed, down the hall.

Medford was sitting up in a mammoth four-poster bed, a white shawl over his shoulders. The newspaper photos I'd seen of him had been taken sixty years before at the time of the big hurrah created by Rene Shaw's charge that Simon's life had been terminated with prejudice by his allegedly greedy son. In those photos, Price was a solemn, handsome young man with a pencil-line moustache and dark, pomaded hair. Now, a withered fourscore and five, his moustache was gone, and his scanty hair was as white as the sheets on his bed. His face, inset with pale, moist eyes, was haggard.

"This is April, Price," Bell said, then indicated me. "And Mr. Cage, a friend of hers." We were standing just inside the door. The old man's eyes never left April, appraising her. He finally raised a thin, splotchy hand, gesturing to her to come to his bedside. She crossed the room slowly. He evaluated her again.

"You were right, Nicholas. She resembles Julia." He took her hand. "Thank you for coming." His voice was fragile, raspy.

"Thank you for seeing me," April murmured.

Medford patted the edge of the bed, and April sat on it. "I made a terrible mistake. Your grandmother knew it. She tried to tell me. But I wouldn't listen. I wanted only the best for your mother, and I was hurt and angry when she married that . . ." he checked it ". . . when she married Alex Tyson. I couldn't forgive her. Not until it was too late. Then I employed a private detective to find her. Or any children she might've had. I'm told you know that now."

"Yes."

"When Nicholas told me you were in Los Angeles and wanted to see me, I was afraid. What could I say to you? How could I explain? How could I ask you to forgive me after the way I'd treated your mother?"

"There's nothing to forgive," April said softly.

"You're a very generous young lady." His eyes searched her. "I want us to know each other. I'm very tired now. I need sleep. But will you come back?"

"If you want me to."

"I do. Very much."

Medford put his head back on his pillows and closed his eyes. April stood up, looked down at him for a moment, turned away, and the brief meeting was over. There was something anticlimactic about it. Something unworthy of the years of emotional turmoil preceding it.

We'd agreed to meet Checkers at Ito's after April had seen her grandfather and were climbing an on-ramp to the Hollywood Freeway before either of us spoke. She stared out into the light-spangled night, appearing drained. Or relieved. Or both.

"Would you take me back to the apartment?" she asked.

I reminded her that Checkers was waiting at Ito's.
"You meet him, will you?"

I agreed, and there was more muteness. I ended it by observing that for having grown up hating her grandfather, she was very tactful with him.

She looked at me. Her expression wasn't cordial. Neither was her tone of voice. "What did you expect? I'd scream at him that he was a son of a bitch for the way he'd treated my mother? He's an old man who found out too late he had a conscience, and now he has to live with it."

"And you're going to see him again?"

"Of course . . . Is there any reason I shouldn't?"

I couldn't find one. But she sensed I was troubled. She asked what was the matter, and I told her the truth:

"I don't know."

I parked near the main entrance to the building, avoiding the garage for being too enclosed, isolated. I escorted her to the apartment, then went off to see Checkers. He was at the bar in Ito's snug tap room, nursing a Kirin and talking baseball with Suzuki, a young man who was studying for a Ph.D. in linguistics at UCLA, paying his way through graduate school by tending bar. I ordered a double bourbon on the rocks. Checkers and I excused ourselves and went to a quiet corner table.

"How'd it go?"

"Fast and friendly," I answered and gave him a report.

He looked pleased. "I'm thinking we oughta get a nice fat finders fee outa grandpa." He chuckled and added, "besides what we bill April for our services, 'course." He drank his Kirin with a calculating squint.

"Unless I miss my guess, Medford's gonna change his will again to include her in it. Maybe leave her the whole wad."

I shrugged. Checkers eyed me.

"What?"

I asked what he meant.

"Something's bothering you."

I nodded and made a stab at articulating it. "From the way Medford talked tonight, I got the impression that slamming the door in Julia's face has been troubling him for a long time. Ever since he changed his will in her favor and tried to find Julia and was told she was dead and there weren't any children."

"So?"

"But when I buttonholed Bell on Medford Lane and introduced him to April, he didn't act one damn bit surprised that Medford had a granddaughter. And when I said she wanted to see Medford, he told us how bitter the old man still was about Julia marrying Tyson. But he knew about Medford changing his will. He knew about the attempt to find Julia. He knew . . . he *had* to know . . . Medford was having second thoughts. But he didn't give a hint that the old man was relenting. All we got from him was sanctimonious shit about how stubborn he was."

"Maybe he was just being cautious," Checkers said. "Maybe he wasn't sure when he got right down to it that Medford would see April, and he didn't want to get her hopes up."

"Look, you were the one who was touting the idea that someone close to Medford was worried about April suddenly surfacing."

"Yeah, but—"

"You thought that's why Bennett was killed. You thought that's why April was in danger. Now you're buying this reconciliation without—"

"It happened, didn't it?"

"And two attempts on April's life happened, too."

He ran a huge hand over his face. "Okay, so I was wrong. It wasn't someone around Medford who killed Bennett and tried to take out April. It don't make sense now. And you've been saying all along that it was Dekoven and Vicari, right?"

I nodded.

"So why you got your balls in an uproar because April and Medford've made up?"

I didn't answer. I couldn't. Not in a way that'd make sense to him, counting—as I knew he already was—the money he'd be pocketing from the April-Medford reconciliation.

"Tug, all April hired us to do was find Bennett. Not who killed him. Or who killed that fella Newkirk. Or when you get right down to it, who'd been threatening her, except if it was someone trying to keep her from getting together with Medford. And tonight proved that ain't the case. So now the way I see it, our job's over. I don't give a shit about whether Dekoven and Vicari've been running dope. That ain't none of our business. Let the narcs handle it. Give 'em the cassette even if it ain't worth nothing legally. And if April's in trouble with Dekoven and Vicari, that's her problem. Let her go to the police."

"That's a switch."

"The situation's changed. April's got Medford in her corner now. With his bucks, he could hire a division of marines to protect her if he had to. What I'm sayin' is, let's get paid for services rendered and forget it."

"It isn't that easy for me," I said. "I've got more to forget than you have."

That was my curtain line.

April was asleep when I got back to the apartment. There was no light coming from under the bedroom door, anyway. I went out on the balcony and sat looking at the lights winking across the marina and tried to dissect my crotchety attitude about April and Medford's rapprochement. Perhaps, I thought, I was trying to cling to something because of my feeling of guilt over Frances' death, and I found myself writhing at the histrionics of playing the avenger. I heard Frances wisecracking. "A helluva lot of good you're doing me now, Buster. Dead's dead." And with that, second thoughts—stealthy vandals in the night—about having elicited the help of Lew Jaffe crept in. I stood up, told them to scat, and went into the den. Lassen had given me his phone number before we'd parted in Seattle. I called it. No answer. I looked up. April appeared in the open doorway.

"I didn't hear you come in."

"I thought you were asleep."

She went to a lacquer box on the desk, took a cigarette from it, and lit it.

"I didn't know you smoked," I said.

"I'd stopped until Newport Beach."

She inhaled deeply, letting the smoke escape slowly, eyeing the glowing tip of the cigarette. She had something on her mind.

"I had a call from my grandfather," she said.

Everything was going around in a circle. "Are you *sure* it was your grandfather this time?"

A reproving cloud crossed her face. "He asked me to have lunch with him tomorrow." She ground out the cigarette. "And he asked if I'd consider staying with him."

"And what did you say?"

"That I'd think about it."

"Have you?"

She nodded.

"And you're going to accept."

"Yes," she replied, bracing herself for my disapproval. But it was unnecessary.

I wished her well.

Cliff Riddell, driving a Cadillac Eldorado picked up April and her luggage at eleven-thirty the next morning. At the door to the apartment, she thanked me. I said think nothing of it.

And she was gone.

I called Checkers and broke the news to him. He was delighted. He invited me to have lunch with him. I remembered this had all started at a lunch with him. I turned him down, saying that I was growing a tad weary of Japanese cuisine.

"No sweat," he said. "Where would you like to eat? You name it."

I told him I'd been looking forward to opening a can of tomato soup.

"Hey, your nose ain't outa joint about last night, is it? About just getting our money and forgetting April?"

"No," I said, knowing it lacked a certain conviction.

"Lemme ask you something . . . you gettin' a hot crotch for her?"

"Oh, Christ, Checkers!"

I didn't have a can of tomato soup so I was scrambling some eggs when Lew Jaffe called to tell me the district attorney's office had secured an eavesdropping warrant from the superior court and he was ready to move when and if I could set up a meeting with Dekoven and/or Vicari.

"I'll get back to you," I said.

I hung up. The eggs had burned. I put them down the garbage disposal and called the Import Bazaar and asked for Dekoven. I was transferred from the switchboard operator to Dekoven's secretary and repeated the routine. After a long wait, the secretary's voice came back on the line. I told her who was calling.

"I'm sorry," she announced, "but Mr. Dekoven isn't available."

"What's that mean?" I asked.

"What's what mean?"

"He isn't available."

"He's out."

"Out to me or out to the world in general?"

She closed the circle. "I'm sorry but he isn't available."

"May I leave a message?"

"Of course."

"Tell him I called. Tell him it's urgent I speak to him. Tell him it's about the cassette."

"The . . . cassette?"

"He'll know what I'm talking about."

I put the phone down and wondered if I should take another run at scrambling a couple of eggs. The decision was made for me. The refrigerator revealed I'd burned the only two eggs extant. So I decided to try Lassen again to find out if he had any information for me about Dekoven and Vicari. The disembodied voice of a phone company operator, every vowel and consonant polished bright, came on with a recorded message that the number I'd reached was not in service. I double checked the number and dialed again. Same operator. Or a clone. Same announcement.

My first thought was that Lassen had reneged on our bargain and was at that moment shearing sheep or cultivating organic zucchini in Idaho. I went to my shelf of "reference" books with its row of Los Angeles area phone directories. With blind luck, I first consulted the San Fernando Valley book and found a Ruth Zenakes listed with an address in Sherman Oaks. I dialed the number.

No answer.

I drove to Sherman Oaks via Lassen's house. There was a real estate agency's for-sale sign on a stick in the peewee lawn. I went to the door, knocked, received no answer, and moved around the deck. Venetian blinds or draperies covered all the windows except one. I looked in. It was a bedroom. There was nothing in it but darker spots of wallpaper where pictures had once hung and against which furniture had stood, shielding against the bleaching sun.

Ruth Zenakes' address was an apartment house. I pushed the button next to her name on the directory in the entry way. Nothing. I rang the manager and a woman's voice, refined as sugar, came out of the intercom.

"Who is it, please?"

I gave her my name, said I was a friend of Ruth Zenakes and had an urgent message for her. "Do you know where she is?"

"She moved yesterday."

"To Idaho?"

"Yes."

I felt like the crown prince of fools for thinking Lassen would keep his end of the bargain, becoming my mole and keeping me posted about what Dekoven and Vicari—knowing I had Bennett's cassette—had in mind for me. It occurred to me at this late date that it would serve Lassen's interest to accept a contract from them to eliminate me. Sure, he'd said he wouldn't. Ho, ho, ho.

As I drove along the San Diego Freeway, I decided I didn't want to go home. Dekoven might've called back if his secretary had given him my message about the cassette. But he might not, choosing to ignore me, having already made other plans for me—a thought that drew my attention to the rearview mirror to see if I was being followed.

I left the freeway at Washington Boulevard and drove to Venice and walked the asphalt "boardwalk" and the pier with its piebald crowd fishermen. And fisherwomen. Or fisherpersons. I examined open-air shops with their geegaw merchandise and browsed a bookstore, buying a paperback private eye novel to see how a *smart* investigator operated. I sat on a bench and read three chapters. It was depressing. The fictional PI, as dumb as a brick wall, was still smarter than I.

I left the book on the bench.

On the way home, I stopped at a butcher shop, one

of an endangered species. It sold only meat. Good, melt-in-your-mouth meat. Aged meat. Some of it old enough to vote. I bought a steak and took it home, thinking I might barbecue it on the small grill on the balcony. But I remembered the last time I'd played steak chef was for Frances, and my appetite left me. I put the meat in the freezer. Dekoven hadn't returned my call. So I made myself a scotch and water and had it for an early supper, another one for dessert, and I poured a third as an after-dinner drink.

I took it out on the balcony and watched the fog drifting in for another night on the town. I thought of what Checkers said. With April united with her grandfather, our job was over. And, although I believe great sins are too frequently committed in the name of pragmatism, I had to admit he was right. As galling as it was to accept, I had nothing—not one shred of evidence—with which to place the guilt for Frances' death at the feet of Dekoven and Vicari. And it appeared I wasn't going to.

The phone rang. I suspected it was Checkers, and I was in no mood to talk to him. I decided to let it ring and check the message—if one was left.

It was Max Polo, live on tape. He hadn't made the call through a secretary. He'd made it himself, giving me a number to call. I did, and he answered immediately. There were no preliminaries. He knew who was calling and said he wanted to see me. I asked what about.

"I don't discuss business on the phone," he replied.

"I didn't know we had any business, Max."

"Can you be here at six o'clock?"

"Where's here?"

"My office."

"What's a busy man like you doing answering his own phone?"

"It's a direct line."

Direct and private and bug proof I thought. A lawyer with his stripe of clientele, he was wise to be wary.

I said I'd be there.

Polo's law offices were in a small, Spanish-style building on the Sunset Strip. Constructed around a garden with flowers, pepper trees, and an ornate fountain, it probably had been an inviting oasis once upon a time. Now the flowers were gone, the fountain bubbled no more, and the roots of the trees had broken through the patio tiles. I wondered why Polo hadn't abandoned these shabby surroundings for a newer, more modish location and felt a spot of respect for him that he hadn't, though I suspected it more a matter of rent than sentiment.

His secretary, a frail woman who appeared elderly enough to make legal secretaries the second oldest profession, escorted me along a hallway separating a half-dozen cubbyholes in which Polo's hired hands, appearing wan and dusty, labored amid hedgerows of filing cabinets. In contrast to these untidy nooks, Polo's office seemed large enough to garage the Goodyear blimp. It was a dim, glowering place. The walls, the woodwork, the furniture and draperies were dark. Dark and old. The office had aged with its occupant.

And less well.

Polo didn't stand to greet me. He solemnly waved a hand at an armchair in front of a desk that dwarfed him. The chair felt as intimidating as a witness stand.

Not unintentionally, I was sure. As soon as the secretary closed the door behind herself, Polo said, "You called Duke Dekoven earlier today."

"So?"

"You left a message that you wanted to talk about a cassette."

"So?"

"Dekoven was leaving town. He asked me to talk to you."

"He didn't ask me to talk to you," I said.

"Anything you had to say to him, you can say to me."

"Then you must know what's on the tape."

"I have no idea," he replied. "Does Dekoven?"

"Didn't you ask him?"

"No."

Which was bullshit. I got to my feet. "We're wasting time."

"I'm authorized to hear anything you have to say."

"I don't give a damn if you're knighted, anointed, and baptized. I haven't anything to say to you. I want to talk to Dekoven. Or Bobby Vicari."

Polo arched his eyebrows. "Vicari?"

"Or both . . . preferably both."

"What's Vicari have to do with this?"

"Call him. Ask him. Or is he out of town, too?"

"To my knowledge, Dekoven and Vicari don't even know each other."

"The cassette says they do." I turned to go. "If and when you hear from Dekoven, tell him I'm still waiting for his phone call."

"Just a moment, Cage." Polo got to his feet and his tennis court–sized desk made him look even smaller. "Is there anything more I can tell him?"

I gave it some thought and decided why not. "Yeah . . . yeah, you can tell him the cassette is for sale. If he wants to buy it, we can get together and negotiate the price. He can name the time and place."

"I'll give him the message."

I said thanks.

An accident had turned the San Diego Freeway into a parking lot. And a cauldron of heat and gasoline fumes. Cars, stalling from vapor lock, lengthened the occluded artery to two or three miles. I muscled the Volvo to an off-ramp and drove surface streets to the marina and settled down to wait for a phone call from Dekoven. It came about nine o'clock.

"Cage?"

"Yeah."

"Dekoven . . . Had a call from Max. He said you want to see me."

"That's right."

"He said you've got something you want to sell me."

"The Bennett cassette."

"Tony Bennett? I'm not running a music store."

"You know what I'm talking about."

"Tell me."

"When I see you."

"You want to come up here?"

"Where's here?"

"My place at Big Bear. Up on Moonridge."

I didn't picture myself floundering around on mountain roads in the middle of the night, especially if Dekoven was planning a surprise party for me. And it was too fast, anyway. I had to make the arrangements for Lew Jaffe to set up a drop on the meeting.

"I suffer from acrophobia."

"What's that?"

"Fear of heights. Especially Moonridge heights at night."

Dekoven laughed. "Look, you name a time and place for next week, and I'll be there."

"Monday. Ten o'clock. Your office."

"You gotta date. See you then."

And he hung up.

I didn't like it. Dekoven was too relaxed, too casual. He knew I was trying to set him up. Maybe he was being flippant for whoever he thought might be listening to—and recording—our conversation. But if he thought the line was tapped, why did he bother to call at all? Then it occurred to me he could've been enjoying a private joke. That he knew something else. That I wouldn't be around to keep our date.

I laughed at that melodramatic possibility and called Lew Jaffe at his home to tell him about the call and share a chuckle or two with him. Only he didn't chuckle. And he didn't say anything for a very long and hollow moment.

"You there Lew?" I asked plaintively.

"It's a possibility," he said.

"Aw, come on!"

"Hey," he said. "What about Bennett? And those guys Newkirk and Condotti you told me about? We've got to consider these things."

"I don't *like* considering these things."

"Then don't go out, lock your doors, and keep away from windows. I'll be in touch."

He hung up, and I felt very lonely. I paced the floor, telling myself how ridiculous he was being. I agreed with everything I said, and wished I believed it. I decided all I needed was a good night's sleep. I checked the front door and the door to the balcony, pulled draperies, and went to bed. If there was any sleep around, it was hiding from me. It was nearly four o'clock by Helen's clock the last time I remembered looking at it.

The doorbell woke me up. Helen's clock said it was eleven-fourteen. I fumbled into a robe and staggered to the door. I didn't have to open it. The second it was off the latch, Checkers burst in like a tornado running behind schedule.
"What the hell's the matter?" I demanded.
"You ain't heard?"
"What?"
"Vicari was blown away last night."

15

Checkers had been driving to his office when he heard the news on the car radio. According to the report, Vicari was shot and killed as he was leaving his Manhattan Beach car dealership about eleven o'clock the night before. The police said he was hit three times by shots fired from a .357 magnum.

"Ain't that the cat's ass?" Checkers asked.

I was too busy digesting the news to respond. Checkers glanced at his watch, said he had an eleven o'clock appointment, and left with only slightly less bustle than he arrived.

I went to the kitchen and tuned the radio to a news station. It was a half-hour later, the coffee had perked, and I was having a second cup of it before the Vicari story was reported. There was a piece of news Checkers hadn't known or had forgotten to tell me. A Manhattan Beach homicide detective said Albert Massi, Vicari's cousin and a dealership employee, was locking up a service bay when he heard the gunshots. He ran to the front of the showroom to see a man get into a car and speed off. But, the detective said, Massi was able to give the police only a vague description of the killer and the car he was driving. The detective did speculate that since Vicari was an alleged organized crime figure, his slaying might be mob related. I was on my third cup of coffee when the phone rang.

"Tug?" It was April. "Have you heard about that man Vicari?"

"Yes."

"What does it mean?"

"It means the world's a little better place this morning."

"Do you think it's just coincidence?"

"For us, yes, but not for Vicari. He who lives by the sword and all that," I said and changed the subject: "How's it going with you?"

"All right."

Maybe it was just me, but I thought her appraisal seemed to lack something in enthusiasm.

"And your Grandfather?"

"He isn't well. Doctor Stangood says it's acute bronchitis." There was a pause, and then she said she wanted to see me. Nothing urgent, she added. Perhaps we could have lunch sometime. I said fine, and she said she'd call and I said fine again.

I started for the bedroom to dress, but the doorbell stopped me and when I opened the door Lew was on the other side of it. His lips wore a musing smile, his eyes were questioning.

He entered, asking, "You heard?"

"I heard."

I offered him a cup of coffee, he accepted, and we went into the kitchen. He sat at the bar, drinking his coffee black.

"Well?" he asked.

"Well what?"

"Is Vicari's murder just coincidence, or is there anything you know about it you'd like to share with me?"

"What're you doing . . . moonlighting for the Manhattan Beach department?"

"This is personal. Just between us. But we're going to have to share the tape with Manhattan Beach. That's going to mean questions. And I'd like to know if there're any answers before I'm asked them."

"The tape I gave you and what I told you is all I know, Lew. Is Vicari's murder a coincidence?" I shrugged. "But maybe not. Maybe Dekoven could tell you something."

"Maybe he could've."

"Could've?"

"There was a bulletin out of the San Bernardino Sheriff's Department this morning. Dekoven bought it last night, too."

My mouth dropped open. Wide. Very wide. So wide I could've swallowed myself.

"He had a place at Big Bear. His caretaker found his body this morning just inside the front door. He'd taken two shots to the head."

I managed to stop gawking and said, "There goes coincidence."

"Any ideas?" Lew asked.

I shook my head. But I tried some speculation, thinking out loud. I said it was possible—even probable—that Vicari and Dekoven weren't the only ones bossing their drug-running operation. That they had partners, and maybe those partners knew about the cassette and were afraid if Duke and Bobby took a fall they'd go down with them.

Lew regarded me with a kindly smile, clearly not ready to buy—or even take an option on—my theory. "You've been away for a long time, haven't you?"

I laughed weakly.

Lew finished his coffee, got to his feet, and said, "Keep thinking."

Over more coffee I scrambled for something that might connect the murders of Dekoven and Vicari with the threat to April and the killings of Bennett and Newkirk. And, perhaps, of Vince Condotti. I came up zilch.

I dressed and wondered why I bothered. I was unemployed. I thought of Larry Simmons, expecting me to go searching for Mona Crane. But I'd decided to let a decent amount of time pass and call him, telling him I hadn't been able to get any sort of line on Mona and to forget it. He wouldn't. But I couldn't carry his emotional baggage for him.

So with nowhere to go, I had to make up a place. I took a copy of *Newsweek* and walked—unafraid that Dekoven or Vicari could reach me from the abode of the dead—to a small cafe called the Foghorn. It had a patio hard by the main channel. I could lunch, enlighten myself about the world's work and problems, and take the sun. I was sipping coffee and trying to read another in the glut of "think" pieces about the Middle East entanglement when a shadow fell across the table. I looked up.

It belonged to Lassen.

He sat down and said, "If you're wondering how I knew you were here, I saw you leave your building and followed you."

"I thought you were in Idaho."

"What made you think that?"

"Ruth's in Idaho, isn't she?"

"She went ahead to meet the moving van. I told her there was one more piece of business I had to attend to. I'm leaving in a couple of hours." A waitress approached and he waved her away. "I guess you've heard about Vicari."

"And Dekoven."

"I saw Vicari and Dekoven when I got back from Seattle. They offered me a contract on you. I turned them down. Vicari said he'd handle it himself."

"What excuse did you give?"

"I said I was retiring."

"I guess that's the only reason you didn't take it."

"Not entirely. You let me go . . . Checkers did, anyway . . . when you had me cold in your apartment. I owed you that. Then we made a deal in Seattle, right?"

"Right."

"And when I make a deal, I keep it." He pinched a cigarette from a pack and lit it. "Do you?"

I nodded.

"Then when I asked you if I could trust you, why'd you say I couldn't?"

I didn't have an answer.

"That worried me, Cage. It worried me a lot. Just because I don't have a record doesn't mean I couldn't be in trouble if you pointed in my direction. I was suspected in a couple of jobs I did. I probably still am."

"You're safe."

"I know," he said. "I made sure of that."

I took a sip of coffee and asked how.

"I killed Vicari."

My coffee cup hit the saucer.

"And Dekoven," he added, his voice as casual as a stroll in the park. "I knew he was going up to Big Bear yesterday, so I paid him a visit last night." He shrugged the rest.

"*Why?*"

"You wanted them. I gave them to you."

All I could do was stare at him.

"And it was the only way I could get out clean." He eyed me narrowly. "I knew your idea of suckering Dekoven and Vicari into some sort of trap wouldn't work. They were too smart for that. And when it didn't work, I figured you'd think I double-crossed you, tipped them off, and you'd give me to the police for killing Newkirk. But let's say it *had* worked, and you'd nailed them. One or the other . . . maybe both . . . might've done himself a favor by implicating me for dropping Newkirk. So you see, I was sort of between a rock and a hard place. But this way, Dekoven and Vicari can't blow any whistles. And if you do, I'll dump on you . . . swear you gave me a contract on them because of what they did to your lady friend."

"If all you were doing was protecting yourself, wouldn't it've been easier just to kill me?"

"We had a deal, remember." An embryonic smile touched his lips. "And I had to consider another thing . . . that you might've planted a time bomb. One of those open-in-case-of-my-death letters that'd shaft me."

I stared at him. "I don't believe what I'm hearing, Lassen. You're not real."

"If you're ever in Idaho, drop around and have another look." He got to his feet and walked away. I stayed at the table.

A long time.

* * *

I went back to my apartment wondering what to do about Lassen. Or that's what I told myself. But it wasn't true. I knew what I was going to do.

Nothing.

I considered the morality of letting him get away with the murders of Dekoven and Vicari and thought of Frances and said to hell with it. The bastards had made murder the name of the game, and they'd blown it. Tough titty, Tilly. I wouldn't lose thirty seconds of sleep because of an itchy conscience. My deal with Lassen had been for him to stay chummy with Duke and Bobby and let me know their next move, if any. I hadn't hinted, suggested, implied, or intimated that I wanted them dead. His reasons for dropping them were self-serving—to prevent the possibility of them dumping on him for Newkirk's murder.

And admitting the murders to me was just as self-serving—to warn me that he'd implicate me if he was nailed for the killings. It wasn't an idle threat. By hearing his admission and doing nothing about it, I was vulnerable to the charge of being an accessory after the fact. That was worrisome.

But I could live with it.

The six o'clock news reported Dekoven's murder. And recapped the killing of Vicari. But it made no connection between the two deaths. Maybe Lew Jaffe hadn't yet given the Manhattan Beach police or San Bernadino County sheriffs the cassette. Or maybe the two departments were, for whatever reason, saying nothing for broadcast or publication. I turned off the TV set and thought about the unpleasant prospect of reporting Lassen's confessional to Checkers. He was, obliquely, involved. In a worst-case scenario, his private investigator's license could be suspended, even revoked, because an employee had withheld information from the authorities.

I went to Checkers' apartment, and he exploded, stomping around his living room, giving me hell in spades. And in hearts, diamonds, and clubs. What'd happened to the smart cop he'd once known? How could I get so stupid in such a short time? I tried to remind him I'd never been as smart as he imagined, but he was in no mood to listen.

"You're an accessory after the fact!" he roared. "You know that, don't you?"

I said I did.

"I still don't know what the hell you thought you was going to accomplish."

I still said nothing about enlisting Lew Jaffe in an attempt to bug Dekoven and/or Vicari. That scheme —whatever its merits, or lack of them—was now as dead as Duke and Bobby. And, anyway, that wouldn't have stopped Checkers. He'd have launched into another screed, and I'd already had enough haranguing for the moment.

"Well, you'd better hope Lassen slips on some sheep shit on that fucking farm of his, fractures his skull and dies."

There was more. A good deal more. But Checkers, realizing he was beating a fait accompli to death, eventually wound down and suggested we go down to Ito's for something to eat. I said I wasn't hungry, and we parted company in the restaurant parking lot. Checkers left me with:

"I take back what I said. You ain't bossing this case any more."

I asked, "What case?"

It was Sunday, and I spent a disproportionate share of it with the *Times*, which spoke of Dekoven as one of Los Angeles' "more colorful characters." The San Bernadino County Sheriff's Department said it was following up on leads that it couldn't discuss. There was a similar but shorter story about Vicari's murder. There was still no reported link between the two killings.

I put the papers aside and was contemplating how to spend the rest of the day when the call came. It was Larry Simmons.

"How are you, Mr. Cage?"

"Uh . . . fine."

"I was wondering if you had any news for me."

"Well, no, not yet."

"I ran across a snapshot I forgot I had. It's of Mona with April Tyson and Mr. Bennett. It was taken here in the Jury Box. I've put it in the mail to you."

I said thanks.

"Have you been able to get a line on Mona's brother?"

"Uh . . . no. No, I haven't."

There was a stillness that stretched from Los Angeles to Seattle and back several times. Why didn't I level with him? Why didn't I tell him I was busy tracking down a covey of KGB agents? Why didn't I tell him that—if the sanitation department hadn't been around yet—he'd find his thousand dollar check reduced to confetti in the trash container on the curb outside his door? Why didn't I tell him to hire Burns or Pinkerton or Wackenhut?

The fact is, I didn't. The fact is, I said, "I was planning to go to Santa Barbara tomorrow and check with the university."

The University of California at Santa Barbara isn't in Santa Barbara. It's in the adjoining town of Isla Vista, which gained a backhanded sort of renown when a Bank of America branch was put to the torch during a student anti-Vietnam demonstration twenty some-odd years ago. I went to the registrar's office, showed my plastic ID to a pleasant lady who appeared at the moment to be navigating her fifties. I told her about Mona Crane's disappearance and said her only living relative was a younger brother named Thomas who was reported to be—or to have been—a student at UCSB.

"I'm trying to locate him to see if he knows her whereabouts."

"One moment," she said and left me standing at a counter, going across the office to use a computer. I could see her face as she worked at it, reading the screen. A deepening frown wasn't a good omen. At length, she made a note on a slip of paper and returned.

"Thomas Crane," she said, "didn't return to school after the winter quarter. This is the latest address we have for him. I hope it helps." She gave me the slip of paper.

The address was on Los Olivas Street in Santa Barbara, a few blocks from the mission. It was a matriarchal-looking house made sprightly by a fresh coat of white paint with doors and shutters trimmed in blue. A small sign on the freshly mowed lawn announced a room for rent. A pretty girl, probably in the latter years of her teens, was sitting on a wooden swing on the porch. It was supported by chains attached to the roof of the porch. The chains creaked as she slowly rocked to music coming from the Walkman to which she was harnessed. When I came on the porch, she detached herself from the radio and gave me a nice smile.

"Hi."

I returned the greeting and introduced myself and said I was looking for Thomas Crane.

Her face grew overcast. "You a bill collector or something?"

I smiled and said it was a personal matter involving his sister. But she wasn't entirely reassured. "Well, he doesn't live here any more. He moved . . . oh, three or four months ago."

"Do you know where he went?"

She shook her head. "It was just a few days after I moved in. I only talked to him two, maybe three times."

"Is the landlady in?"

"No, she's away. Somewhere in Oregon. A sister died, and she went to the funeral."

"Well, is there someone else who might know?"

"Not now."

I thanked her and left the porch, moving to the Volvo at the curb when I was stopped by:

"Mister!"

I turned. The girl hurried to me. "I just remembered. He told me he ran a computer store. On lower State Street, I think he said. He told me the name.

It's . . ." the personal computer behind her eyes conducted a search . . . "it's called . . . the First Byte! Yeah, that's it! The First Byte."

I thanked her again.

It was a couple of blocks north of Highway 101, a rather humble storefront. Its inventory looked skimpy, and its customers were—at the moment, anyway—otherwise occupied. There was a young man engaged in some repair work on a computer behind a high counter at the rear of the display room. I went to him. I put him somewhere in his early twenties. He wore khaki shorts and a T-shirt with lettering that said "The First Byte Is the Best." His hair was long and mussed, and his face was long and dour. He ignored me until I told him I was looking for Thomas Crane. He gave me a pair of eyes reflecting total indifference.

"What can I do for you?"

"I want to buy a dozen Macintoshes."

"We don't handle 'em," he said and went back to doing whatever he was doing to the computer behind the counter.

"What do you handle?"

"Come the first of the month, we're outa business so you'd better go somewhere else."

I told him I liked an honest man and inquired if, by chance, he was Thomas Crane. He conceded he was, and I said I'd sought him out to ask about his sister.

"What about her?"

I again related the story of Mona taking her unannounced leave of Seattle and Larry Simmons' feeling she might've been murdered. Crane gave me the sort of smile one reserves for a child making up a story about the boogeyman.

"That's a pile of crap . . . I saw her about a week ago."

"Where?"

"Right here. She just walked in, said she was passing through town, and looked me up. I was pretty surprised, you know. First time I'd seen her or heard from her in about three years. We never went for that loving big-sister, little-brother routine."

"What did she say about leaving Seattle?"

He shrugged. "Nothing except she'd kissed it off."

"Did she say why?"

He flipped his shoulders again. "Just said she'd got fed up with the place."

"Well, did she say where she was going?"

"She didn't know for sure. Said she might go to Chicago."

"Where'd she been?"

"San Diego, she said. L.A. and San Diego."

"Do you know where she's staying in Chicago?"

He shook his head.

"Do you have any relatives there?"

"Nope."

"What about friends your sister might have?"

"If she's got any, I don't know about them. And she might not've gone there. There's a lot of gypsy in Mona. Once she told me she was going to Boston, and the next I heard from her she was in Baraboo . . . You know where Baraboo is?"

"Never heard of it."

"Wisconsin."

"Where's Wisconsin?"

Crane was polite. He smiled at my joke.
Weakly.

* * *

I had a crabmeat omelet for lunch in the restaurant on Stearn's Wharf. As I left Santa Barbara, I turned on the radio to a news station, only half listening to it until I reached Ventura, where the newscaster got my undivided attention by reporting that federal agents and the police in Los Angeles, San Francisco, Portland, and Seattle had raided Import Bazaar warehouses, finding hidden in crates of merchandise—and in the merchandise itself—both cocaine and heroin with a street value of fifty million dollars. The authorities announced that the raid had been prompted by undercover information following the murders of Dekoven and Vicari—killings they now attributed to a quarrel between the dead men and their partners in the drug-smuggling operation. Fourteen Import Bazaar employees in the four cities were being held for questioning in the drug-running operation as well as the murders of Dekoven and Vicari.

You listening, Lew Jaffe?

The message light on my answering machine was winking at me. I answered it. Jasmine's voice, imperious as a chainsaw, commanded me to call Checkers.

I did, and he grumbled, "Where you been?"

I repeated the story of Mona and Larry Simmons, including the fact that Larry'd given me a check for a thousand dollars.

"How come you didn't tell me anything about the job?"

"Because it's a freebee."

"I don't get you. What about the check the guy gave you?"

"I tore it up."

"You *what*?"

Checkers' end of the line was dead while he fought off a heart attack. Then he asked, "Why?" He sounded as if he were being strangled with a piano wire.

"Because I didn't want the job, but I felt sorry for Simmons."

"Well, if you're into charity work now, forget I called."

"What's that mean?"

"It means I picked up a check for twenty-five thousand from Woodman this morning."

"Twenty-five thousand?" Now it was my turn to beat back a coronary. "How come?"

Woodman called, Checkers explained, saying that Price Medford wanted to show his appreciation for what we'd done for April, and he had a check for twenty-five grand for us. Did Checkers want to pick it up, or should he put it in the mail?

Checkers was out the door.

"I figured we'd split it ten and ten with the other five for expenses. I got a check waiting for you, but if you're tearing 'em up, I'll just—"

"I'm there."

It was the first check for ten thousand I'd ever seen with my name on it. And it might be the last. I thought about having it photocopied and framed for hanging. Checkers, too, was content—to a point. The point being that when April came into her share of her grandfather's money, there'd be another—and perhaps even more lucrative—payday.

It was too late to deposit the check, so I took it home and admired it some more. Then I steeled myself for the unpleasant task of talking to Larry Simmons. I placed the call, hoping someone else would answer and tell me Larry'd thrown all his cares to the winds and had taken off for Katmandu. No such luck. Larry answered, and I told him he could relax.

"I located Mona's brother in Santa Barbara," I said. "He saw her a week or so ago. She was passing through town."

"Where'd she been?" He sounded as dreary and suspicious as ever.

"She told her brother San Diego and Los Angeles."

"Did she say where she was going?"

"Chicago. But her brother said not to count on that. He said she's a gypsy. She might wind up anywhere."

"When're you leaving?"

"Leaving?"

"For Chicago."

That did it. My patience went out the window—head first—and a big glob of my sympathy for Simmons followed close behind. I wasn't going to be a soft touch a second time. Larry and I had arrived at a moment of truth.

"I'm not," I said.

"But—"

"Look, Larry, you said all you wanted to know was whether or not Mona was alive and well. Her brother says she is and since he's seen her, he's a pretty good authority. Let go of whatever you're trying to hang on to. I think you're more in love with being in love than you are with Mona."

"Maybe you're right," he conceded, though he

didn't sound convinced. "And thanks for what you've done. I'll send you another check."

"I don't want another check. I didn't want the first one. I tore it up."

"Aw, you shouldn't have done that."

I said goodbye.

16

I went back into hibernation, and before I noticed it July left, and August arrived with unseasonable Santa Ana winds, ready for a brush fire it could fan into an inferno and burn a few thousand acres of brush and at least scorch a few neighborhoods. Temperatures rocketed. I lived in shorts and a pair of mellowly mature huarachis.

The mail brought me the snapshot of Mona that Larry Simmons had said he was sending. It included Bennett and April and had been taken as they sat in a booth at the Jury Box, Bennett in the middle with an arm around each of the women. Mona, her black hair worn short, was on the plus side of pretty but short of being noticeably attractive. There was an aura of blandness about her. Larry had characterized her as happy. The photo belied it. She looked withdrawn, melancholy. April and Bennett, on the other hand, were beaming brightly. I put the snapshot into a desk drawer.

But my mind kept returning to Mona. Not because of Larry's neurotic concern for her but the fact that she was, according to her brother, an untethered spirit who had the guts to nurture her wanderlust.

I envied that.

After my return from Vietnam, I'd indulged in some tramping around the countryside. But then I'd met and married Helen, whose life was strewn with anchors, holding her fast to a conventional existence centered on home and hearth, bringing my fling at vagabonding to an end. I contented myself with reading books by others who'd explored the other side of distant hills. Now, with the vision of ten thousand dollars in my bank account pirouetting in my head, the desk, chairs, and couch in the den were obscured by road maps as I dreamed and plotted a cross-country course, not on the interstate system, but on forgotten roads and byways. I'd engaged in such hankerings before. This time I'd really convinced myself I would make the wish a reality. Then, the next day, my temporarily quotidian life closed in.

April came calling.

She'd come to get her rental car. It had been parked in the basement garage, running up a bill I was grateful I didn't have to pay.

"I hate being without a car," she said.

I sympathized, poured canned lemonade, and we went out on the balcony. She seemed distracted, and I was certain it wasn't concern for the tab on the rental.

"How's it going?" I asked.

"Grandfather went to the hospital day before yesterday."

I registered surprise. Not entirely over the fact that he required hospitalization but that he would permit himself to be removed from his house.

"He flatly refused to go at first but finally gave in."

"What hospital is he in?"

"Doctor Stangood's."

"Stangood's?"

"The Stangood Medical Center. It's in Pomona."

"Why would he go there?"

"Stangood's his doctor and—"

"Still . . ." For some indefinable reason, the qualms I'd felt about the sudden reconciliation between April and her grandfather came tiptoeing back. April waited for me to go on, but I didn't.

Although it was in the shade and sheltered from the feverish winds, the balcony felt as hot as an open-hearth furnace. We went inside, and I turned up the air conditioner. April sat at the breakfast bar, and when I put more lemonade in front of her she stared into the glass, moody as a foggy night.

"I want to ask a favor."

She looked up. I waited.

"Would you come to the house and stay until we see what happens with grandfather?"

"Why?"

"I don't like being there alone."

"What about the Riddells?"

"Oh, don't know . . . I feel as if they resent me. My being there. They're so cold, impersonal. And, my God, the arguments."

"Arguments?"

"The Riddells. Almost every evening. I hear them all the way upstairs, screaming at each other."

"What about?"

April sighed wearily, distressed. "His drinking. And I gather he's using something . . . coke, I think . . . and there's some woman he's been seeing. And from what I hear, she isn't the first. He goes out at night and gets back . . . sometime . . . three, four in the morning, and they start yelling at each other again.

Last night it sounded like he was slapping her around. And during the day I have the feeling that—"

She stopped, groping for it.

"What?"

"That they're always watching me. And everytime I've been in grandfather's room, Mrs. Riddell's found some excuse to be there, too. I can't help thinking there's something they don't want me to know."

"Why don't you get out?"

"I wanted to. Before he left for the hospital, I told grandfather I thought I should get a place of my own. He didn't understand. I couldn't explain. I didn't try. He asked me to stay at least until he came back. I said I would . . . Will you come?"

I wondered if she was imagining things. Not about the Riddells' fights. Being watched. Was she just self-conscious about being a stranger in a strange place?

"Let me think about it."

"I can pay you if that's what's stopping you."

It wasn't. But I didn't tell her that. And I didn't tell her about the twenty-five thousand from Woodman. That was Checkers' business.

"How?" I asked.

"Mr. Woodman and Reverend Bell came to see me yesterday. They said grandfather'd told them he wanted to set up a trust fund for me . . . a hundred and fifty thousand dollars a year for the rest of my life."

I gulped at the figure. And even though it was only a snippety percentage of Medford's net worth, it seemed generous. Very generous. And as with the reconciliation, very sudden. Too sudden? Too generous?

"What did you say?" I asked.

"I told them I hadn't expected grandfather to do anything like that. I said I wasn't sure I wanted him to. They asked me to think it over, and I said I would."

I was relieved she hadn't jumped at the offer.

"Will you stay at the house?"

I asked if the Riddells knew of the invitation.

"No."

"Don't you think you should tell them?"

"I intend to if—"

She stopped. She could read in my expression.

I went to the garage with her and sent her off in the rental. I said I'd be along in a couple of hours. I returned to the apartment, packed a small bag, and called Checkers' office. A pleasant feminine voice, unknown to me, answered.

"Checkers and Associates."

"This is Tug Cage."

"Oh, yes, Mr. Cage," she responded, sounding as if she'd been breathlessly awaiting my call.

"Who's this?" I asked.

"Diana Norton."

"Where's Jasmine?"

"Who?"

"Never mind. Is Checkers in?"

"I'm sure he is to you, Mr. Cage . . . one moment."

It was about that before Checkers' voice came booming through. "Hiya, Tug!"

"Who the hell is Diana Norton?"

"New secretary. You should see her." He smacked his lips.

"What happened to Jasmine?"

"She wanted a raise. I wouldn't give it to her. So she quit. Gone to work for some collection agency."

"A marriage made in heaven," I said.

He laughed. "But Diana's just temporary. Jasmine will be back."

"You just *un*made my day."

He laughed again and asked what was on my mind. I told him.

"A hundred fifty thousand for life?"

"That's what she said. But she hasn't made up her mind to accept it."

"Why not? A hundred fifty thou a year ain't unsalted peanuts."

"And that could be the catch."

"Whaddya mean?"

"What if something happened to her a month or a year from now?"

"You said the trust is the old man's doing."

"That's what Bell and Woodman told her. But she has only their word for it."

Checkers fretted.

I went on. "Let's say April's life *isn't* in danger. Let's say the trust's just a way of buying her off. In that case, I'd bet that there's a stipulation in the trust agreement that she has to give up any claim to the Medford estate."

"Has she signed anything?"

"Not that I know of."

"Well, for Christ's sake, don't let her. Not until a lawyer's seen everything they give her. Break her arm if you have to."

I said I didn't think that would be necessary.

"With that young lady, you never know," he said.
I gave him that.

The Santa Ana was catching its breath as I drove to the Medford house. Mrs. Riddell didn't say a word when I announced myself over the intercom at the gate. Cliff Riddell and a Latino gardener were conferring at a flower bed bordering the parking area. Riddell watched stonily as I climbed out of the Volvo with my bag. I said hello. He made a vague gesture in reply. I went to the door and rang the bell, and Mrs. Riddell responded, regarding me with the indifference she might reserve for a plumber arriving to fix a leaky faucet.

"She's in the living room," she announced.

I thanked her and crossed the entry hall under her apathetic surveillance. One of the double doors stood open. I knocked on it and entered, closing it behind me. April turned from a French door to a side terrace and thanked me for coming.

"Sure."

"I'll show you to your room."

"Later." I put my bag down. "I have a question . . . Have you signed any papers in connection with the trust fund your grandfather is setting up for you?"

"No," she said and saw the relief in my face. "What is it?"

I told her.

Her face clouded.

"Your grandfather's a very wealthy man and a hundred fifty thousand a year, even if you lived to be ninety, would be a cheap payoff if Woodman and Bell've been dipping into the till."

"But if I don't sign, I won't get the money."

"No, but you could contest your grandfather's will. So far there's only Woodman's word . . . what he told Mr. Lenox . . . that the will favoring your mother was changed by your grandfather."

"But what if he did and I sued and lost? I'd wind up with nothing."

"That's right. But there's one way you can protect yourself."

"How?"

"Talk to your grandfather. Ask him if he authorized the change in his will."

"But if he told Mr. Woodman to establish a trust for me, he must have—"

"*If*," I said. "But if Woodman and Bell could switch wills without your grandfather knowing it, they could set up the trust without his knowledge. I think you should go to Pomona tomorrow and talk to your grandfather."

She obviously didn't care much for the idea. She turned back to the French doors to the terrace. The Santa Ana was back, hammering the house. "I don't know. It seems so . . . crass."

"It's a crass world," I told her. "But you wouldn't be going to ask for money. All you'd be going for is to get the truth. Did he withdraw the will leaving his estate to your mother? If he did, fine. If he didn't, he should know that Bell and Woodman did."

April continued to look out the French doors, watching the wind slam through the garden, rage at the trees. Then she turned to me.

"Will you go with me?"

I said I would.

* * *

April told Edna Riddell we'd be having dinner out, and we went to La Scala on Canon Drive. It was a self-conscious supper. We both fumbled around for small talk, but every topic we cobbled up disappeared like smoke. I drove back to the Medford house via Beverly Glen and Mulholland Drive, the sinuous spine of the Hollywood Hills. The hoydenish winds were still running free, sweeping the dark sky clean. From the mountains to the sea, it was the night of a million lights.

I occupied a Spartan second-floor room. The mattress on my bed felt as if it'd been stuffed with pea gravel. I slept fitfully and awoke early. The Santa Ana had blown itself out. The house was silent. I dressed and went looking for a cup of coffee. En route, I paused outside the door to Medford's bedroom. I pushed it open and looked in. The large bed had been stripped, and the other furniture had been covered with white sheets, leaving me with the thought that someone wasn't planning on the old man's return.

I went on. In the entry hall, I crossed to the single door facing the doors to the living room. I opened it and looked into a different world, a place of chintz and prints and Chantilly lace, a woman's room, airy, colorful, radiant—so antipodal to the rest of the ungarnished house. It had been, I was sure, Lora Medford's refuge. I circled it, stopping at a cabinet displaying glass figures of birds—robins, jays, hummingbirds, an eagle, a hawk, gulls, pelicans. Why this collection? Was it an expression of Lora's desire to take wing and flee this monastic place?

I suppressed any further curbstone psychiatry and

moved to a graceful desk standing in front of a window with a view of a flower garden on the side of the house. The desk held a studio photograph of Price in middle age and another of a lovely girl in her teens. I guessed the latter was of April's mother. There was little resemblance to Price. Yet Julia must've been as strong-willed as her father to go off with Alex Tyson, forsaking the Medford fortune. April had told me so little about her mother. Or herself.

I left the room, feeling I was exiting a time capsule. I crossed the entry hall, entered the dining room, and pushed through the door to the kitchen. It was large and well equipped enough to serve a modest restaurant. But who had they fed from here except themselves and a solitary old man?

A door led to a large butlerless butler's pantry. Another to a screened porch. A third one opened onto a black rectangle beyond which I saw—when my eyes adjusted to the darkness—stairs into the cellar. As I stepped back and closed the door, I was startled by:

"Looking for something?"

I turned. Cliff Riddell, clad in his western garb and holding back the swinging door, stood in the entrance to the dining room. He swayed slightly, and I wondered if he'd just got up or had just come home. His voice wasn't friendly. Neither were his bloodshot eyes.

"I couldn't sleep, and was hoping to find some coffee," I replied.

"I'll make some."

He crossed to the service island festooned with stainless-steel pots and pans hanging from hooks above it, put water and coffee into a large percolater, and plugged it in while I searched for some small scraps of conversation I could use. What I came up with was, "Is there any news about Mr. Medford?"

"No."

He crossed to the cellar door, opened it, snapped a light switch on the wall, and surveyed the cellar from the top of the stairs, then looked at me.

"What're you doing here?"

"I told you. Looking for a cup of coffee."

His eyes were glued on me, flat and skeptical.

"You seem to have something on your mind," I said. "What is it?"

"You're a private detective."

"So?"

"Miss Tyson brought you here for some reason."

"That's right."

"What?"

"I'll answer that if you'll answer a question of mine."

He didn't agree. But neither did he object.

"Why does my being a private detective bother you?"

"Because Miss Tyson had no right to bring you in here to snoop."

"I didn't know what I was doing was snooping."

"That's what I call it."

"Do you have something to hide?"

"Look, this is Mr. Medford's home. It's been his home all his life. Except for Doctor Stangood, Reverend Bell, and Mr. Woodman . . . and Mr. Lenox before him . . . Miss Tyson's the first person who's been in here in over ten years. Then Mr. Medford goes to the hospital, and the first thing she does is bring you in. I'm responsible for this house, and I want to know why."

"Fair enough . . . She asked me to come because you and your wife make her feel like an intruder even though Mr. Medford invited her to stay here. She said she felt there's something here you don't want her to know. I thought it was her imagination. Now I'm not so sure."

We eyed each other for a beat or two, and I excused myself.

The coffee was still perking.

The Stangood Hospital was on a broad shelf of land in the lower San Gabriel Mountains north of Pomona. It was housed in a sprawling, adobe-style building, white as an undertaker's shirt. The sun ricocheted off the walls, adding points to the hundred-degree temperature. The lobby was as cordial as a fifty-pound cake of ice. We crossed a half-acre of black tile to an information desk, where a vacuous, saucer-eyed young lady, looking as if she were hovering somewhere between dumb and stupid, was stationed. April told her we wanted to see Mr. Medford.

"Mr. Medford?" She looked as blank as a fresh sheet of paper.

"Does he work here?"

"He's a patient," April informed her.

Her lips made an "O," and she punched a button on a computer and the screen came to life with a list of names. She frowned at them and announced there was no patient named Medford.

"There's some mistake," April told her.

The receptionist didn't dispute the fact. Or accept it. She just looked at us, as neutral as a Swiss bank. And then with what couldn't have been anything less than divine inspiration, she suggested checking with the admitting office. I felt I should applaud. But it was just as well I didn't. Price Medford's name didn't appear on the admitting office's roster either.

"Is Doctor Stangood in?" I asked, wanting to be helpful in any way I could.

The young lady replied that she didn't know.

"Could you find out for us?"

"I could call his office."

Feeling such logic should be rewarded, I replied with an enthusiastic "great!"

She used a telephone and asked someone if the doctor was present, then hung up.

"Yes."

"In his office?" I asked.

"She didn't say." She started to reach for the phone.

"Never mind," I told her. "Where's his office?"

She pointed to the mouth of a corridor. "Down there."

I thanked her for her help.

Stangood was conferring with his secretary when we entered his reception room. He looked annoyed when he saw us and managed only a pithless smile.

"Miss Tyson."

Stangood was in the vicinity of fifty, a stout man with a large face about as distinctive as a tub of lukewarm bath water. His hair was thin and in full retreat. He wore a white lab coat over gray trousers and a pale blue shirt with a polka-dot tie. His eyes skulked behind tinted glasses.

"You're here to see your grandfather."

"Yes."

"She was told at the front desk he isn't here," I said.

He looked at me. I was sure his eyes, if I could see them, were asking who the hell I was. April introduced us. He offered his hand. I took it. It was as firm as a surgical sponge. His glasses went back to April, and I assumed his eyes went with them.

"If I'd known you were coming, I would have told you that your grandfather was admitted under a pseudonym."

April looked puzzled. "Why?"

"Because his retreat from the world has made him grist for the news media's mill, and we didn't want to risk attracting its attention." It sounded rehearsed.

"May I see him?" April inquired.

His glasses passed over me and returned to April. "Of course, but . . ." His face grew somber. "I don't want to alarm you, but your grandfather is very ill. He's developed a viral pneumonia. We have him on oxygen. I also gave him a sedative, and he's sleeping now. You can look in on him."

"But not talk to him, right?"

"I'm afraid not," Stangood replied. "Of course, if you care to wait . . ."

I looked at his glasses with what I thought was a disarming smile. "How long?"

Stangood considered the question. "Five or six hours, I'd say."

"I'd like to look in on him," April said.

"Of course."

Stangood led us out of his office and down a corridor to a large, private room, its sterility relieved by pastel yellow drapes at the windows and upholstery on the chairs. Medford slept—peacefully, it appeared—with an oxygen tube making a blue-green see-through moustache on his upper lip. April went to the bed, looking down at him for a moment while Stangood and I stayed just inside the door. When she turned away, Stangood asked her if we were going to wait until he was awake.

She said no.

I drove down the road from the hospital to the floor of the San Gabriel Valley and along Indian Hill Boulevard to the San Bernardino Freeway, heading west toward Los Angeles before April spoke.

"I think he's dying," she said, looking at me.

"Maybe not."

I sounded more sanguine than I felt. April looked away, staring out the window, occupied with her own thoughts. And I was busy with mine. About Stangood. He'd seemed irritated but not surprised by April's arrival, and I wondered if he'd been forewarned. April had told Edna Riddell where we were going. Had she contacted Bell or Woodman and one or the other had alerted Stangood, telling him to sedate Medford, worried that she might ask about the will naming her mother as his beneficiary? And was it for the same reason that Edna Riddell was always in Medford's bedroom whenever April was with him?

April gave me the card key to use on the electronic gate. And handed me the key to the front door when we found it locked. As we entered, Edna Riddell was coming out of the living room and told April the Reverend Bell called and asked if April would call back as soon as she came in. The message delivered, she disappeared without asking about Medford.

April went into the living room and called Bell at the Soldiers of God Temple. The call was brief and one sided in favor of the reverend. After a couple minutes of listening she said, "I'll be there," hung up, and turned from the phone.

"Be where?" I asked.

"Mr. Woodman's office at ten in the morning. The trust agreement is ready for me to sign."

"Are you?"

She looked troubled. But before she could answer, Edna Riddell reappeared and asked April if we'd be going out for dinner. April glanced at me. I said yes, and Mrs. Riddell disappeared again.

I looked at April. "Well?"

"I'm still not sure."

But there was something—in her voice, the way she averted her eyes, something—that made me uneasy.

"Then why're you going to Woodman's office?" I asked.

"To find out if I have to give up any claim to grandfather's estate."

"And if you do?"

"I don't know, Tug!" she snapped.

I backed off. "Let's talk about it at dinner."

She agreed and went upstairs. I went to the living room and called Checkers' office. Diana Norton answered exuberantly and put me through to Checkers immediately, and for a brief moment I found myself lonesome for the choleric Jasmine. As usual, Checkers came on the line with roar, and I told him April was still in a quandry about whether or not to accept the trust Medford allegedly established for her.

"How you think she's leaning?"

"She's seeing Woodman in the morning," I answered, "and I've a hunch she might sign even if she has to waive any claim to Medford's estate."

"Well, I don't know anything we can do about it."

"I'm taking her to dinner at Ito's. We'll be there about seven. You be there, too. Maybe we can convince her to forget the trust if she has to sign a waiver."

"How do you talk someone outa taking a hundred fifty thousand a year?"

"Are you going to be there or not?"

Checkers just grunted.

"And there's something else you can do in the meantime."

"What?"

"See if you can find out anything about Cliff Riddell."

"Who's he?"

"Medford's straw boss."

I noticed a change in April the Irresolute as we drove to Ito's. There was something that looked suspiciously like determination in her eyes and the set of her jaw. There was also an emanation of displeasure when I told her Checkers was having dinner with us.

I'd asked Checkers, thinking that his intimidating, with-the-bark-on approach, might cower April into seeing things our way. But now I wasn't sure it was *our* way any longer. That Checkers, given time to think about April receiving one hundred and fifty thousand a year for life, had perhaps concluded that he stood more to gain financially if our client took the money and ran rather than gamble on suing for a share of Medford's estate.

Ito gave us an isolated tatami room for privacy, and a waitress—a Madame Butterfly named Ureshii—

brought us cocktails. Checkers was charming, or a dim facsimile thereof, relating some of the amusing situations he'd found himself in during his years with the department. I'd heard them all before. I didn't laugh. April hadn't heard them before. And she didn't laugh. But Checkers didn't seem to mind. He went from one story to another until Ureshii returned, and we gave her an order for another round of drinks. Then, irritated by the clear signal Checkers was sending— that he wasn't going to support me in trying to persuade April to refuse the trust fund—I took the bullshit by the horns.

"Okay, you've broken enough ice," I told him.

He tried to look puzzled. I turned to April.

"Are you going to sign that trust agreement or not?"

"I told you—"

"I know what you told me. That you don't know. But that's crap. You're going to sign, but you're afraid to say so."

"Why would I be afraid?"

"Because you're not really sure it's the right thing to do. Because you're never sure. You can't face up to anything. Instead, you run. You ran from Bennett's murder. You ran from Frances'. And when you haven't run, you've lied. Or left out something you should've told us."

April looked horrified. I didn't know whether she was going to cry or spit in my face. She did neither. She got to her feet, threw open the sliding door, snatched up her shoes, and disappeared. Checkers went after her in his sock feet, passing Ureshii delivering the second round of drinks. I downed mine in a couple of gulps and held up my glass.

"Bring me another one. A double."
"*Hai.*"

Checkers came back as Ureshii was serving the double. He asked her to bring him one and sat down, stuffing his feet into the leg well under the low table, eyeing me caustically. I asked him if April had left.

"I offered to drive her back to Medford's, but she told me to get lost, she'd take a cab. And she said she was gonna sign the trust agreement regardless of how it reads."

"Did you tell her you were on her side?"

"I ain't on anybody's side."

"Except your own."

"Yeah," he replied. "And maybe yours now and then."

"Tonight sure as hell wasn't *now*."

"Okay, so when you told me about the trust and maybe her signing away her right to sue for Medford's estate, I thought like you did . . . that she shouldn't do it. But then I got to thinking. If she had to sue, Christ knows how long it'd be before it was settled. Three, four, five years. And then maybe she'd lose and we'd be sitting around with nothing in our pockets but our hands."

"Horseshit," I said. "If Woodman and Bell switched Medford's wills and were cooking his books, the last thing they'd want to do is walk into a courtroom."

"Maybe."

"Maybe, hell."

We didn't eat. We argued. And drank. It was ridiculous—a casebook example of a study in futility.

We were locking the barn door after the bird had flown the coop. When Ito stuck his head in and politely asked us if we wanted to sign a year's lease on the room, we took the hint. Checkers went to the bar.

I went home.

17

I parked in my assigned space near the elevator shaft, a concrete structure in the center of the garage, and was locking the Volvo when I heard the crack of a gun and felt the sting of a thousand killer bees as a slug plowed a furrow of flesh on my left side in the vicinity of my rib cage. I staggered back against the car in the next stall and looked around to see where the shot had come from. I saw the figure of a man step out from between two cars in the next aisle. The revolver in his hand, looking as big as a grenade launcher, was leveled at me. I dived behind the front of the car a second before the gun exploded again. The bullet hit something at the far end of the garage. I galumphed behind the elevator shaft.

I heard the gunman's running footsteps coming after me. I continued around the shaft. On the far side, I saw the metal fuse box and pulled it open. There were three master switches. I threw them all. The garage's dim lights went out. Except for the pale wash of light coming through the ramp, it was as black as a witch's cat. I ran to a row of cars parked against a far wall, taking refuge behind them. My side hurt like hell, I felt light-headed, my heart pounded, and my stomach churned. The gunman, still a shadow, came around the elevator shaft, alert, listening.

A hunter on the prowl.

The ramp was to my right, a dozen cars away. I moved, crouching, to the next car and paused. The gunman didn't see me, but he moved in my direction. I took the loose change out of a pocket. It included three quarters. I threw one of them toward the other side of the garage. It hit something and made a small metallic sound. The gunman whirled, moving gingerly toward the sound. I made it along the line of cars to the one parked next to the ramp and was about to make my escape when the gunman stopped and turned back. I threw another quarter toward the far end of the garage. It made a click against the concrete floor behind him. He spun. I climbed on to the ramp and ran up.

The gunman heard me. And I heard him come after me. As I reached the top of the ramp, I was blinded by the headlights of a car entering the garage. I threw myself out of the way, tripped, and fell on my stapled knee. More pain cut through me. I heard a shout, a squeal of tires, a thump, and a strangled scream. I got to my feet and looked at the ramp. The car had come to an abrupt halt halfway down. The driver jumped out and rushed to the gunman lying face down at the bottom of the ramp, the headlights holding him in their glare. The driver knelt beside him, turning him on his back. He flopped over, limp and lifeless. I recognized him.

Al Massi.

The driver climbed slowly to his feet. He hadn't seen me. Instinct, not reason, told me if I stayed there it meant talking to the police, and that could mean trouble—being asked more questions than I wanted to answer if I was identified as Massi's potential victim. I moved out of sight and hobbled to the front door of the building. I didn't wait for an elevator. I crossed to the stairwell and climbed the six flights to my apartment and sank into a chair, my side burning, my knee throbbing, and my mind searching for a reason why Al Massi would try to kill me.

I was shaking.

When I stopped, I left the chair and went into the bathroom, shedding my blood-stained jacket and shirt, and took a large beach towel from a cabinet. I folded it several times and wrapped it around myself, covering the wound, holding it on with the belt from a robe, digesting the irony that Massi, my candidate for the killer of Frances, had himself been killed by a car.

As I left the bathroom, sirens began to shriek in the distance, coming closer. I went out on the balcony. A sheriff's black and white sped up and stopped at the entrance to the garage. It was followed by the paramedics and another sheriff's car. Other tenants began to populate other balconies. A small crowd gathered around the mouth of the ramp. I went inside to give my own problem some attention. I needed a doctor to dress my wound—one who wouldn't feel compelled to report a gunshot wound.

I called Doc Hooper.

When he answered, I asked, "Are you sober?"

"Who's this?" he grumped.

"Tug."

" 'Course I'm sober," he replied indignantly. "What makes you think I'm not?"

I didn't want to get into that. And he sounded like

he might be telling me something approximating the truth. I asked him if he could come see me. I needed him.

"What's the matter?"

"I'm hurt."

"How?"

"Gunshot."

"Holy Jesus! . . . I'll be right there."

I poured a straight Jameson, filling a water glass and went back out on the balcony. The paramedics were wheeling Massi's covered body to the ambulance. As it drove off, my mind again dug around in quest of an answer to why Massi wanted to kill me. I kept turning up Lassen's name. Was he involved? I didn't see how. Or why. But the need to find out was too strong to ignore.

I went into the den, got the area code for Willow River, Idaho, and called long distance information, asking the operator if she had a number for a Harry Lassen. She did. I dialed it. The phone rang a half-dozen times before it was answered.

"Hello?" It was a woman's voice.

"Mrs. Lassen?"

"Yes."

"My name's Tug Cage. I'm calling from Los Angeles. I know it's late, and I'm sorry to bother you, but may I speak to Harry?"

"He isn't here."

She didn't recognize the voice of "Stan Roberts." I asked if he was somewhere I could reach him. "It's important."

Her voice was a tight whisper. "Harry's dead."

"Dead?"

"He was murdered."

At present long distance rates, I must've spent two or three dollars on stunned silence.

"Who . . . killed him?"

"No one knows. I'd gone into town. It was day before yesterday. When I came home I found him on the living room floor. He'd been shot twice . . ." there was an audible gulp ". . . in the head." She started to sob and hung up.

My doorbell rang.

Doc Hooper came in trailing the faint odor of a damp bar rag and carrying a satchel large enough to hold a case of Jack Daniel's. The Tennessee sour mash was his favorite whiskey. But the Doc wasn't persnickety. If Jack Daniel's wasn't available, he'd drink anything of eighty proof or more.

Doc wasn't drunk. Or completely sober, either. He removed my improvised bandage and sniffed when he saw my wound. He wasn't impressed. He had, he said, seen cat scratches that were worse.

He'd finished dressing the wound when the doorbell rang again, sounding as assertive as a dentist's drill. Doc answered it, and Checkers came steaming in.

"What're you doing here?" I asked.

"Doc called me. Said you'd been shot." He saw the bandage. "What in Christ's name happened?"

Before I could answer, Doc asked if I had anything in the apartment to drink. I directed him to the bottle of Jameson in the kitchen.

"What *happened*?" Checkers demanded again.

"You want a drink?" Doc asked me.

"No, thanks."

He looked at Checkers. "How about you?"

"No!" Checkers bellowed.

Doc shrugged and disappeared into the kitchen.

"Well?" Checkers pleaded.

I told him. He looked bewildered.

"Al Massi? Why would he wanna waste you?"

"I'm not sure," I replied. "But it might have something to do with Harry Lassen."

"Lassen? What about him?"

I told him that, too.

"For Christ's sake," he said and lowered himself into a chair. "You think there's a connection?"

"Maybe," I answered. "When Vicari was killed, Massi told the police he saw a man run to a car and drive away, but he couldn't identify him."

"So?"

"What if he was lying? What if he knew it was Lassen and didn't say so because if Lassen was arrested it'd open a can of worms, including the fact that Massi might've been the one who drove the car that killed Frances?"

"You think he was?"

"I think I more than *think* it," I said. "I think I *know* it."

"What's that got to do with him gunning for you?"

Doc came back from the kitchen before I could go on and said he'd stop by in the morning to see how I was doing. I thanked him, and he picked up his satchel, hiccuped, and left.

"But there's one person Massi *would* tell," I continued. "His uncle . . . Lug Wrench. And it's possible . . . given the old man's reputation for wanting blood for blood . . . he told Massi to get Lassen."

"Could be," Checkers said. "But I still don't see how you fit in."

"There's only one way," I said. "If Massi was

following Lassen, waiting for the right time to take him out, he may have seen him meet me at the Foghorn and concluded that I'd given Lassen a contract on Bobby and Dekoven because of Frances. And Massi told his uncle, and Lug Wrench ordered him to get both of us."

Checkers shook his head skeptically. "I dunno."

"I don't *know* either. But it's the best I can do. Massi may have lost Lassen then tracked him to Idaho. It wouldn't have been hard. He could've gone to the real estate dealer who had the listing on Lassen's house, pretending he was interested in buying it, and found out where Lassen had gone. Massi went to Idaho, killed Lassen, and came back here to take care of me."

"You're guessing."

I admitted it.

"And you could be wrong."

"Or I could be right."

Checkers looked at me with all the portent of a doctor about to inform a patient he had a terminal disease. "Well, if you are, you're still in trouble. Unless Lug Wrench's made the biggest switch of anybody since Saul of Tarsus, he'll keep giving out contracts until he hands you your head."

I reluctantly conceded he was probably right.

"Probably, hell. I *know* I'm right." He gave me a gimlet-eyed look for a lingering moment, then asked, "Bobby hadda wife and kids, didn't he?"

"What's that got to do—"

"Didn't he?"

"Yeah."

"Well, I think I'll pay Lug Wrench a visit . . ."

"What?!"

"... and go over a few facts of life he may've forgotten. Wanna come?"

"What the hell've you got in mind?"

"You'll find out if you feel up to coming along."

I didn't. But I did.

Luigi Vicari lived in a rambling house in Pacific Palisades that looked like it had been built by somebody suffering from an acute attack of afterthoughts. Dim light showed at two downstairs windows. Checkers rang the doorbell and knocked, making doubly sure Lug Wrench knew he had visitors. Checkers had obtained the old man's address with a phone call. He'd also learned Lug Wrench had a young flunky to attend to his domestic needs. The old man was a widower, his late wife being one of the few Vicaris who hadn't died a violent death.

The flunky answered the door. He was in his twenties, a pointy faced sort of fellow who saw the world through perpetually suspicious eyes. He wore a black suit, white shirt with black tie, and black tassled loafers. His jacket had a bulge, indicating his apparel included a revolver in a shoulder holster. I wondered if he knew they'd gone out of style. Shoulder holsters. Not guns. Checkers asked if Lug Wrench was home.

"Who're you?" the flunky asked.

"I'm Checkers, and he's Cage," Checkers replied, "and if you're gonna make a crack about it sounding like a comedy team, don't. And tell Lug Wrench he'd better see us or he'll spend the last few years of his life wishing he had."

The young man glared and told us to wait. He closed the door, locked it, and we waited. Not long. Five minutes, maybe, and he was back, escorting us to a room so crowded it resembled a furniture showroom out of the Thirties. The flunky closed the door and stood in front of it. Lug Wrench sat in a high-back chair, holding a cane in front of him as if it were a scepter. His face, broad and with a nose broken sometime during the course of his violent fourscore years, had become out of place on his shriveled body. His hair was incongruously black, and he needed a shave. He glanced at Checkers, then pinned his eyes on me, remembering I'd arrested his son for killing the call girl and was apparently offended by the fact that I wasn't somewhere else, lying in a pool of blood. He finally gave up trying to stare me to death and looked back at Checkers.

"So you're Sergeant Checkers," he said in a phlegmy voice with a slight accent. "I've heard about you." It was the old refrain.

"You know Cage."

In reply, Lug Wrench again gave me that stare of his.

"I'm not with the police any more," Checkers said. "And neither is Cage."

"Then what're you doing here?" he demanded irritably.

"You've heard about your nephew?"

"Yes." He sounded more resentful than grieved.

"He was trying to kill Cage when he was hit by that car."

"That isn't what I hear."

"Well, that's what you're hearing now. And you gave Massi the contract on Cage."

"Did I?" he asked in a tone suggesting he was complimented by the accusation.

"But if you're smart, you won't buy another one."

"Are you threatening me?"

"No, not you. You're too old to threaten. You're not gonna be around that long. But Bobby hadda wife. And a coupla kids. Your grandchildren. Your name. Your blood. So if anything . . ."

Lug Wrench, leaning heavily on his cane, hoisted himself to his feet, trembling.

". . . happens to Cage, you'll spend the rest of your life going to family funerals."

Lug Wrench continued to shake. Inside, he was still a degenerate killer. Outside, he was a pathetically warped old man.

"If you touch one of them, I'll—"

Checkers cut him off: "You'll what?"

Lug Wrench raised his cane as if he were going to lash out with it. Checkers stood his ground.

Lug Wrench lowered the cane. "You're bluffing." His voice was quivery too.

"Call me and see," Checkers challenged in a voice that was menacingly flat, then he turned and went to the door. I followed. The flunky didn't move. Checkers looked over his shoulder at Lug Wrench.

"Whistle for your dog."

Lug Wrench gestured feebly, the flunky moved aside, and Checkers and I strode from the room and the house. Outside, I congratulated him on his performance, and he smiled modestly.

"But the whole thing was ridiculous," I added.

Checkers looked hurt. "Whaddya mean?"

"If you think you scared him off, you're whistling Dixie off key. I'm surprised he didn't fall down laughing."

"I'll bet you anything you want he backs off."

"What's the use of betting? If I win, I won't be around to collect."

But Checkers' theatrics were unnecessary. A week later, I read in the *Times* that Lug Wrench suffered a heart attack and was rushed by ambulance to the UCLA Medical Center.

He was DOA.

I spent the next week being kind to myself. Doc Hooper stopped by every morning to dress my wound and partake of the supply of Jack Daniel's I'd laid in for him. On some days he drank conservatively, others not, spending hours guzzling sour mash and berating the medical profession.

"Hippocrates called medicine an art but doctors today are nothing but damn mechanics. Their patients aren't anything but chunks of meat they can hook up to a machine. Art? Shit! They can't diagnose an ingrown toenail without a couple of million dollars worth of equipment."

And on he'd rant. Fortunately, it was a monologue, so I could read or retire to my den, wistfully studying my road maps, plotting my meandering course across the country on forgotten roads, even though I felt such an idyllic journey was becoming more and more remote.

I was relieved, of course, to learn of Lug Wrench's demise. I could now go out into the world without the nagging fear that someone was lurking in the wings to make me another entry in the city's homicide statistics. And I also felt the need for human companionship other than that of Doc Hooper. Or Checkers. I thought of Diana Norton. Even though I'd never seen her, I felt certain a lady who treated me with such laudable deference on the telephone must have some physical virtues. I called Checkers' office.

"Checkers and Associates!" The voice was like a blast from an enraged pipe organ. It was Jasmine. She was, as Checkers had predicted, back.

"Hello!" she trumpeted and I hung up, suddenly feeling as antisocial as a coyote.

The phone rang. I hesitated picking it up, thinking Jasmine guessed I was the caller and had phoned to verbally trample me for hanging up on her. But I convinced myself that was highly unlikely, and so I answered.

"Mr. Cage?"

I recognized the voice and almost wished it had been Jasmine.

"Larry Simmons."

I gave him a paper-thin "hi."

"I'm in Los Angeles."

"Oh?"

"Been attending a reunion of some of the guys I was with in Korea. I'm leaving in the morning, and I thought if you weren't doing anything we might have dinner."

I thought fast. "I'm sorry, Larry, but I was just leaving to meet some friends."

"Too bad . . . Well, look, do you know how I could get in touch with April?"

"Larry, if you're still looking for Mona—"

"No, no, it's not that. I just thought I'd call and say hello."

"Just a minute."

I found Medford's number and gave it to him. He thanked me, told me to be sure to stop by the Jury Box when I came to Seattle, we hung up, and I realized how little I'd thought of April since the night she left Ito's in high dudgeon and I had been stalked by Al Massi. I didn't want to think of her now and picked up a book to try to occupy my mind. But the phone rang again.

"This is Larry."

"Did you reach April?"

"No," he replied, "I talked to some woman who said April wasn't in. When I asked to leave a message, she said April wasn't there any more and didn't know where she'd gone."

I tensed but tried to hide the fact from Simmons. I said I hadn't seen April or talked to her lately, so I wouldn't know anything about it. I thought I sounded cool.

"Well, if you see her, say hello for me."

I said I would, broke the connection, and called Checkers' office, telling Jasmine before she could let out a peep that I wanted to talk to Checkers, and I wasn't in the mood to take any shit from her. She harrumphed, Checkers came on the line, and I asked if he'd talked to April lately. He said no, asked why, and I told him I had a report that she left Medford's and Mrs. Liddell was saying she didn't know where she'd gone.

"Have you checked it out?" he asked, sounding anxious. And with reason. April hadn't paid him.

"No," I replied, then thought of a reason to go to the Medford's house, and added:

"But I'm going to."

Cliff Riddell answered my ring from the gate. I announced myself and said I'd come to pick up the clothes I'd left after my overnight stay at the house.

The gate opened, and I drove in and parked. Riddell was waiting at the door with my bag in hand. His face reflected his leeriness of me.

"Edna packed it," he said, handing me the bag. "We wondered when you'd be coming for it."

"I've been busy," I replied. "Sorry if I inconvenienced you."

He put a hand on the door to close it.

"I'd like to see April."

"She isn't here."

"It's rather urgent. Do you know when she'll be back?"

"She won't."

I looked surprised, puzzled. "You mean she isn't staying here any more?"

"That's right."

"Where did she go?"

"We don't know. When she left, she said she'd let us know where she was, but we haven't heard from her."

He closed the door.

The dome of the Soldiers of God Temple rose above a layer of smog and haze—dirty as a sewer outfall—blanketing the San Fernando Valley. I left the Ventura Freeway and drove a winding road to the church. It was late afternoon or early evening, depending on your point of view, but the temple's acres were a busy place. A small army of gardeners was busily grooming the already immaculate lawns and gardens. A surprising number of young people hurried along a crisscross of walks, tying up—I assumed—the last odds and ends of their daily work for the Lord. From the temple itself came voices raised in song. "In the Sweet 'Bye and

Bye." Choir practice. It was soothing if you needed soothing. I stopped and asked a young lady where I would find Reverend Bell's office.

"The administration building," she said, pointing.

"Thank you."

"Bless you," she said and bustled on.

The administration building was an impressive structure that must have decimated several marble quarries in its construction. I found the reverend's office on the top floor. His reception room housed enough secretaries to paralyze the U.S. postal system if they put their minds and word processors to it. Bell's private secretary had an office of her own. She was an economy size woman of indeterminate age, and a nameplate on her desk identified her as Elsa Mueller. She looked down her large nose at me, a panoramic view on which I felt I was but a bug on the horizon. With an unmistakable lack of enthusiasm, she announced my presence to the reverend.

Elsa, meet Jasmine.

Bell's office was bigger than a breadbox and slightly smaller than the lobby of the Biltmore. His desk looked like it had been converted from the flight deck of an aircraft carrier. The furniture was equally massive. The color scheme was blue and, on a guess, boasted every shade known to man. And a few that were still in the developmental stage. The room was two stories in height with a library on a balcony. Hundreds of books boasted the same leather binding, leading me to suspect they'd been purchased by the yard. At his desk, Bell was framed by two flags on standards behind him. One was the Stars and Stripes, the other was the Soldiers of God banner—a blood-red cross overlaid on two crossed sabers against a field of white. Bell came around from behind his desk and hiked over a half-acre of blue carpeting to greet me with plastic Christian warmth, saying he was delighted to see me.

"For any particular reason?" I asked.

That threw him off balance. He managed a weak chuckle and gestured me into a chair sized for an overweight King Kong. He hiked back to his desk and eventually arrived at his chair. I wondered why he didn't have a golf cart for trips such distance. He sat down, leaned forward on his elbows, and asked what he could do for me.

"Tell me about April."

His forehead wrinkled questioningly.

"The Riddells say she's left her grandfather's."

He nodded.

"And she didn't tell them where she was going."

"That's true."

"Do you know where she went?"

"No," Bell answered. "I haven't seen her since we met at Donald Woodman's office to sign the trust agreement. That was . . . what? . . . a week ago yesterday. However, she did call Donald two or three days ago."

"From where?"

"She didn't say."

"And Woodman didn't ask?"

He ignored the question.

"Does Medford know she's gone?"

"No."

"Have you or Woodman done anything to find out where she is?"

"No." he replied, his voice growing impatient, querulous.

"And you're not concerned?"

"Why should we be?"

"If you don't know, I can't tell you," I said. "But I'll try. She's Medford's granddaughter. When he went into the hospital, he asked her to stay at the house, and she agreed, according to April. You're his friend. His *only* friend. You're the one who's going to have to tell him she's gone."

"I'm aware of that."

"Then what're you waiting for? Are you hoping he'll find out from someone else? The Riddells? Or are you hoping he'll die and you won't—"

"I resent that," he said, getting to his feet.

I shrugged and asked, "What do you think Medford's reaction will be when you tell him she's disappeared?"

"She didn't *disappear*, Mr. Cage. She *left*. And quite frankly, I'm not surprised. I suspected her only interest in her grandfather was whatever money she could get from him. Well, she succeeded in getting one hundred fifty thousand a year for life. And when she did, she had no more interest in him, so she left." He made the long journey around his desk. "And may I add that I resent you injecting yourself in something that's none of your affair. You no longer represent Miss Tyson, do you?"

"No."

"Then I suspect your only concern for her is to somehow use this situation to get more money out of Mr. Medford."

I climbed out of the corpulent chair. "Even an expert can be wrong, parson."

"What does that mean?"

"That when it comes to getting money out of Medford, you wrote the book. You have yourself appointed the trustee of his estate and this religious dodge of yours named the beneficiary. And when Medford changed his will so everything would've gone to April, you and Woodman scrapped it without Medford knowing it."

"That's a lie!"

"And it wasn't Medford's idea to set up a trust fund for April. It was yours and Woodman's. It was a buyout. A payoff. A temporary solution until you can arrange a permanent one. Like a fatal accident, maybe."

"This is scandalous!" the parson roared. "You have no basis . . . no proof . . . for such a charge!"

"I'll tell you how we can get the proof. Let's go see Medford. Let me ask him if he knew about the change of will."

"No! . . . Price is an extremely ill man. Too ill to be subjected to the emotional confrontation your scurrilous lies would provoke. Nor am I going to listen to any more of your slander." He went to the door and pulled it open. "I'm asking you to leave, if you'll be so kind."

I was so kind.

At Stangood's hospital, the young lady with the eyes as large as manhole covers and as empty as a synagogue on Sunday was behind the information desk. She paid no attention to me as I passed her. Nor did the nurse at the desk at the head of the corridor to Medford's room. When I pushed the door open, a head of white hair turned toward me, showing an age-ravaged face of a woman. She seemed a little unnerved. I thought I'd entered the wrong room. But I knew I hadn't. I excused myself, backed out, and went to the nurse at the desk.

"Where's Mr. Medford?"

She looked blank.

"Room 104."

"Oh, you mean Mr. Johnson."

"Whatever."

"He's been discharged."

I gaped at her. There had to be some mistake. But before I could correct her, a voice behind me said, "Mr. Riddell took him home day before yesterday."

It was Stangood.

"But when Miss Tyson and I were here—"

"I know." He gave me something that was more of a grimace than a smile. "You're surprised by his recovery. So was I. Actually, there was nothing unusual about it. He's still a sick man. But he was very unhappy here. Very fretful. He wanted to be in his own home. In his own bed. And I decided he might be better off . . . certainly psychologically and, perhaps, physically . . . at home. Mrs. Riddell was a registered nurse at one time. And I'll be constantly available, of course."

I thought of a lot of questions to ask. But it would've been as rewarding as spitting into a high wind. So I skipped them.

"Of course," I said.

18

On the drive back to the marina, I had a fatherly talk with myself. The subject was April. So she'd disappeared again. So what else was new? It didn't mean anything had happened to her. Dekoven and Vicari, in pursuit of Bennett's incriminating tape, had been the physical threat to her, and Lassen had erased that. Granted, she'd been more than a tad worrisome to Bell and Woodman and, conceivably, they might —to save a hundred and fifty thousand a year—have ugly plans for her. But they'd have to leave what might be called a decent interval before they made a lethal move. Maybe April'd figured that out. Maybe that's why she'd left while the leaving was good. And maybe she'd worked out a way to collect her monthly checks without revealing her whereabouts.

So say goodbye to April, son. Say it and mean it this time. And while you're at it, bid adieu to Bell and Woodman. So they're crooks. The world is full of them. Bankers, doctors, lawyers, politicians, labor bosses, corporate presidents, chairmen of the board, defense contractors, stock brokers, car dealers, real estate agents, the guys who knock down on their income tax, the ones who pad their expense accounts.

And preachers. Their name is legion. So why worry about two out of a multitude? It was a good talk. It made sense.

I was convinced.

Until I closed my apartment door. Out on the freeways, preoccupied with staying alive, I could talk to myself without listening. Now I was alone. Just me with me and no distractions. All that fatherly talk was the horseshit that all fatherly talks usually are if you're not the father. I began to fret and fume. I wanted to know where April was. And I wanted to find a way to stop Bell and Woodman from robbing a sick old man whom they'd moved around—home to hospital, hospital to home—as if they were hiding the first prize in a scavenger hunt. It wasn't that I really gave a damn about Medford. And it wasn't a matter of the principle. It was ego, badly bent if not broken. Woodman and Bell had occupied a big chunk of six weeks of my life, and I wasn't going to watch them ride off into the sunset to continue their plundering, leaving me with the platitudinous egg on my face.

I had to stop them.

But how? I didn't even have to think about it. There was no way. I wasn't going to prove anything without getting to Medford to find out if he'd ordered the change in his will. And I couldn't get to him—not as long as he was behind the electronic gate, the high brick walls, the barred windows, and the deadbolts on the doors of his hermitage.

I went into the kitchen. There were a few dirty dishes in the sink. I put them in the dishwasher and turned it on, then poured some Jack Daniel's from a bottle Doc Hooper had overlooked and went into the den. I sat at the desk. There was an Arkansas road map on it. I'd been charting my coast-to-coast odyssey, trying to travel blue highways exclusively. So far I'd failed in California and Arizona, made it as far as Tucumcari in New Mexico, bombed in Oklahoma, and was stuck in a town called Lower Creek in Arkansas. I was debating whether to surrender in Arkansas when the phone rang.

It was Checkers, asking if I'd been able to get a line on April. I told him I hadn't, Bell and Cliff Riddell claiming they knew nothing of her whereabouts.

"Well, what the hell," he said. "So maybe she screwed us. But we did okay with that check from Medford, right?"

"Right."

For Checkers to be so philosophic about losing money was as rare as the Kohinor diamond. He asked me if I wanted to come to his place for a drink. I looked at my watch. It was after ten. I asked for a rain check and was going to hang up when I remembered something.

"Did you find out anything about Cliff Riddell?" I asked.

"Oh, yeah," Checkers replied, apparently having forgotten my request, too. "I got some notes . . . here they are . . . three arrests . . . two of 'em for driving under the influence . . . got off with fines . . . one for aggravated assault . . . year's probation . . . He says he's an actor . . . I called a casting director I know. Said he's heard of Riddell, and he ain't no Barrymore. Says he's worked as a stunt man and done some bit parts in Westerns in movies and TV. And that's it."

I hung up and put the Arkansas map aside and went into the living room. The bag I'd picked up at the Medford house was on the floor beside the front door.

I carried it into the bedroom to unpack. The extra jacket I'd taken had been stuffed into it and was as wrinkled as gift wrappings on Christmas afternoon. I decided it'd have to be sent out to be pressed. I started to check the pockets. And that's when I found them. April gave them to me when we came back from Stangood's hospital, and I hadn't returned them—the key card to the Medford gate and the key to the Medford front door.

The keys to Medford.

It was after twelve when I left the Volvo near the junction of Medford Lane and Vermont and walked to the gate. It was a clear night. A gibbous moon watched me, aloof and nonjudgmental. I wasn't armed. I'm not a gun lover. It's a hangover from Vietnam, where I discovered guns had a tendency to kill people. When I retired from the department, I deep-sixed my service revolver late one night off the end of the Santa Monica Pier. I felt a ton lighter.

The Medford house, what I could see of it from the gate, was dark. I inserted the key card into the slot. The gate swung open, squeaking and groaning. I'd forgotten how much noise it made. I held my breath, expecting the house to suddenly erupt in a blaze of light. It didn't. In a pair of crepe-soled shoes I'd dug out of a closet for my role as a footpad, I moved soundlessly to the front door while the gate creaked shut. Inside, the house was as murky as an abandoned mine shaft. But I'd come equipped with a penlight and used it for navigational purposes. I climbed the stairs slowly, freezing when the grandfather clock in the foyer struck the half-hour, the bong reverberating in the thither-most cranny of the house.

I went along the upper hall to Medford's room,

hoping the old gentleman wouldn't suffer a stroke when he awoke to find me at his bedside. Or worse, if he panicked and started shouting for help, bringing the outsized Riddell scrambling to his rescue. I put the penlight away and opened the bedroom door slowly, deciding that since I couldn't predict Medford's reaction, I'd have to take a chance he was less excitable than I feared. I closed the door and stood with my back to it, letting my eyes tune in on the deep shadow falling across the bed. And when they did, I saw nothing. Nothing, that is, but the bed.

No Medford.

He hadn't gone to the can. Nor had he crept downstairs for a midnight raid on the refrigerator. The bed was the same as it'd been when I'd seen it before—stripped bare. And the sheets were still over the furniture. He might be somewhere else in the house. In another bedroom. But I couldn't go stomping around yelling "Hey, Medford, where are you?"

I stood in the middle of the room for a few moments, up to my ass in frustration, then decided to pretend that Medford was lodging somewhere else in the house and make a surreptitious search of it. I went back into the hall. There were three more bedrooms on the second floor, including the monkish cell where I'd spent a night. I stealthily opened the door to the first two and glanced in. They were unoccupied and looked like they never had been. The third was April's. I entered and looked it over, hoping—vainly, I knew—to find a clue to where she'd gone. But she'd left nothing behind. Not even the scent of the perfume she wore.

There was a door at the end of the hall. It opened on stairs, and I climbed them to an attic. It was a template for every attic that ever was. Or should've been, if it wasn't. It was filled with nearly eight decades of discards—furniture, clothes, rugs, steamer trunks, books. And boxes in which God only knew what'd been packed. And had decayed, probably. I simply glanced around and left the musty place in its own time warp.

Back on the first floor, I scouted the late Lora Medford's hideaway and went down a hallway that opened off the foyer under the circular stairs. It was short, ending at a door. I opened it carefully. It was a small sitting room, scantily furnished without distinction. I entered gingerly. Floor-to-ceiling draperies covered one side of the room. I peeked through them into an alcove bedroom. Edna Riddell was sleeping soundly in one twin bed. The other was undisturbed. And that raised a question, to wit:

Where the hell was her husband?

I retreated and continued to rummage around the ground floor. I ended up in the kitchen and crossed to the cellar door, opening it and pitting the feeble beam of the penlight against the black hole. It gave out after a couple of feet, and I found a switch beside the door and snapped it. A bulb with a green metallic shade dangling from a dropcord glowed, and I descended the wooden stairs.

When you've seen one cellar you've seen them all. A furnace-cum-air conditioner dominated the decor. The cellar was small, a fifteen-by-fifteen-foot hole in the ground. There was no exit to the outside. Nor any ground-level windows. An array of pipes hugged the ceiling. The floor was concrete, cracked and worn except for comparatively new patches where some repair work had been done. There was a double sink against one wall. It'd been used for laundry in a time before washing machines. A tall cabinet stood over a large cement patch in a corner. I opened the doors. It contained an arsenal of gardening tools and supplies waiting to be called into action. Against another wall was a workbench with an array of hand tools displayed on a rack above it. If asked, I would've accused Cliff Riddell of being proficient with them. He looked the type. A type with which I, having ten thumbs, had little in common.

I left the cellar to do what cellars do best—just be there to flood when the rains come—and returned to the foyer, feeling as empty handed as a beggar in Bangladesh. Staring at the front door, I suffered a severe attack of false courage, deciding to wait for Riddell to return and demand to know where he'd taken Medford after his discharge from the hospital. Facing down Riddell—two inches taller and thirty or so pounds heavier than I—was not the stuff of which pleasant prospects are made. But I had to have the courage to do it even if I would end up in traction.

Which I might.

I felt someone behind me. I turned with a start. Edna Riddell, wearing a white terrycloth robe over pink pajamas and holding a .25-caliber automatic, stood in the entrance of the hallway to the Riddells' living quarters. She took a couple of steps toward me, the hand with the gun shaking slightly.

"How did you get in?" she demanded, and her voice was as shaky as her gun hand.

"I'm saving my secrets for my memoirs," I said, thinking a nip of humor, dog-eared as it was, might having a calming effect on her. It didn't.

"Miss Tyson isn't here."

"I know."

"Then what do you want?"

"I was looking for Mr. Medford," I answered, "but he doesn't seem to be here either."

The trembling of her gun hand increased slightly, but her voice became firmer. "Get out of here."

"Where is Medford, Mrs. Riddell?"

"If you don't leave, I'll call the police."

"Fine . . . Maybe I can interest them in asking you where Medford is."

"I don't know."

"You're lying, Mrs. Riddell." I tried to sound reasonable about it, keeping the accusative tone in my voice to a minimum. "Doctor Stangood told me Medford was discharged from the hospital day before yesterday, and your husband brought him home."

"He's lying!"

I shrugged and said, "We're not getting anywhere, so why don't I wait for your husband? Maybe he'll be more cooperative."

The gun sagged in her hand, and I went into the living room. I snapped on a lamp and made myself comfortable. Mrs. Riddell came in, putting the automatic in a pocket of her robe. Her face was as hard as armor plating.

"If you're going to wait for Cliff, you're going to be here a long time."

"Where is he?"

"In Beverly Hills screwing Cadence Moore."

I raised my eyebrows. I knew the name. I had, some years before, seen a film in which she'd costarred, proving to the world—if not to herself and the motion picture industry—that if there was anything she wasn't, it was an actress. But that was a minor impediment for Cadence, supplied as she was with the chutzpah of a grizzly bear and equipped with an eye-filling body that four wealthy ex-husbands had paid handsomely to sample. So in modern Hollywood, the Vatican of loose definitions, her few screen credits had crowned her a "star." I didn't wonder why Cadence was interested in a plebeian ex-stunt man. Sexual conjunctions in Movieland were often inexplicable—even by the participants.

"He may get home sometime this morning. Maybe not. I never know. But this time I'm not going to be here when he does."

"You're leaving him?" I asked, interested only because, if true, the Riddells' marital shattering could be the wedge to pry out the information I wanted.

She sank onto the couch, nodding.

"When?"

"Today . . . this morning . . . I'm already packed. I'm going home."

"Where's home?"

"Denver."

She bit her upper lip, trying to fight back tears. She lost. She buried her face in her hands, crying, "The bastard! . . . the dirty bastard!"

I left the chair and crossed to the couch, standing over her. "You're not going anywhere unless you tell me where Medford is."

I waited. She didn't answer. She didn't look up.

I pulled up a hassock and sat in front of her. "Listen to me . . . I know Bell and Woodman've been playing fast and loose with Medford's money. I know Medford made out a will that would've left his estate to his granddaughter."

"I don't know anything about any will."

"Yes, you do. You know because Medford supposedly changed his mind and went back to the original will leaving everything to the Soldiers of God. But there had to be a codicil revoking the will favoring April Tyson. And you and your husband witnessed Medford's signature to it." It was a low-risk guess.

She looked up, her face tear-spotted. "We didn't."

"That's right," I said, "you didn't witness Medford's signature, because he didn't sign it. His signature was forged."

"I don't know what you're talking about!" She jumped to her feet, wiping away tears with her hands. "Now leave me alone."

I stood up. "Who're you protecting? Bell?"

"I'm not protecting anyone!"

"Woodman? . . ."

"I told you—"

". . . your husband?"

"I never want to see him again! . . . Never!"

I didn't know whether she meant it or not. But I played it as if she did. "Then protect yourself."

She turned to leave the room. I took her arm, stopping her.

"If you don't, no one else will."

She looked at me with noncommittal eyes, pulled her arm away, and wandered around the room, her arms clasped tightly over her breasts, looking at everything, seeing nothing

My eyes followed her, and I said, "I'll take you to a lawyer I know. He'll go to the district attorney with your story and tell him you'll testify against Bell, Woodman . . ." I paused, not certain what her reaction would be " . . . and your husband . . ." she didn't bat an eye . . . "in return for immunity from prosecution."

Say Goodbye to April

She stopped her walking tour of the room and faced me, her arms dropping to her side. I could see some of her tension leave her. Her eyes went past me, looking into nothingness for what again seemed a long, long time. Then she said, "All right."

"Good . . . Now where's Medford?"

She stiffened.

"Well?"

"In the cellar."

"The cellar?"

"He's buried down there."

19

She didn't have to tell me where in the cellar he was buried. I remembered the large cement patch underneath the cabinet. I measured it in my mind. About three feet by six. The size of a grave. But there was, I knew, one thing wrong. I went to the cellar. Edna followed and stood at the foot of the steps. I crossed to the cabinet full of garden tools and pointed to the floor beneath it.

"Here?"

She nodded.

"He couldn't be," I said. "This patch has been here for years."

"He died about five and a half years ago."

I rolled with the punch. "How'd he die?"

"A heart attack."

I must've looked as skeptical as I felt.

"It's true. Doctor Stangood—"

"Stangood?"

"Yes."

"He knows Medford's dead?"

"He was here when he died."

"Who was the man pretending to be Medford?"

"Harlow Taft. Cliff knows him. He's an actor. Or

was. Never did anything but bit parts. Makes his living coaching poor slobs who come here thinking they're going to get into pictures. They pay him a few bucks an hour to attend his classes. Cliff hired him when Mr. Woodman told him to get someone who . . ." Her voice faded.

"Where did Cliff take him after he picked him up at the hospital?"

"His place."

"Where's that?"

"In Hollywood. On Barton, just off Gower."

"All right, go get dressed, and let's get out of here," I said.

"Where's the lawyer you mentioned?"

"He lives in Hancock Park."

"We going there now?"

I looked at my watch. It was ten after two. I shook my head. "Not at this hour."

"Then where are we going?"

"My place," I said.

Shades of April.

Edna went to dress, and I stood looking at the slab under which Medford was buried, considering the elaborate plot Woodman and Bell had concocted to conceal the death of the old man—whether from natural causes or not—and their embezzlement. They'd hired Jack Matson to find Medford's daughter and children, paying him to fail. Charles Lenox said it was three or four years ago that Woodman telephoned to tell him about the fruitless search and the change in Medford's will, again making the SOG Foundation his beneficiary. That, if Edna was telling the truth, was a year or two after Medford'd died. Then April arrived, wanting to see her grandfather and—with the hiring of Checkers and me—appeared disinclined to take no for an answer.

Damage-control time.

Apparent cooperation became the game plan. Hire an old, down-at-the-heels actor, install him in Medford's bedroom. Bring April in. She'd never seen her grandfather. She wouldn't know Price Medford from Price-Waterhouse. Then, to show they had nothing to hide, have her ersatz grandfather invite her to stay with him. But don't overdo it lest the charade start to show at the seams. So off goes the bogus grandfather to the obliging—for a high price, unquestionably—Doctor Stangood's hospital, a critically ill man. Then the pièce de resistance—the hundred-and-fifty-thousand-a-year-for-life trust fund if she gives up all claim on the Medford estate. How can she turn it down? She can't. And then she gives our imaginative embezzlers an unexpected bonus. She disappears.

With April out of the way, Bell and Woodman's pilfering of the Medford estate was back on track. But there'd be one more itchy problem down the line. The deceased Medford would have to "die" some time. If he lived forever, someone might notice. But I was certain the preacher and the lawyer had thought of that. They might have Riddell cast Harlow Taft to reprise the Medford role in which—with the help of Doctor Stangood—he'd play a very realistic death scene. Or better, a skidroad derelict might be enticed into service. There would be an announcement that the old recluse had finally gone to his reward, and his corpse would be delivered to a crematorium.

Edna's cry was short, muffled, but unmistakable. I started up the cellar steps but was brought to an abrupt halt in midflight by the appearance of Riddell and Edna in the open doorway to the kitchen. He had her in front of him, holding her with a hammerlock on her right arm. She was wincing with pain, pleading with him to let her go. He held Edna's automatic. It looked ridiculously small in his ham-hock hand. Or it would have if it hadn't been pointed at me. Riddell was drunk. And maybe he was on something more than booze. He weaved. The gun wavered. His eyes were muddy. His voice slurry.

"Get back down there," he ordered.

I backed down the steps.

"Cliff, please," Edna pleaded.

"Shut up!"

He pulled her back and slammed the door. I galloped up the steps, reaching it just as the lock clicked. Riddell's liquor-marinated motive for locking me in the cellar baffled me. I instinctively looked around for another avenue of escape even as I knew there was none. But he'd forgotten the tools on the rack above the workbench. I selected a large chisel and a heavy hammer and climbed the steps to the door. I listened for sounds from the kitchen. There were none. I started driving the bolt out of the upper hinge. I worked slowly, hammering and listening. The bolt was obstinate. It took time. Forever, it seemed, but it finally came out. The middle hinge was easier to uncouple and the lower one easier still, perhaps because by then I considered myself a seasoned bolt extractor. But now, unexpectedly, I had on my hands a door that clearly wasn't longing to be free of its anchorage. So I returned to the workbench, found a crowbar, and resumed my labors, prying the door free of the jamb. It took another eternity. But suddenly, with a screech, the door was torn from the lock. As it fell from the doorway, cartwheeling down the steps, it admitted a cloud of grayish smoke carrying the smell of gasoline.

The smoke was blinding with red, angry tongues of flame crackling through it, resembling lightning in a black sky. I ran down to the laundry sinks, turning the taps, stripped off my jacket, soaking it, then draped it over my head, doused my handkerchief, held it to my face, and mounted the stairs, moving gingerly through the doorway to the kitchen. Flames blocked passage to the rear door, leaving a dash for the butler's pantry the only alternative. I made it. The pantry was dense with smoke but free of fire. I pushed into the dining room. Flames engulfed the archway to the foyer. And I could see fire raging in the foyer itself. Riddell, in some insane, doped fury and drunken rage, was willing to destroy the house to incinerate me in the cellar and cover the fact that Medford was buried there. And kill his wife, too. Knowing she had talked to me, revealing Medford was long dead and entombed in the cellar, he wouldn't take the chance that she'd not repeat the information to someone else. If she wasn't already dead and left behind as more fuel for the flames, maybe I could get her out of the inferno.

I rushed to the windows at the far end of the room, threw one open, scrambled out and hippity-hopped to the French doors of the living room. Flames were dancing hellishly in there, too. I moved on, circling the house, coming to the windows of the Riddells' bedroom. More flames. More smoke. If Edna Riddell was in there, there was nothing I could do for her. As I turned away, a window exploded. Shards of glass flew like shrapnel. They missed me.

I ran.

Or what I call running. Around the house and down Medford Lane to where the Volvo was parked on Vermont and climbed in, tasting the smoke I'd inhaled. I had to cough to breathe, and my heart was pounding as if trying to wrestle itself free of a vise. I heard the howl of sirens in the distance, coming closer. Someone had reported the fire. I watched as first one truck and then another pounded up Vermont and turned into Medford Lane. They were followed by an LAPD black and white. And above the tall eucalyptus trees I could see the flames reflected on the smoke roiling in the night sky.

I put the key in the ignition. But I didn't turn it. I just sat there. I don't know how long. Time was no longer linear. It was a a wheel, a vortex. Lights appeared in houses, and residents came out of them. More fire equipment rumbled up Vermont and into Medford Lane. Another black and white. And still I sat, my mind as fertile as a polar icecap, trying to decide where to go, what to do. Decisions, decisions. I was sick of decisions. But I made one. I started the car and drove off.

To the marina.

I showered, had a drink, poured another, and took it into the den and sat in the recliner. I knew I couldn't sleep. But when I awoke it was daylight. The drink was on the table beside me, untouched. I looked at my watch. Ten-fifteen. I knew the fire had happened too late for the story to make the final edition of the *Times*, so I went into the kitchen and turned on an all-news radio station and started coffee perking and waited. It wasn't long.

"A spectacular fire destroys a Los Angeles landmark in the Los Feliz area, claiming one life," the announcer said. "Details after these messages." There were commercials for a rug-cleaning company and a chiropodist, and the news returned. "A fire in the early hours of this morning destroyed the eighty-year-old mansion of Price Medford, taking the life of a woman tentatively identified as Edna Riddell, the Medford housekeeper. She was apparently alone in the house. The whereabouts of Price Medford, a wealthy recluse who hasn't been seen in public for more than ten years, is unknown, although it is possible, according to fire officials, that he, too, died in the fire, and his body is buried in the rubble. Also missing is the dead woman's husband, Clifford Riddell, who was also employed by Medford. The Reverend Nicholas Bell of the Soldiers of God Temple, a longtime friend of Medford, had this to say when contacted by K-Six News." Bell's voice, unctuous as chicken fat, came on: "This is a tragedy beyond dimension. I pray my old and dear friend somehow escaped and will be found alive and well. If not, I'll find comfort that our maker, in His infinite wisdom, had a plan—"

I couldn't take any more of his sanctimonious bullshit.

So Edna was dead. And Cliff Riddell, if he was sober enough to realize it, was not only an arsonist but a murderer. And someone had to know that. I started for the telephone to call Hollywood Division and talk to Captain Gabrysiak, but I was ambushed by a hammering on the door. And hammering meant it was Checkers. I opened it and stepped back and he came in like a runaway bulldozer.

"Why'n the hell don't you answer your phone?"

"I guess I was asleep."

"Then you don't know what happened."

"I know," I said, waited a beat or two and added, "I was there."

He gaped. "Whaddya mean?"

I said I was in the Medford house when the fire started, told him what'd happened, and when I was through he said "Holy Christ!" and asked me what I was drinking.

"Coffee."

"Shit!" he grumbled and stomped into the kitchen. He found the liquor and poured three fingers—*his* fingers—into a glass and downed it. The sun was always over some yardarm somewhere as far as Checkers was concerned. He was having more sauce as a chaser when I said I thought someone—Captain Gabrysiak, for instance—should be told what I knew. He almost strangled on his drink, coughing and sputtering.

"Why?" he demanded. "And what do you know? I mean *really* know? You don't *know* that Medford died five years ago and was buried in the cellar. All you know is what the Riddell woman *said*. You know Riddell locked you in the cellar. But that'd be your word against his. But you don't *know* he torched the house. You didn't see him do it. Sure, the arson boys ain't dummies. They'll find out the fire was set. And if Riddell don't show, the cops'll go lookin' for him. And when they get him, maybe he'll talk. But maybe he won't. Maybe Bell and Woodman'll pay him enough to shut him down."

"You're forgetting what'll happen to them if Medford's body is found in that cellar."

"No, I ain't. And I ain't forgetting that we don't *know* . . . we ain't got no *evidence* . . . that Woodman and Bell switched wills. Nobody knows except Bell, Woodman, and Riddell and maybe that Doctor whatever-the-hell-his-name is. And shit, maybe Woodman and Bell'd come up with a paper from the old man saying that's where he wanted to be buried. God knows, the old guy was enough of an oddball to have an idea like that. So burying someone in the basement might be against a zoning law or something. But all they'd get is a fine. Or maybe they *will* get into deeper shit. But that don't change the fact that Bell's still the trustee of Medford's estate and that foundation of his is still the beneficiary. That's what we gotta do somethin' about."

"What do you mean?"

"You gotta find April. Get her back here."

My temperature started to rise, and Checkers knew it.

"Listen to me . . . I ain't saying Bell and Woodman're gonna get outa this free and clear. They can't. Not about changing Medford's will, anyway. Or about giving April that trust fund, saying it came from Medford."

"So what?"

He rolled his eyes impatiently. "Think, will you? Think! Somewhere down the line some judge's gonna throw out the will favoring Bell. And the waiver April signed, too, saying they were forged. But if a court says April's entitled to her grandpa's money, she's gotta be here to collect, ain't she? Christ, everybody in the country with the name of Medford'll say they were related to the old guy somehow. Everybody'll be suing everybody else. They'll have to hold court in Dodger Stadium. Might be fifty years before the dust settles. Or worse . . . If the will leaving Medford's money to Bell's foundation and April ain't found, all of Medford's money'd go to the government. You've heard about that, ain't you? It's called escheat or some lawyer word like that. So you *gotta* find April."

"*You* find her!"

"Tug—"

"All I've done for nearly two months is say hello April, goodbye April. Goddamn it, you were ready to settle for the twenty-five thousand we got from Woodman. Now you see a chance for another payoff . . . a bigger one . . . and you—"

I suddenly shut up, realizing there was no point in arguing. I couldn't win. So why not give in? Or pretend to.

"Okay, okay," I said, sighing resignedly.

Checkers relaxed. "That's better." He frowned. "Where the hell you think she is?"

I shook my head. "I don't know. Let me think about it."

"Okay." He glanced at his watch. "I gotta make a phone call." He headed for the den and closed the door behind him.

I waited, wondering how I could con him into thinking I was looking for April. I might have to go to Seattle. Or Hawaii. I smiled, thinking of Mai Tais on the patio of the Moana Hotel.

On Checkers.

A front page headline in the early edition of the *Times* read "Los Feliz Hermit Buried in His Cellar." The story said police and firemen, acting on an anonymous tip, had uncovered the skeletal remains of Price Medford from a decaying pine box buried under the concrete floor of the fire-destroyed Medford mansion. The skeleton was removed to the morgue, where an attempt would be made to establish the cause of death.

My eyes went back to the words "anonymous tip," and I wondered about the phone call Checkers had made from the den—behind a closed door. But I didn't wonder too long. Or too hard.

I didn't have to.

The *Times* headline was the start of it. Over the next week, other stories exploded like a string of firecrackers . . . Cliff Riddell was sought on suspicion of arson . . . Bell was questioned about Medford's death . . . Bell said he could explain . . . On advice of counsel, Bell refused to give an explanation . . . Doctor Stangood was interrogated and claimed cardiac arrest was Medford's cause of death . . . Stangood disclaimed any knowledge of Medford being interred in the cellar . . . Funeral arrangements weren't *his* responsibility . . . Why hadn't he filed a death certificate? . . . No comment . . . Cliff Riddell was arrested in Cadence Moore's bedroom while sleeping off a drunk . . . "What fire? I don't know anything about a fire," he said when he was sobered up and could talk with some coherence . . . The coroner's autopsy on Edna Riddell's body revealed she'd died from a gunshot wound to the head . . . Her husband was held, charged with first-degree murder . . . Charles Lenox, quoted as Medford's former lawyer, said he suspected fraud and embezzlement by Bell and Woodman . . . In reply, Woodman claimed complete innocence . . . The district attorney announced a grand jury investigation into the handling of Medford's financial affairs . . . The coroner reported that no exact cause of death could be established in the case of Price Medford.

I talked to Checkers on the phone after the first story broke. I wryly observed how fortuitous it was that an unknown tipster had broken the l'affaire Medford wide open. He quickly changed the subject, asking when I was going to start my safari in the quest of April.

"You expect me to leave *now*," I said, amazed. "I want to see what happens."

"Nothing else is gonna happen. It'll take weeks, months before they corner Woodman and Bell."

"So what's the rush?"

He couldn't answer that. He grumbled, hung up, and the rest of that week and part of the next went by without seeing or talking to each other. And then the letter arrived.

> Tug,
>
> I have been reading about what's been happening there. About my grandfather, the Reverend Bell, and Mr. Woodman as well as Mr. and Mrs. Riddell. I was right that they were hiding something from me, wasn't I?
>
> I am sending you this check for $2,000 because I don't know Mr. Checkers' address. This is all I can spare right now. When I heard my grandfather had been dead for five years, I knew you were right. The trust fund was a "buy-out." I returned the first check I received to Mr. Woodman.
>
> Tell Mr. Checkers to send me a statement of

what I owe him. He will get every dollar of it—even if I *do* have to live forever to make that much money.

I'm staying here temporarily while I decide where I want to settle down and try to put my life back in order.

April

The letter was postmarked Santa Barbara and written on the stationery of the White Sands Motel. I got the phone number, called, and asked for Miss Tyson's room. She didn't answer. I pulled open a desk drawer to put her letter in it.

But I didn't.

The White Sands was without pretensions, looking tidy, comfortable, offering a view of the beach and the white sand from which it took its name. April still wasn't in. I went outside to wait for her. I watched a fountain gurgle and kids playing in the swimming pool. I looked in the coffee shop and the quiet bar. I sat in a chair on the patio, grew restless, and wandered across Cabrillo Boulevard to the beach. And that's when I saw her. She was sitting on a beach towel, wearing a white swimsuit, her black hair falling free, gazing moodily out at the water. And beyond—as if she saw something no one else in the world could see. I went to her. But she was unaware of me until I said,

"Hello, Mona."

20

Her head jerked around. Her eyes grabbed mine. The sounds of the other people on the beach went away. Even the surge of the ocean licking the shore seemed to tiptoe. The world was a vacuum, and Mona Crane and I were the only two in it. She rose to her feet. Slowly. She didn't have to ask the question. Her expression—disbelieving, quizzical—asked it for her.

How?

I took two letters from a pocket. "From the letter you, April, wrote me," I said. "And the letter you, Mona, wrote to Ross to prove Mona was alive if someone started asking too many questions about why she'd dropped out of sight. I had it in a drawer of my desk. It didn't take a handwriting expert to tell they'd been written by the same person."

I offered them to her. She didn't take them. She just stared at them. Just stared. She took in a deep breath, exhaled it, and picked up a short robe of blue terrycloth and put it on. Slowly, deliberately. She folded the beach towel carefully and put her feet into a pair of sandals. Thinking. Knowing her impersonation was over.

"You want to know why."

"That'd be nice," I said.

She replied, "Yes, it would," and I wondered if she said it for my benefit.

Or hers.

We went to her room. Mona sat on the edge of the bed, huddled within herself, gazing blankly out a window. I was patient. I had no better place to be. Nothing better to do. Back in Los Angeles, it was the beginning of the end for Bell and Woodman and Cliff Riddell. Doctor Stangood, too, probably. And here in a motel room in Santa Barbara, the end for Mona Crane alias April Tyson had already arrived. I couldn't see the ending. Its size, its shape. But it was here. Waiting. As patient as I was.

After several minutes, she said, "I don't know where to start."

I thought about the skeleton of the woman found in Kirkland, her teeth bashed out to prevent identification, and Ray Simmons wondering if it was Mona. Now I wondered if it was April.

I said, "How about this? . . . Is April dead?"

"I don't know."

She saw I wasn't buying it.

"It's true! I don't!"

"She's dead," I said—flatly, with certainty.

"How do you know?"

"Bennett and Newkirk wouldn't have let you play at being April if they didn't know where she was. She might've shown up in the wrong place at the wrong time. They wouldn't take that chance."

She didn't say anything.

"Would they?"

She sighed. "No." Her voice was soft. Pianissimo.

But colorless. "I didn't know what'd happened to her. Ross said they had an argument, and she packed up and left. He said he didn't know where she'd gone."

"Do you know what the argument was about?"

"It'd been going on for a long time. Ever since Ross found out who her grandfather was. How rich he was. He wanted her to go to Los Angeles and try to see him. She wouldn't. She'd talk about her grandfather a lot. And about her mother and what'd happened. When she did, you could see the hate. Feel it."

"And you believed Newkirk? That she'd just gone away?"

"I wondered about it at first. Ross said he was sure she'd come back. And when he went to the police and told them she was missing, I didn't believe he'd have done it if . . . anything else had happened to her."

"How did he explain her leaving her and her mother's birth certificates and the other papers behind?"

"He didn't."

"And you didn't ask?"

"No."

"What did Bennett think?"

"He agreed with Ross."

"How did he fit into this?"

"He knew Ross. Paul handled something for him once. Something about a boat attached for money Ross owed on it. They became friends."

"How did you meet April?"

"Ross and I were living in the apartment next to her mother's while he was fixing up the houseboat. Then Mrs. Tyson died, and April came to Seattle, decided to stay, and we got acquainted. Ross'd been working on the houseboat, doing some remodeling, and when it was ready, he moved into it. April wanted to go with him but he wouldn't let her. Said it was too small. Said she wouldn't like it. Gave all kinds of excuses. I think he was punishing her for refusing to try to see her grandfather."

"And because he didn't want any more people to know they were close? Because he was already planning to get rid of her? Kill her? Hide her body?"

"I don't know."

She knew. But it didn't matter. Newkirk was dead. Bennett was dead. It didn't matter at all.

"So Mona Crane disappeared and became April Tyson and moved in with Bennett," I said. "Why did you leave Ray Simmons hanging out there? Why didn't you just tell him you were quitting?"

"Ross told me not to. He knew how Ray felt about me. He said he'd keep after me to come back to work for him."

"So you moved in with Bennett."

"That was Ross' idea, too. And Paul's. They said the people I knew in Seattle wouldn't come looking for me there."

"You lived with Bennett but you were in love with Newkirk, weren't you?"

She left the bed and went to the window, her back to me. "I suppose I was."

"And then he dropped you for April—"

She whirled angrily. "I don't want to talk about it. It doesn't have anything to do with . . . with anything." She came to me. "You know all you need to know. I pretended to be April. I lied. I took money. I'm a thief. I didn't want to be. I told Ross and Paul I wouldn't do it. But they wouldn't listen. They kept after me and after me and after me. They wouldn't let up. Finally I said all right . . . all right, I'd do it."

She put her hands to her face, sobbing, and rushed into the bathroom, shutting the door behind her.

I stood at the window. The sun was setting, and in the distance the shadows on the Santa Ynez Mountains were deepening and lights in the houses on its slopes came on. Now one, now another, seeming smug, self-complacent. Look at us, they seemed to chide with sickening bovinity, not a care in the world on this lovely summer evening.

And I said bullshit.

I paced the room. I could hear the shower in the bathroom. Was Mona trying to wash her sins away? And if so, which sins? I believed she didn't want to impersonate April. Believed she had only because of the hammering from Newkirk and Bennett. A human soccerball, going the way she was kicked, bouncing crazily. She was congenitally weak, vacillating, irresolute. But was that an excuse? A defense? She had sent back what money she'd received from the trust fund.

Give her that.

The sound of the shower stopped, and in a moment Mona came out of the bathroom. She wore only a bath towel. Her hair was wet, glistening. She asked if I was going to call the police.

"I don't know."

She moved to me, raising her face close to mine. For a moment we held a tableau, then my arms went around her, pulling her to me. She loosened the towel. It dropped to the floor.

"Come to bed," she whispered. "Please . . . come to bed."

"That wouldn't change anything," I said.

"I don't care."

Her lips ground against mine.

"I need you."

She was abandoned, fierce, insatiable. It was as if she was trying to purge herself of something. Or devour me. Or both of us. We had each other once. And again. Then we rested in each other's arms, and I asked why she'd run away from the Medford house and come to Santa Barbara. Was it because her brother was here?

"Tom's gone," she answered. "I don't know where he is . . . Why did I run?" She thought about it. "Just because I couldn't take it any more, I guess. Being April. Being afraid. Doing something I knew was wrong. Because I wanted to be myself again. Just be Mona again."

I said nothing, and then we slept.

When I awoke, feeble daylight peered into the room. I left the bed and dressed while Mona continued to sleep. I sat in a chair, watching her. I'd said going to bed with her wouldn't make any difference. But it had. And I should've known it would. So she was a thief. But she'd stolen—or tried to steal—from thieves. From a lawyer who, as Estevan had said, thought corners were made to be cut. And a self-anointed man of God whose real calling wasn't the propagation of the faith but the greedy gathering of the sheaves of personal and political power.

And who was I?

I was the guy who'd made an alliance with Lassen, a hired killer, even after he'd admitted killing Newkirk. I was the guy who'd protected himself by saying nothing, doing nothing when Lassen told me he'd murdered Dekoven and Vicari. An accessory after the fact to murder. I'd said it wouldn't bother me. It hadn't. And that was what was frightening. I'd lived by the dogma of our times—take care of number one.

Why shouldn't Mona?

I left the chair and went to the door to leave when I heard Mona ask where I was going. I looked back at her. She was showing no false modesty. Her breasts were beautiful.

"Back to Los Angeles," I said.

I didn't have to tell her what that meant for her. Her future was in her own hands—to make or break. She started to get out of bed. I stopped her by holding up a hand.

"Let's leave it at wherever it is."

"I just wanted to tell you . . . I woke up last night and decided where I want to go."

"Good."

"It's a place in—"

"Don't tell me."

Our eyes looked deep into each other for a brief moment.

"Goodbye, Tug."

I said goodbye.

21

I drove too fast going back to Los Angeles, as if I could outrun the memory of the past two months. Especially the memory of the dead. Of Frances, mostly. But of Bennett, Lassen, Newkirk, Dekoven, Vicari, too. Even Massi and Edna Riddell. And April, a woman I'd never seen, never knew. It was a KIA list as long as some I'd seen after a firefight in 'Nam.

And as pointless.

I went to Checkers' office and told him how April wasn't April any more. He sat behind his desk looking as if the world had made a sharp left turn and he'd been thrown off. It was the longest silence I'd ever encountered in his presence. Finally, he sighed resignedly and said, "Well."

I said, "Yeah."

He looked at his watch. "You want some lunch?"

"No."

"How about a drink?"

"No."

"I guess I don't either."

"I'll see you later," I said.

But I never would.

* * *

A guy named Friedrich Von Logau said the mills of God grind slowly, yet exceedingly small. Maybe so. But the mills of justice grind slowly, period. The case of Cliff Riddell was the exception. He was bustled through a preliminary hearing and trial almost before he'd sobered up. And a few weeks later he was convicted of first-degree murder and arson and given life in prison without possibility of parole.

But it was six months before the grand jury returned indictments against Bell and Woodman. It was another month before they were arraigned. They entered not guilty pleas to twenty-six counts of embezzlement, forgery, falsifying evidence, and perjury. Both defense lawyers and prosecutors predicted it would be another six months or longer before the two were brought to trial. And then another six months or more to try them.

Time, where is thy sting?

Woodman posted a fifty-thousand-dollar bond. Out of toadyish regard for his political clout, Bell was released on his personal recognizance. And although the court assumed jurisdiction over Medford's estate, nothing else had changed for the reverend. In the end, Medford's fortune would probably go to the state and federal governments, and there'd be loud wrangling about their fair share.

Bell returned to his pious hustle, saying he wore a crown of thorns, blaming his adversity—to the raucous, foot-stamping applause of his zealous flock—on left-wing, un-American, anti-God radicals who were conspiring to silence him, destroy him.

The money changer was back in the temple.

* * *

But I had other things on my mind. A decision to make, for one thing. What would I—approaching the tag-end of my thirties—do with the rest of my life? I'd come full circle from that barren time after my forced retirement from the department over four years before. I hadn't made a decision then. But I had to make it now. Time wasn't going to wait until I had. And, after long hours, I did.

It wasn't easy. I was going to desert the debatable charms of Los Angeles. I wasn't going to make my blue highways hegira. That would be more drifting, more flight, filled with the fantasy that I might unexpectedly meet Mona at the crossing of some unremembered byway and lost road. I was going to Berkeley and apply for admission to Boalt Hall, the University of California law school. It was late. Too late, perhaps. But my life had never really offered me a new beginning. It owed me one. Or I owed myself one.

Whatever.

I made a reservation to fly to the Bay Area for a day's visit to the university, was driving Hollywood Way to Burbank Airport, and noticed "Arnie's" neon sign. It was as jittery as before. Something nudged me. I didn't know what. Maybe it was because it was there it had all started the night Checkers and I argued about "April" going to the police. Now I knew that even though she may have thought she'd go, she wouldn't have. With Bennett dead, she'd have given up. Gone away. Gone back to being Mona Crane. But then she'd received the call from "Medford" and had stayed, because Checkers and I represented protection. Of a sort, anyway.

I was early. My plane wouldn't leave for over an hour. I turned around and went back to the neighborhood bar. The neighbors were out in force this time. A Dodgers game had replaced the Cactus Men movie on television. I guessed that since Arnie's was still here and I was still here, the Cactus Men had lost their war of the worlds. But maybe, being the sly creatures they were, they'd left behind an earth-shattering bomb, timed to explode when they'd returned to their own safe nook somewhere Out There. Maybe they were chortling over the fact that we here on earth were living in a fool's paradise. If so, the joke was on them.

We'd beaten them to it.

I shouldered my way to the bar and ordered a beer. The bartender—Arnie?—reported that the Dodgers were playing the Giants, and the score was tied in the last of the ninth with the Giants coming to bat. But my interest, what little I had, roamed from the television set to the table Checkers and I had occupied several decades ago. Or so it seemed. It was vacant, and my attention returned to the bar. A bubble of realization rose to the surface. I asked the bartender if he had a pay phone.

"Got two," he said, not taking his eyes off the game. "One in Men's and one in Ladies'. Take your pick."

I picked Men's, slotted coins, and dialed the number.

"Checkers and Associates!"

Ah, Jasmine, I thought, how nice to hear your hog call one last time. I asked for Checkers.

"Who's calling?" she asked as if she didn't know.

"A voice from the past," I replied, my voice sepulchral. I was dripping nostalgia.

"Huh?"

"It's Tug!" I bellowed. "Now cut the horseshit, and give me Checkers!"

I got Checkers. "Hiya, fella. Been tryin' to reach you. Don't you answer your phone any more?"

"No."

"Where are you?"

"Arnie's."

"Arnie's? . . . Where's that?"

I reminded him.

"What the hell're you doing there?"

"Never mind," I replied. "I called to tell you I know who made the phone call to April . . . Mona . . . pretending to be Medford."

"Yeah? . . . Who?"

"You, you bastard."

"What're you talkin' about?" I could see his expression—the wide eyes and arched eyebrows of pure innocence.

"You went to the bar. You ordered another drink. Then you went into the men's room, made the call, and—"

"Now why would I do a thing like that?"

"To convince me . . . and 'April' . . . that she was in danger. To keep her on the hook."

He started to protest. I dropped the receiver, letting it dangle from the cord. I could hear Checkers' voice but not what he was saying. I stood there thinking that if Checkers hadn't made that phone call, none of it might've happened. None of it. I went back to the bar. The place was subdued. The game was over. The Giants'd won.

I was glad someone had.